HAPPILY HAUNTED AFTERS

A ROMANTIC COMEDY

BRITTANY KELLEY

HAPPILY HAUNTED AFTERS

BRITTANY KELLEY

1

EMMA

The worn couch in the restaurant's cramped office beckoned me. Five minutes in there, and I could nurse my digital addiction and rest my feet. My drug of choice? Realtor. Dot. Com. Oh *yeah*, the good stuff. My me time between tables demanding more coffee and orange juice, and, and, and...

Ducking into the darkened room, I caught Lena's eye and tapped an imaginary watch to let her know I was escaping the bustling brunch hour between tables. She rolled her eyes, which I staunchly ignored. *Good for me.*

I exhaled, a grin curving my lips. The cushions sank under my weight, and I dug my phone out of my apron. Time for my fix. I tapped the red app, and exhaled, tension smoothing from my muscles. There it was: the white whale of my personal dreams. *Suggested based on my recent searches*, the app exclaimed under the listing header. Yeah, recent searches, uh-huh. Or *maybe* because I clicked on this particular link five times a day over the past year. Watching it. Waiting.

Forty acres outside New Hopewell, Texas. Piney woods setting, lakefront property. Owner's cabin: two bedrooms, one bath. Historic hotel included, in need of TLC. Buyer responsible for all permitting. Sold as-is.

A breathy sigh escaped my lips, my finger skating over the screen, reverent. Now for the pictures. Cottagecore to the extreme, vibrant salvia and sunflowers crowd for space next to the cabin's front porch. God, it was straight-up country house porn. Though the pictures of the inside were blurred, a fine mist covered the camera in certain angles. Odd, but I'd fantasized for the last twelve months on exactly how I'd decorate it. Make it a home. Make it *mine.*

I tapped again and again, letting the images float across the screen.

The lamp behind me flickered. Frowning, I reached a hand back. Totally non-descript, though probably saddled with some unpronounceable Swedish name that made it seem twice as exotic at a bargain bin price. Faulty discount wiring or not, it cast forlorn outlines on the wall, ghostly shadow puppets playing across the walls.

Ghosts were everywhere these days.

Great. Now I was wasting my break watching shadows when I should be halfway to housing nirvana. The couch creaked as I leaned back into the cushions. *Ah, the perfect place.*

The perfect size for me, a party of one.

Recently reduced in size from two. Single, single again.

My chest hitched at the memory, and I swallowed, choking it back. I wasn't going to let the ghosts of relationships past ruin my five—nope, two minutes. Besides, work might be the worst place to mull over my boyfriend humping someone else. Oops. Forgot a prefix. Ex-boyfriend. *Exest of all exes that ever did ex.*

Occasionally, my brain dubbed new music to the memory. A nightmarish TikTok vision of him pumping into some chick set to the latest Dua Lipa song. Maybe later I'd get buckwild and remix it to Sara Bareilles and cry into a bottle of two-dollar André Spumante from the Valero gas station around the corner. You know, keep it casual.

Just like he'd wanted to.

Anger flared, and I tapped again, wondering why my zen was nowhere to be found.

I needed to take the plunge. Buy it. What did I have holding me back, anyway? Not Dan, who found one of fifty ways to leave his lover. Not a *career*. Not... anything.

Because there it was, the pièce de résistance, the abandoned hotel.

Condemned. No trespassing.

Goosebumps pebbled along my arms, and I stared hard at the old place. Shutters sagged, wood shingles dangling off like a snake's half-shed skin. Fixing it up would be a whole 'nother kettle of fish. Or was it a barrel of monkeys? I frowned. *Whatever.* I could manage it.

A coat of paint. Okay, several coats of paint. New shutters, obviously. Verdant boxwoods and ivy in black planters flanking the rejuvenated double doors. A dreamy smile curved my lips, and I zoomed in on the image. Black sconces would be perfect *there*—with flickering gaslights, a row of white rocking chairs beneath them. Rocking chairs filled with people happy to escape from their busy lives. Happy to have a vacation, to live for a few days without worrying about cleaning or cooking or laundry. And I'd be right there, checking them in, making them feel welcome. At home. Because I would give them space—a place to shed their worries at the door.

Give them something I couldn't seem to give myself.

My throat tightened. I'd been that once, anticipating needs and wants and delivering an ideal vacation. Delivering a dream. Worked alongside one of the best in the biz, folks leaving my boss' boutique hotel with memories they could pull out and hold close when life got rocky, until they could escape into our care again.

This hotel—this massive property—could be something incredible. Retreats. Canoe rentals at the lake. Maybe add horses and give trail rides eventually. I could see it. The idea was so close and clear and yet... if I reached out and tried to grab it, the whole thing might slip like sand through my fingers.

I squinted at the screen. Something white clouded one of the windows. Maybe a ratty old curtain, or a sheer? Shadows in the dark folds of fabric could make that odd shape. Unease threaded through me, and I brought the phone closer to my face.

A hand landed on my shoulder, and I practically levitated.

"Ah!" I yelped, my heart racing.

"Calm down, it's just me... are you *really* creeping on that beat-up place again?" My older sister stood over me, jolting me back to reality. The noise of the restaurant came back full force, the heady scent of fried food wafting from the kitchen.

"Maybe." I'd been stalking this damn listing for a year, since the real estate market crashed. The *same* crash that lost me a job I adored, and sent me packing back to my hometown, working at my parent's restaurant. Living above their garage. *Ugh.*

I tapped again, relaxing into a rhythm of images and serotonin. Lena huffed in irritation, then settled down next to me. I didn't care.

"You thinking about revisiting your criminal past, or what?" She poked me in the hip.

"Caught me." I shrugged my shoulders. But it stung. I'd never stop hearing about that dumb night. Even though it happened over a decade ago, Lena would always see me as a teenage fuck up. "Wouldn't be trespassing if I bought it."

I adjusted the collar of the white shirt we all wore,

smoothing the stained fabric, and Lena fixed me with a serious look.

Great.

"There's no way you could afford that. You know I love you, Em, but running a business is hard work." She wrinkled her nose at me, not needing to finish the sentence. *Em and hard work didn't mix.* "You've seen how much mom and dad put into this place, know it pisses off the other staff when you hang out in their office, and you want to run a business, but you can't even..." She trailed off, eyes darting in my direction and then back to the tables full of customers. "Listen, I know you loved working at a hotel, but working at one isn't the same as owning it."

She didn't need to say anything else. As always, her words hit the mark.

Emma Cross, forever leaving everyone disappointed.

I turned my attention back to the siren call of real estate. There was nothing I could say to change her mind. Arguing would only prove her point. *I wasn't ready.* Lena peered over my shoulder, her mouth pinching to the side in disgust.

"I don't know what you see in that place. It looks like a money pit. Can you imagine what it would do to Mom and Dad to have to *bail* you out again?"

Irritation flared, and I sat up, scraping the toe of my Keds across the white pine floors. I raised my chin, ready to argue. *It had potential.* It just needed a little elbow grease. Okay, an entire truckload of elbow grease. Just like me.

But I could do it.

"Girls," my mom sang out, fixing us with a stern look as she swept by. "Enough chit chat. Your tables are trying to get your attention." Sure enough, my five minutes were up.

"Okay, okay," Lena and I mumbled at the same time, sharing a furtive glance. I tugged my ponytail, trying to secure my thick hair before going back on the floor.

Lena had already scurried off, flashing a brilliant smile and pouring steaming coffee with a practiced air. She threw me a glance, and I pasted on my own smile. Once, I'd loved this, talking to people, chatting them up. Making them laugh, making them happy. But Lena only worked weekends, helping out because mom needed her, not because *she* needed our parents.

Unlike me, the family fuck-up.

My thoughts swirled as I slogged through refilling water, tea, coffee. Taking plates. Taking orders. Updating the restaurant's social media between tables with colorful snaps of wildflowers in vases, perfectly plated fruit and waffles. Loved my parents, but *good grief* did they need a millennial's touch on their online presence. Geocities just weren't gonna cut it in this day and age. Trying to explain it to them was harder than just taking it over, a fact that made them roll their eyes in exasperation.

I slapped our brunch bestseller onto a table.

"Eggs sunny side up, side of bacon, side of grits, side of sourdough with butter, lightly toasted." The order rattled off my tongue. "Anything else?"

"Where's your head at today, missy?"

I paused, a hand landing on my hip. Ah, it was Jimmy. Oops. I hadn't even registered him. Crinkled eyes, bald spot I could nearly see my reflection in, and glasses that were cool when I was a toddler and had somehow come back into fashion. I was ninety percent sure he'd worn them the entire thirty years.

"Mr. Jim." I flashed a smile. "How'd it come out?"

"Well, you forgot my Tabasca sauce and my extra sugar." Jimmy always said it like that.

I winked at him. "I'll be right back with it."

"You've got something on your mind," he said, before I could spin away and retrieve his condiments.

"Why do you think that?" I cocked my head, eyes narrowing.

"It's not like you to forget. And you've got a look about you, like my wife used to get before she'd hand me a honey-do list a mile long."

"Maybe I do have something on my mind." I grinned.

"Is it a boyfriend?" he pressed, making a grand show of slathering his butter on the toast, one eye on me.

"It surely is not." I wrinkled my nose.

"It's something important though. Hmmm." He crunched into the bread, crumbs scattering onto his shirt. I handed him another napkin, smiling at him. "A mystery."

"There's a house." I waved my hands, trying to articulate the massive amount of land. "And an abandoned hotel. I want..." I trailed off. Why was I telling him this?

"You want a change, huh? Have a big dream. You've got a look in your eyes. Sure it's not a boy?"

"I do, and trust me, I'm sure." I winced.

"Know what I want, Em?" He fixed me with a serious look.

"Tabasco and sugar."

"Got it in one." He took another bite of his toast, dismissing me.

I choked out a laugh and scrambled to get his condiments. For a second, part of me thought maybe he'd give me some grand advice, from a long life well-lived. Something sage and remarkable that would light a cayenne flavored fire beneath me.

As I snagged his 'Tabasca,' Lena twirled between tables, stopping to make small talk with our regulars. She was good at everything. And here I was, living over the garage of my parent's house, working for them. Dependent on them. No wonder Lena couldn't see who I wanted to be—who I *was*. Not when I was right back where I was a decade ago.

I was sick of it.

But I needed one critical piece to make my plan work: *money*. Sure, I'd saved some, easy enough when you leeched off your parent's generosity, but with student loans and car payments and insurance... It wasn't enough. Money. I needed it. Or someone who had it.

An investor. Excited butterflies filled my stomach, but I took a few deep breaths. I had to think this through. Do it right.

The tables cleared out after the lunch rush, and Jimmy waved to me as he ambled out the door, finally sated on a ridiculous amount of sugar grits. Good for him. Only one table left. I swept his check from the table, glancing at it before tucking it into my apron.

I did a double take.

Old Mr. Jim tipped me a hundred dollars. My hand fluttered to my mouth. Surely not. He must have added an extra zero on accident. Or the decimal was in the wrong spot.

My heartbeat sped up, and I swallowed. There was a note with it. I squinted at the spidery handwriting, lips moving as I read silently.

"I know this isn't near enough what you might need nowadays to make your dream happen. Take it from this old coot—dreams won't wait forever. And don't make me wait until my eggs are cold to bring the hot sauce next time. -Jim"

My vision grew watery, and I leaned against a wall. That grumpy old codger. I knew he was hiding a heart of gold. He was right though; a hundred dollars was a drop in the bucket. But maybe this was a sign. A sign to get my ass in action, to finally get something right.

I pushed an errant curl out of my eyes.

It was time for a change. I was *great* at change. First things first, I needed an investor. A muscle twitched in my temple.

I knew the perfect man for the job.

Thought of him every time I sat down to daydream about the property, making lists for what I would do, the place it could become. Reveled in the memory of his dimpled smile, his dumb jokes. Oh, I had the perfect man in mind. I'd known him nearly all my life. *Just not the past five years.*

Rubbing my apron strings, I stared at Jim's now empty chair, the worn wood seat likely still warm. I squeezed my stinging eyes shut. The noise of the restaurant faded against my thoughts racing in time with the staccato beat of my heart. Jim, for all his grumpy charm, believed in me. Even when I forgot his dang Tabasco, he saw what I could be. And I believed in that run-down property. Saw what it could be.

Maybe I *could* do this.

Opening my eyes, I narrowed them at my reflection in the massive front windows. I swallowed against a lump in my throat. I would do it. It was about damn time.

Now I had to do something I wasn't great at.

Commit.

2

JACK

The small velvet box was easy to return. Easier than it should have been. Dark blue, satin interior, a small sad look from the saleswoman who put the money back on my card, twinkling rocks winking slyly up at me like they knew how I really felt from the glossy display cases.

I shoved the card in my wallet with unnecessary roughness.

"Better now than later, huh?" The joke fell flat, and the woman behind the counter managed a small smile.

The door flung open, and the heat of a summer that wouldn't quit even into the fall blasted my face. I rubbed a hand over my stubble.

I wasn't sad.

Irritated. That's how I felt. Like an itch I couldn't quite scratch between my shoulder blades. Like I'd performed poorly on a test I thought I was going to pass. Like I'd lost a mediocre account.

Conversation ebbed and flowed around me, business here finally picking up. *Good sign for the economy.*

Shit. I'd just returned the ring, and I was thinking about the *economy*?

That's not what I should be thinking about after calling it quits with Caroline. I should feel angry. Or sad. I'd sunk the last three years of my life into her. I should feel something. Not mildly irritated. Second ring returned. First, I'd thought my college sweetheart, Beth, was the one.

Now, Caroline had turned me down. Dappled shade cooled the heated skin of my neck, compliments of palms and pine trees competing for space. Another perk of the landscaped-within-an-inch-of-its-life outdoor shopping development.

Taking in the brand name shops and glossy signage, showy foliage and designer clothes, I calculated the probable cost for the place out of sheer habit.

My phone buzzed in my pocket.

Aiden: you on for tonight? Or are you wallowing

I tapped out a reply, deleted it.

Aiden: I have a new cider, you'll like it

Aiden: It's not as pretty as your ex-girlfriend, but it might cheer you up

I snorted, then sobered.

Me: You're an ass

Aiden: you know, it's not too late to pull the stick out of yours and have some fun. We on? We could come up with a new recipe, just like old times

I sighed, my fingers flying over the phone screen. Aiden and

I had been college roommates. Best friends. He pursued his dream, a dream we'd once cultivated together, brewing beer in our ratty rental house, testing out yeast and putting his chemistry degree to good use. And he ended up living his hops-flavored dreams, while I... didn't. I pursued money. Financial stability. Crossing off achievements like life was a boring video game. Now he was a head brewer at a local craft brewery, and I was the asshole in a suit.

Me: maybe next week

Aiden: sure

I put the phone back in my pocket. Great, now my only friend was pissed at me, too.

Couples clustered around small iron tables populated the venue next door. The smell of fajitas and fried chips permeated the area. A man held a woman's hand, rubbing a thumb over her wrist. Smiling, laughing. I scowled.

I could use a cold beer.

What I really needed was a good workout. Let off some steam, vent my irritation. Maybe get some sleep. I crossed the street, focused on that. Better *that* than focusing on the fact I clearly didn't care enough about my would-be fiancée—about us—to be more than irritated when she turned me down.

"I just don't think you love me. You're the perfect boyfriend, don't get me wrong, Jack. I just..." Caroline *trailed off, pushing her long blonde hair over a shoulder and squirming in her chair. "I just don't think you're the one. You don't act like you care about anything but work. And I don't think you care about me, either."*

I turned the corner away from the restaurant and towards the parking lot, a muscle in my temple starting to twitch.

What the hell was I supposed to do with that? And when I

hadn't argued, just stared at her, she'd given me a small, sad smile. And all I felt was... *irritated.*

Probably because she was right.

In my pocket, my phone rang. *Good.* Work. Hopefully the Chevalier deal was coming through.

"Jack, it's Robert."

"Talk to me." I winced, hating the way my voice sounded, the way the words came out. Caroline's accusation rang in my ears. *Cold.*

"There's been a steep price drop on a property out in East Texas."

Adrenaline surged. I might not love the corporate talk, but I liked making deals. My company was snatching up foreclosed properties and land all over the state at the lowest prices seen in over a decade. Once the real estate bubble popped, it was a developer's dream.

"There's a condemned hotel on site, so we'd have to run the numbers on bulldozing it, but it's forty acres of lakefront real estate in Piney Woods country. Good location for another development."

I glanced around the swanky outdoor mall full of self-important people, bodies bared in the lingering heat, hallmark of the Texas fall.

"Piney Woods, huh? Sounds like we'd have to price more than bulldozing just the hotel." Heavily forested areas required razing, save for a few choice trees to market the developments as "*natural.*" I rolled my eyes skyward. High white clouds dotted the blue expanse.

"You know the drill. That's why I'm sending you."

I paused walking. A butterfly flitted across a nearby planter, and despite its gracefulness, the brilliant reds and oranges were aggressive against the greenery.

Reminding me of her.

I swallowed down the still-vivid memory.

"You there, Jack?" Something creaked in my ear, probably Robert swiveling on his old-school chair. Peaking his fingers together, watching the people of Houston skitter below his high seat.

I ignored the butterfly as it winged away.

"Sending me?" Unusual. Most business we did over the phone. "Want me to look at it? Sweet talk the owners?" I could usually negotiate the price down even further. I clenched my teeth. Talking desperate people down from money grated on me. But forty acres of lakefront?

I doubted these owners were hurting, despite the economic downturn.

"You got it. They've turned down ten potential buyers and then lowered the price. Turned us down twice already. Something smells off about the whole deal. Owner said they would only sell to the right person, something about the place being special. I definitely need some feet on the ground." *Feet on the ground. Like real estate was some kind of macho operation.* "Probably just one of those old school country folks. Get out there, schmooze them, wine and dine them, whatever it takes. This could be the deal to make you partner. We see real potential in you, and, more importantly, in this acreage."

My heartbeat sped up. *Partner.* That shiny silver sports car across the way could be mine. Another achievement unlocked.

I frowned. Not that I'd abandon my old Bronco.

Too many memories.

"Make 'em love you, make an offer, and make partner," Robert continued, and I imagined his expensive Italian loafers now perched on his desk. "You know the deal. Charm 'em, like you always do. I'll send you the details and we can circle back later."

Sure enough, my phone vibrated as an email arrived.

"When do you need an answer?" I narrowed my eyes and double-timed it to my Bronco.

"Sooner the better. I hear your holiday plans got canceled. Sorry about that."

I inhaled deeply, fighting the urge to call him on his bull-shit. He couldn't care less about anyone's personal life.

Cold. Just like Caroline said *I* was.

"Go down there this weekend, over the Labor Day holiday, stay in town, and get it done. Use the company card for expenses."

It was an order. *Partner.* My goal was in reach. Finally.

"You got it. I'll swing by my condo and be on my way." A redhead sauntered past, face hidden under a wave of glossy curls. My head swiveled to her automatically, autopilot initiated. She glanced away from her phone, a coy smile curving her lips.

It wasn't her.

I frowned. The woman's grin faded.

"Good. I'll expect a progress report on Saturday." With that, he clicked off the line. I stared at it for a moment, then shook my head, eyes tracking the woman's flaming hair.

When would I stop seeing her everywhere?

Not five seconds after I shoved the phone in my back pocket, it rang again.

"What do you need, Robert?" I pulled the keys to my old truck out, business voice fully deployed.

"Hey, it's me."

My hand froze, inches from the Bronco's handle. I would need a winch to pick my jaw off the pavement.

"Um, Em." My voice was too high. I swallowed. "Emma." It came out a gravelly rasp.

My pulse picked up, and I leaned my forehead against the Bronco, immediately regretting it as the hot surface scorched my skin.

"I know it's been awhile, but—"

"What do *you* want? How did you get my number?" I

managed, rubbing a hand across my burning forehead and cutting her off. Damn it. I sounded like a dick. Like I was still mad at her. Maybe I *was* still mad at her. The phone vibrated again; the office was calling.

I ignored it. A breathy exhalation cut through the vibration, sending chills down my spine.

"Oh. Lena gave it to me, uh, I hope that's okay. I didn't know you guys still talked... Um. Anyway, I'd like to proposition you."

"Excuse me?"

"I mean, I have a proposition *for* you." Emma squeaked out a laugh. Something in my chest hurt, and I rubbed at it with my empty hand. That was her nervous laugh. She'd be doodling, her long graceful fingers clutching a pen or pencil so hard her knuckles would be white. I could just imagine her long legs bouncing against the floor. Where was she?

"Jack?"

"What is it?"

"I want to be partners."

I swallowed. *Partners.* That word was getting thrown around a lot today.

"I mean, I'd like to pitch you on a property renovation and business opportunity." She paused, and the weight of the sudden silence hung between us like a muggy day. "You're still in real estate, right?"

Business. I could do business.

"What're the terms, where's the property, do you actually have the liquid assets for something like this?" My voice sounded clipped. Professional. Cold.

The memory of Caroline's voice echoed in my head.

You don't care about anything but work.

She was right. I was a stone-cold asshole. I closed my eyes, a surge of sadness finally breaking over me. But not about losing her. Not that. About realizing Caroline might have a point.

"I have a plan." The grin in her voice nearly broke me. She

always had some hare-brained plan. Discarded them as quickly as her string of boyfriends in college. "But I want to see it first. And I want you to see it with me. You know, get your professional opinion." Her words were rushed now, excited. My memory dredged up her bright eyes and flushed cheeks, the way she always looked before she got us into trouble in high school. And then college. And then the last night I'd seen her, nearly six—or was it five?—years ago. "I booked us a stay at the place over the long holiday weekend."

A weekend I initially planned in my head to spend with Caroline, looking for wedding venues. A holiday weekend that now stretched before me with absolutely nothing to do but work.

"I have a work trip planned in East Texas."

"*Oh.*" She sounded disappointed. "Oh. Of course you do. Okay."

Jesus. A whole weekend in Emma's orbit. What could possibly go wrong?

More like what could possibly go right?

I closed my eyes, letting myself imagine.

"Jack? Are you still there? Listen, I know I haven't—" Her voice was twinged with regret, or anxiety, and my heart squeezed. We'd both fucked up. But I wouldn't let her do it again. I wouldn't let *myself*. Business. "Wait, where in East Texas?" Her words tumbled out. "That's where I'm looking. Where are you staying? Maybe you could head out and meet me. That is, if you have time for an old friend." Her voice was wheedling. How many times had I heard that same tone?

Nothing good would come of this. I squeezed my eyes shut, rubbing the back of my neck as the keys jangled against my skin. What did I have to hold me back? What harm could it do to meet her for coffee? Go hear her out, at least.

I owed her that much.

"Text me the address and I'll meet you there. How about

Thursday?" Couldn't be that far from where I'd be. Distance in Texas was relative anyway, measured in hours instead of miles.

"Are you sure?"

I paused, rubbing a hand across the back of my neck. It wasn't like Em to consider how sure I was. Or anyone beside herself.

Then again, what did I know? We hadn't seen each other in years.

This was a bad idea. Going into business with friends rarely worked out, I'd seen it explode enough times. Not that we *were* friends, not anymore. Acquaintances. Lena texted me gifs occasionally, or small-town gossip, but we hardly mentioned Em. An unspoken rule.

But what could it hurt to meet up with her and see this property? Didn't mean anything.

"I'll meet you there, but that's all I'm agreeing to until I see your business plan and the property. Is your boyfriend coming?" A shot in the dark. Em was never single. Not that I cared.

A short bark of a laugh was the only response. "No. No, Dan is not coming." A beat of silence. "And he's not my boyfriend."

"Oh." My chest clenched. Because this was a bad idea. She was single. And knowing her, probably on the prowl. Not that I was in any condition to be looking for a rebound. And rebounding with Em? Terrible fucking idea. Was she humming Dua Lipa?

"What about you?" Em asked, briefly breaking off before quietly singing the chorus. With my luck, it would be stuck in my head all day now.

"I'll see if Caroline can come." I smacked my forehead against the driver side window of the Bronco. A woman walked by, concern and apprehension etched on her face. And then the alarm sounded, a series of sirens and beeps.

Idiot. My phone beeped, the office trying to reach me again.

"I have to go, Em. See you soon." I found the de-arm button for the car alarm and tripped it, but it didn't stop.

"Okay, love ya, bye."

Love ya? I stared at the phone, watching the screen light up as my office continued to ring through. *Love ya.* The car whined and howled, and a few people stopped to stare. I whacked my palm on the hood, and the alarm fizzled out in a bizarre cacophony.

Em didn't mean anything by it. She never had and never would.

3

EMMA

Pine trees lined the road, evergreen limbs clawing the sky. Night threatened to fall any minute. It would definitely be dark as shit once it did, seeing as how there weren't any lights out here in yeehaw East Texas. And I'd definitely forgotten to pack a flashlight.

The thought never crossed my mind, actually.

I'd been too busy planning. Putting together a spreadsheet, even a PowerPoint presentation highlighting my main points, as though a slide deck and Excel would be enough to convince Jack to be my partner, after all I'd put him through. Ha. I'd put my ancient laptop through its paces.

I hated Excel. And yet, there I'd been, watching tutorials on how to make it fancy and pretty and make the numbers do things I didn't know spreadsheets could do. After watching the yawn-worthy tutorials, I had a new, post-Dan motto.

Be the Excel spreadsheet you wanted to see in the world.

Neat rows and columns and data tied up in a tidy package

and tuned to any color in the color wheel I wanted to be. Organized. Optimistic, but real.

Not the vapid mess of chaotic energy and mind-numbing, shallow relationships I'd strung myself out over the past decade or so. Enough of my family's quiet concern and brutal disappointment. Or in the case of Lena, not so quiet.

Be a spreadsheet and spark joy. I was going to Kondo my damn life. I had everything to gain. Besides, what did I have to lose?

Savings? Who needs 'em!

If everything went according to plan, I'd be the proud owner of a fixer-upper hotel and an eventual fledgling business. Something that was mine. Something that would show everyone exactly what I was capable of. Excited butterflies exploded in my stomach at the thought.

My phone vibrated in the cupholder, and I chanced a glance at the screen before picking it up.

"Hello?"

"Hello, this is Emma, yes?"

"This is she." My good ole southern manners mother had drilled that response into me as soon as I could speak.

"Oh good. It's Susan, the seller's agent again. Just wanted to let you know the house is clean and ready for your stay, fresh sheets, and my client put some things in the fridge for you. She wanted me to remind you of the terms of the agreement." A heavy, put-upon sigh followed this, and I smiled in spite of myself.

"I remember."

"Well, they wanted me to call and tell you again." Another long exhalation. Susan sounded completely over it.

"Go for it."

"The term of the stay is three nights, three days, to begin at sundown this evening and end at noon on Saturday. You are to stay the entire night at the property, but may leave during the day to see the town. You must stay in New Hopewell. If you meet the terms of this agreement, the owner or I will meet with you to discuss a discounted price and wrap up the sale, if you're still interested."

"Susan, I could recite this by heart." I'd only read the email a hundred times in the last week. I gripped the steering wheel tighter. The razor's edge of hope was nearly too much; I'd either actually make this happen, or I'd screw it all up.

"Emma, I'm glad to hear it. I'll be glad to get this deal done. Trust me." The sound of a clacking keyboard filtered through the speaker.

"Anything else I should know?"

"Well—" She paused, the typing suddenly stopping. "I don't know if I should tell you this—"

"Tell me what?" Tingling anticipation wound through my body. There had to be a catch.

"There's not a whole lot of restaurant choices."

I laughed, relief coursing through me.

"Be safe out there, talk to you soon."

And with that, the line went dead.

Sudden movement jerked my attention back to the road, and I screeched, along with the brakes on my beat-up old Toyota. The seatbelt pulled across my chest, a tight reminder that I needed to keep my thoughts and car from careening out of control. A deer bounded across the road, and I gulped, choking air down.

Adrenaline kicked in, sending tingles down my arms and legs, and a high-pitched laugh burbled out of my mouth.

Just a deer.

"You're so dramatic, Emma." My imitation of Dan was pitch-perfect, and I grimaced at my reflection in the rear-view mirror.

I shoulda dumped him way before. And now he wasn't my boyfriend and he could go get a UTI with his new chick.

A car horn sounded behind me.

"Yeah, yeah, I hope you get a bladder infection, too." You get a bladder infection, you get a bladder infection! *Everybody gets a bladder infection.* Well, hopefully not me. Oprah would *never*. I flashed a toothy smile and waved at the dude behind me. Never can be too polite. Never know who's packing in good ole Tejas.

I eased the car back into first gear. The clutch on the darn thing was sticky as hell, but there was something really satisfying about wrenching the stick into place when I was angry.

The car behind me flew by me on the shoulder, middle finger salute out the driver's side window.

A wrinkled print-out lay next to me in the empty passenger seat. "Beautiful, quiet retreat. Deep Piney Woods setting, lakefront property. No need to ever leave." It proclaimed, in obnoxious Comic Sans. I had it memorized, knew it by heart. Staring at it during every break the past year would do that to a girl.

Gripping the stick, I rammed the car into second, then third, reciting the words I'd read so often over the past twelve months.

Come hell or high water, I was making it to the damn property. A frown turned my lips down. Even if my trusty Toyota was acting weirder than usual.

"Shit." The car jerked as I hit the rumble strip, jarring my teeth and practically dislodging a filling. A reminder that if I was going to pull this off, get Jack's help, I had to focus on one thing at the time. No more flighty Em. Only focused Em.

The rumble strip reminded me of something else, too: I needed to pee.

The seatbelt cut against my collarbone as I squirmed, scanning the distance for an exit.

A quick look at the GPS told me there was a gas station a few miles ahead. Mile marker after mile marker flashed by, the sun setting in a brilliant display of peach and orange. And only five more miles to New Hopewell, the small town and closest city to the cabin. New Hopewell.

If only it would live up to its name.

"Mile marker forty-one." I took the exit, expecting the blinding lights and garish yellow and reds of another big chain gas station.

What I got was a beat-up old rickety place. A sign screamed, "GAS LIVE BAIT SANDWICHES." Punctuation must not be a priority around here. Either that, or I didn't want to try the sandwiches.

Paint peeled off the exterior, a faded blue and white. A single rectangular window showcased a dusty interior, a yellowed lace drape half pulled across it. In the new half dark, it didn't inspire confidence. Creepy. I half-expected a banjo to twang in the distance.

Two old-fashioned pumps rose out of the pock-marked asphalt. My nose crinkled.

They didn't even look like they'd work.

Shrugging, I turned off the engine and popped the gas cap. No reason not to fill up while I stopped to pee. I squeezed my eyes shut. Just thinking about peeing made it so much worse.

"Hey there."

My eyes flew open, and I screamed. I'm not proud of it, it just happened. My heart thudded in my chest, so fast and furious, I slapped it to try to get it to stop.

"What the hell, Emma? What's wrong with you?"

I choked, half coughing and half laughing. "Jack, you scared the shit out of me. Not literally."

But almost literally, considering how badly I had to use the bathroom.

Jack. I swallowed a sigh. He'd always been handsome. Ridiculously so. But I'd get used to it, being around him was like breaking in a pair of new shoes. My reaction to his hotness would wear off. Probably.

But right now, he was shiny and new again, dark hair and dark eyes and tanned skin and so, so tall.

A small sigh escaped my mouth, and his lips curled up in a smile. Dazzling. White teeth. Straight, thanks to the years we both spent in braces. Even had the same dentist, though my smile wasn't nearly as show-stopping as his. Dentists only get you so far.

His eyes flitted away from mine to the back seat.

I swallowed again. What did he see back there? A box of crackers, an empty soda can, a box of candy I ate on the three hour drive out here.

A mess.

"Same old Em," he said.

I patted a curl back into place, masking disappointment. But this bladder wasn't gonna make it much longer. The red bull had been a mistake. As had the water and every other liquid I'd ever drank *ever*.

Jack still smiled, his eyes crinkling up playfully. That look. The same expression that egged me on for years.

It was like coming home.

I snuck a look at him, but his smile had evaporated into blankness.

"It's good to see you, Jack. I've missed you." I was so wrapped up in watching the progression of expressions, his arms caught me by complete surprise. He folded me into his chest, and I caught his familiar scent. All the anger melted right out of my body, and I sagged into him. "How're your parents?"

His body stiffened against me, and I bit my tongue. Should've known better than to ask.

"They divorced. Finally." His grin vanished. "Wish they'd done it years ago."

He let me go, the hug lasting a moment too long. What would his girlfriend think? I frowned.

"I gotta pee." I hauled away from him, reeling from the hug.

Just a lil squeeze between friends. "I can't believe you still wear Axe." I breathed him in.

"Hey, wait, Emma."

"I gotta pee." It was too awkward already. And my bladder was about to explode. I closed the distance to the rickety old building. It didn't inspire confidence. Swallowing, I grabbed the rusted handle, nearly losing my balance as it opened on its own.

It squeaked inward, fluorescent lights flickering overhead.

"Hello?" A cautious step propelled me onto the filthy linoleum. My feet knew what my mind didn't want to acknowledge—my bladder was out of time. *You get a bladder infection!*

There was no hope for it. I was going in.

Code Yellow.

It was *find a toilet now or make one in my pants.*

4

———————

JACK

Emma. So much the same about her, from the smart-ass grin to her absolutely mind-boggling ability to never plan bathroom stops. Her body was as graceful and athletic as I remembered, her hair untamed, unruly, unstoppable. Just like Em herself.

And yet—changed. Her eyes still shone, full of life and light, but she carried herself like a woman who knew how to guard herself. Like she expected to be hurt. Brittle.

My throat constricted, and I let out a long sigh, cracking my neck and taking stock of the absolute shit hole of a gas station. Long yellowed shelves were sparsely populated by boxes and cans all covered in a thin film of grim and dust. Thin fluorescent lights swayed overhead, one flickering intermittently and emitting a low droning hum. And no one was around. Did anyone even work here? Something about the whole place seemed off.

Hell, this whole trip was off.

I should've known when she suddenly initiated contact that

this had a fifty/fifty chance of evolving into a complete shit show.

But here I was, ever at her beck and call, five years later. Sixty some odd months since our friendship imploded as gracefully as a frag grenade, shrapnel embedded so deep it still ached.

Business. I swallowed.

A mirror behind the gas station counter caught the expression on my face, and with the bristly five-o'clock shadow—it wasn't a good look. A ragged sigh dipped deep from my chest, and I folded my arms across it, as though that would stop another from escaping.

I was an idiot for thinking it would ever be different between us, that we could be acquaintances. One sidelong glance at her, and I was right back to college. And high school.

Original goal for the weekend? Help Emma out. Not go into business with her, but help steer her the right way. Never go into business with her.

No way was I making the same mistakes my parents did.

But I could make up for everything... everything that had come between us. The way I'd cut her out of my life. A neat amputation, considering how close we'd been. Screened her phone calls, said things I could never take back. Tried to pretend she didn't exist, as though two decades worth of memories were easily scrubbed from my brain.

Pulling out my phone, I scrolled past our tentative conversation over the past week. Checking the text she'd sent with the property address, still disbelieving.

The same address Rob tasked me with buying. The property that could help me pass the finish line on my career goal. My heart pounded, loud even against the rumble of the ancient AC window unit, spitting to life.

I could make *partner.*

I swept a palm over my face. Caroline accused me of being cold. I didn't know I had this much ice in me.

Originally, I'd thought maybe I could make amends. Get closure, heal from the implosion of our friendship.

Maybe.

New goal? Survive her. Play my cards close to the chest. Talk her out of the property, convince her it would be too much work. She buckled down occasionally, but only when it was something she really wanted. Which hadn't been often. Surely she hadn't changed. Like I had forgotten how often she'd copied my work in high school, and then even in college.

The memory of Em's red-gold hair falling over the curve of her cheekbone at my old dorm, as she copied down answers after pulling a double at the hotel she'd worked at. "Why work hard when I can work smart?" she'd say, with that signature grin. "Homework is a waste of time. Besides, I'm fixing your mistakes too; you should thank me." With a shrug and a quick wink, she'd leaned back over, pencil scratching out the answers.

If she were in my shoes, she'd do the same thing.

My stomach churned. I ran a finger along the counter-top, only to quickly regret dredging it in what had to be a year's worth of dust and grime.

The churning had to be hunger. The protein bar I'd gobbled after my morning workout was not enough. I eyed the slim pickings. I should've brought something with me to eat. God only knew what they'd have stocked at the B&B I'd booked, the only hotel in a fifty-mile radius.

I swallowed, my throat dry. God knew Em wouldn't have thought to bring food, unless she'd had a major personality change in the last few years. And learned to cook. My cheeks hurt, and I realized with a start I was grinning at the memory of burnt toast, her special.

Though it had damn near been long enough. Who was I to assume?

My fist pounded the counter, and I squeezed my eyes closed. This was a mistake. I'd made one terrible assumption after another.

I'd assumed this could be fun, for one thing. I'd assumed we would both be here with our respective fiscal responsibilities, a business-barricade between the two of us. We'd circle each other like moons, the gravitational pull of a potential professional relationship keeping us safe.

She always exerted her own gravity, though. A pang surged through me.

I'd missed her. But... better not to engage. How many times did I need to travel down that primrose path?

I massaged a tense muscle in my forearm, pausing to adjust the band on my watch. Uncomfortable. In the mirror behind the counter, my eyebrows rose, and my throat bobbed as I swallowed.

For a grown man, I felt like a scared teenager. Totally thrown off my game.

I shouldn't have come.

I shifted my weight, searching the dump of the convenience store. If the whole town looked like this, she wouldn't need convincing to drop her hare-brained hotel scheme. I snorted. It was so like her, to fly by the seat of her pants and land in the middle of nowhere for a long weekend.

I sighed, pinching the bridge of my nose. It could be fine.

Maybe it could be fun.

Maybe *we* would have fun.

My feet moved of their own accord, toward the bright light trickling out behind a door marked 'ladies.'

Toward Emma.

5

———————

EMMA

Jack was the first thing I saw when I opened the bathroom door. I shook the excess water from my hands, and a half smile tugged the corner of his lips. Dark brown hair fell over his forehead, careless perfection. One of my oldest friends, and here I was, ogling him like he was some bare-chested dude that used to roam the Abercrombie and Fitch store in our hometown mall. The hometown I still lived in. Ugh.

"Checking on you." His eyes roamed my face, and nervous butterflies flipped in my stomach. Nah, that couldn't be right. Probably hunger pains.

"Is there anything better than that instant relief when you've been holding it for hours?" Yup. That was a safe conversation.

Talk about pee with your super-hot ex best friend, smooth move, Emma.

He threw his head up, a bark of laughter ricocheting off the pocked drop ceiling. I smiled to myself, triumphant at making him laugh. Not that it was hard. Jack was sunshine, always smiling, always laughing. Being in his beam warmed me from the inside out.

"I can think of a few things that are better." He waggled his eyebrows at me, a move I'd always been jealous of. How dare he be handsome and kind *and* be able to move his face like that? Rude.

"Don't be lewd." I slapped his arm, and he threw an outrageous wink at me. Huh. That was new. His arm felt like a steel beam.

"You started it," he said.

"Don't make me finish it." My brow furrowed, my hand still on his bicep. His new-to-me hard-as-a-rock bicep. Clearing my throat, I removed my hand from his arm like I'd been burned.

What do I do with my hands? What are hands? Hands?

There was no good place to put them, so they dangled in front of me like jellyfish tentacles, floppy and weird and awkward in front of Jack, of all people.

Had he noticed how awkward I was? Or was I always this awkward?

Maybe I'll just stare at my blue toenail polish for the rest of eternity.

"Where's your girlfriend?" I gestured around the poorly lit convenience store, spotting cobwebs in one corner. "Here kitty, kitty, come out, come out."

Jack's girlfriends were all the same. Short, curvy, brunettes. The bigger the boobs, the better. The literal opposite of me. Flaming hair, though at least it had softened from the burnt orange of middle school into a more acceptable red. Luckily, I'd also grown into my long legs since then.

His girlfriends were knockouts. He'd had one who went by Kitty, and now they all did. According to me, anyway.

"Em, don't do that." He swatted my hand from where I'd perched it on my brow, standing on my tiptoes to look over the rows of canned and boxed food. "Let's get out of here. This place is... gross."

I scrunched up my nose. "Don't change the subject, Jack. Where is she?"

He shrugged. "She had to work."

"It's a holiday weekend." I squinted at him, waiting for the punchline.

"Her job is pretty serious."

"So it's just you and me." I stared at him, the enormity of that sinking in. The last time we'd been alone together for more than a couple hours... I could hardly remember it. We'd always had a buffer of a Kitty or one of my loser boyfriends or Lena or our parents or...

My heart skipped. Great. I needed to take care of myself. I was probably dehydrated from the Great Pee Event of the Century.

"And the cabin." The voice came from nowhere. Disembodied. Dry as gravel, sandpaper on rusted metal.

I screeched, my arm flailing out. A moldering box of Cheez-Its flew to the ground, skittering under the dusty face out.

Jack's hand flew across his mouth, his eyes squeezed shut. Probably trying not to laugh. I'd always startled easily. Didn't mean it was funny.

I glared at him, doing my best impression of our tenth grade English teacher when she'd catch us texting in class.

"Scared ya, didn't I?"

Slowly, I turned on my heel.

Grey was my first impression. Everything about the old man was faded, like an antique photograph that had been passed down for generations. Wrinkles completed the comparison, lining his face, an Etch-A-Sketch drawn by a demented toddler. A dozen grey wisps shot from his age-spotted baldpate.

"Y'all musbe the newcomers, yup." His watery grey eyes roamed over the two of us, and Jack stepped closer. "Musbe,

musbe, only city folks would be dumb enough ta stay all the way out there. In *that* house." He shook his head, a wad of chewing tobacco adding an additional hurdle to understanding his thick southern speech. "Mmhmm."

"Oh, okay." I edged away from the man. I was too close—the size of the wad of chewing tobacco meant I was still firmly placed in his splash zone.

His hand shot out, grasping my bare wrist. The strength of his grip surprised me. Jack took a step closer to the old man, his shoulders back. Small hairs at the back of my neck stood up.

I should shave them off. They drove me crazy, always curling when I wore my hair in a ponytail.

"We don't want any trouble." Jack raised his hands, waving them at the old man.

"What are you doing, directing air traffic?" I hissed at him. He abruptly stopped, narrowing his eyes at the question.

"Trouble, trouble. Tha's all y'all will be in for." The man shook his head, his eyes wide. They practically bugged out of his head, round and way too big for his face.

"Okay, well, sorry about the crackers, you know what? I'll buy them, okay?" I shot a glance at Jack, who side-eyed me.

The old man's hand finally retracted, and he muttered something under his breath.

"What?" I caught Jack shaking his head from the corner of my eye.

"I said, you young people these days. Millennials, all avocado toast and almond milk. What's wrong with cows, anyway?"

"Cows?" I echoed dumbly. A fluorescent light flickered again, and I blinked against it.

"No respect," he continued, ignoring the interruption. "I tol' her, I tol' her not to rent that damned cabin. I tol' her it wasn't fit for people. And now yer here," he paused, staring at me in disbelief, running his hand through the wisps on his head.

Ooooookay.

"Is there anyone I can call for you sir? Are you all right?" I asked, while Jack covered his face with his hands, still shaking his head.

"Nope. Jus' me, all by my lonesome. And you two. No one else for miles," he answered.

And that wasn't creepy at all. I pursed my lips.

The old man cast a meaningful look at the box I'd knocked off.

"How much do I owe you?" I fished around in my purse, pulling out a wadded five-dollar bill. At this point, I'd make it rain to get the Cheez-Its and get the hell out of there.

"Now you lissen, an' you lissen good. You got yerself a feller, an' they appreciate that, down there. But lissen."

I leaned forward, and Jack did, too. We could *listen* all we wanted, but that didn't mean we'd understand a word from his mouth.

"Can you, maybe, I don't know, I don't want to be rude—but could you maybe spit that out?" I pointed at his cheek, where the tobacco lodged. "I can't understand you."

His cheeks blew up like a bullfrog, and his mostly-bald head turned a shade of puce best left to designer runways and models paid to wear it.

"Y'all lissen, I said."

I clamped my mouth shut before I could tell him to get the eff on with it. Jack's hand was suddenly on my lower back. And just like that, POOF! My train of thought derailed completely.

"Things happen up at that property. People wanna have fun out there." He pranced around, sticking his chest out. "That place ain't for fun. That dog don't hunt, if you catch my drift."

Jack's hand was on my back, Jack's hand was on my back, Jack's hand...

"I said that dog don't hunt!" he rasped. "That's not what hunts up there." He leaned even closer, and his eye twitched like something was in it. Oh, he was winking. "If ya catch my meaning."

"Uh..." I did not, in fact, catch his meaning. And as weird as this situation was, the urge to laugh bubbled up in my chest. I didn't dare look at Jack. Laughing right now seemed like a recipe for disaster. I clamped down on my cheeks.

Jack took a firmer grip on me, his hand sliding around my waist, gripping me towards him. The urge to laugh died completely as heat spread through me at his possessive touch.

"I'm sorry, we're not going hunting." Jack's arm now urged me towards the door. "And we didn't bring a dog, so we'll just be going now."

"Take one of these." Hands shaking, he withdrew a small flashlight from his back pocket. The tobacco moved from one cheek to another. "It gets right dark out there, ya hear me? Never can be too careful."

"Aw, thank you so much, that's so sweet of you. Really." I flashed my best charming smile, the one I saved for performance reviews and first dates.

"Mmhmm. That'll be twenty dollars."

"Wait, what?" That smile always worked on old Jimmy at the restaurant.

Jack nudged me again, and I handed the old man the five fisted in my palm.

"Here." Jack shot me his patented *what-the-fuck* look before getting a crisp twenty from the money clip I'd given him for Christmas a decade ago. He still used it?

I swallowed, a new lump forming in my throat.

"I'll take some M&Ms, too." He grabbed the sharing size of almond M&Ms from a nearby hook, then pushed me out the door. I eyed it, suddenly starved. Sharing size my *ass*. I could down that bad boy in five minutes flat.

"Y'all best be right careful up there." His eyes bored into

mine, and my smile wavered. He was officially giving me the creeps. "Don't let them bedbugs bite."

"Thanks so much, okay, bye now," I managed, the Cheez-Its Jack shoved into my hands a shield between us.

Jack pushed me towards the door, and I looked over my shoulder at the old man.

"Bless yer hearts, y'all won't last a night." He gave a little wave, chuckling or coughing as he wiped the counter with a greasy rag.

The door swung shut behind us, a bell jangling merrily over the jamb.

"That guy was weird." Jack rubbed his temple, his dark eyes wild. His hand was still on my back, guiding me back to my car.

"Yeah, right? What's the point of cleaning if you're going to do it with filthy wipe? Totally didn't make sense." Yeah, okay he was weird, but I wasn't about to admit it out loud. I'd seen horror movies. I knew how that went. "He's harmless." I crossed my fingers behind my back.

"Are you kidding me? I know you've got a soft spot for grandpas, but come *on*, Em, he was a creep."

"He blessed our hearts."

"You know that's not a compliment, right?"

I shrugged, reaching for the car keys. "It's better than fuck you, you idiot."

"That's exactly what it means."

"Yeah, but he chose not to say it." I could hear his eyes roll. Didn't even need to turn around to look. My lips quirked up.

"What do you think he meant about the cabin?" I asked.

Jack's long legs meant he beat me to my car, and he opened the driver door so I could clamber in. *Just like he always did.* "I think he meant we're dumb city millennials and we shouldn't go hunting." He rubbed his temple, twisting his lips up to the side.

"Maybe," I answered, staring at the still flickering light inside the station.

The Cheez-Its deposited on the passenger seat, I stuck my keys in the ignition. The engine clicked, then sputtered.

"Shit."

"What?" The scent of Jack's signature evergreen body wash filled the car as he leaned over me, and he turned the keys.

I threw my hands in the air. "What, like it's going to start up for you and not me?"

He turned his head slightly, so that our faces nearly touched.

"Things get turned on around me. You'd be surprised." He gave an exaggerated wink, and for a moment, my heart stopped. I was going to die and haunt the gas station for an eternity. Heat crawled up my chest and to my cheeks.

"You're such a dork," I choked out.

The engine clicked, then sputtered, then died. Jack's face fell.

"Uh-huh. Tell me again about how things get turned on around you?" I shoved his arm. Damn. Had the dude spent every day in the gym? This was not the Jack-bod I was used to.

"All right." He checked his watch. "Get in my car. We'll come back when it's light tomorrow and deal with this. I'll drop you off at the cabin and you can stay there tonight."

"I'm not going back in there to tell that old man we're leaving it here." I hissed. "The whole gas station is giving me a serious case of the get-me-the-fuck-outta-heres."

"Uh-huh." He eyes narrowed as he appraised me. "I knew you were playing it cool. Once a scaredy cat, always a scaredy cat. Fine. Get in the Bronco. I'll lock it, and I'll be right back."

"Am not. Okay, I am. Fine." Despite the warm air, goosebumps pebbled my arms, and I hopped back out, practically sprinting towards Jack's truck. The sound of gravel crunching and the bell ringing told me Jack closed the distance to the store already. Damn his long legs.

Ah, the old Bronco. I climbed in, slamming the door behind me. The whole beast of a car smelled like him. He'd had it for a decade now, easily. Since right after we graduated high school. I ran my fingers over the dash, humming to myself, remembering all the time we'd spent in it.

Something swelled in my chest, and I swallowed again. He hadn't traded it in for a flashy Audi? Or a beemer? Whatever rich bros bought. I glanced at my Toyota. I wouldn't know. The dashboard shone, signs of a recent Armor-All spree. Not a speck of dust. Clean floorboards, new upholstery on the seats.

The engine roared to life, and my lips split into a grin. He tinkered with this thing like it was his baby. He must have installed remote start. Country music filled the cab. My shoulders relaxed.

Safe. I was safe here.

My stomach growled.

Shoulda grabbed the Cheez-Its.

I eyed the distance between my sedan and the Bronco. Not worth it. I might be safe in here, with some starry-eyed country singer perv crooning about checking his date for ticks, but no way was I getting back out of the car.

What the hell had that old dude meant? That dog don't hunt?

What dog?

A fist rapped on the window.

"Son of a bitch, Jack," I yelped.

He rewarded me with a smile, mouthing, "gotcha" through the glass.

I was still shaking my head when he landed in the driver's seat next to me.

"Well?" I pressed. "What did Methuselah say?"

"He wasn't in there. There wasn't anyone in there."

"Shut up." Fear, cold and primal, sluiced down my back.

He scratched his chin, staring at the run-down convenience store.

"What is it?" Dread spread through me, and I recognized the look on Jack's face. He was scared.

The beginnings of a grin twitching the corners of his mouth. "The old man was out back. He said it was fine."

A small growl escaped my throat. "I'm gonna get you back for that."

"I grabbed your Cheez-Its and your M&Ms."

He thrust the box into my lap. The bag of candy plopped on top of it.

"Your offering is accepted." I narrowed my eyes. "With extreme prejudice."

"That doesn't make sense, Em." His dimple appeared in his cheek, the one that only came out when he really thought something was funny.

"Sure it does. I am accepting the peace offering, but I also am retaining my prejudice against you. In an extreme manner." I pushed imaginary glasses up the bridge of my nose.

"Suit yourself." He threw an arm around the back of my chair, and I stiffened. His head turned, the tractor beam of his grin drawing me in. And that damn dimple, like a Death Star of temptation. I leaned into him for a second, inhaling his Jack-Axe smell. On anyone else, it would smell like bad teenage choices.

On him, it smelled like a sexy woodcutter dressed in a kilt and wielding a giant axe ready to deflower maidens. On second thought, maybe that wasn't an axe he was wielding.

Jack leaned closer, and my breath hitched.

Then he looked over his shoulder and put the car in reverse.

Oh. He was checking his blind spot.

Not checking me out.

6

———————

JACK

The Bronco shook. *Rumble strip, check.* Next to me, Em gripped the 'oh shit' bar, shooting me dirty looks.

"Sorry. Was thinking about something else." *And the lie detector test determined that was a lie!* What I was thinking about was about a foot away from me, brow furrowed, a skeptical look on her face. Carefully, I corrected the steering wheeling wheel.

The sky purpled, the last remnants of pink and gold disappearing behind the shaggy tree line.

"I can't believe you still wear that cologne."

The corner of my mouth crept up. I'd stopped off before getting on the highway and picked up a bottle.

"Same one you gave me for Christmas ten years ago." *Another lie.* And for what? To make her feel guilty? *Maybe it was.*

A soft punch landed on my bicep.

"You're such a liar."

Truth.

"You remember that Christmas?" I took my eyes off the

road, glancing over at her. She tucked a leg underneath her, holding one close to her chest. "Don't sit like that."

She rolled her eyes. "If you paid attention to where you're going, I could sit however I like. But noooo, can't get *comfy* because somebody might wreck."

We'd had this argument so many times. I shrugged. The white slashes on the road flew by, turning reflective in the headlights.

"Of course, I remember that Christmas. I gave you a bottle of deodorant and a pamphlet about puberty, and you gave me a pretty silver locket. You made me feel like a total asshole."

"You said it, not me." I snorted and was rewarded by another punch. Along the treeline, fireflies began flashing. "Nobody made you give me that. You made yourself the asshole, thank you very much."

Em shifted, drawing her arm away from the handle and hugging herself.

Damn it. That statement had landed. And not playfully, either. I'd hurt her. Again. God, with all her posturing, I forgot how sensitive she was.

I made a fist, stretching my hand before putting it back on the wheel. Not how I wanted this to go, dammit. I was going to talk her out of the property and we'd make amends. Period.

"Tell me about this place you've conned me into dropping you at." A quick glance told me Em's lips thinned. Pissed. Good. At least she could be mad at me instead of beating herself up over the past. We were both to blame. There was enough guilt to go around. Hell, we could fill the car with it.

"Yeah, yeah, 'poor Jack, always doing what Emma wants.'"

"How is it that you can still do Mr. Truman's voice perfectly?"

"Probably all those days in detention with him. *Emma*." She mimed writing on a chalkboard. "If you just used your brain for good instead of evil, you might just live up to your potential."

A chuckle started low in my chest, and a smile played around her lips before twisting into a grimace, as if the words of our old teacher hit home.

Potential. Em had it in spades. Had she ever seized it? Was that what this property was to her? I frowned.

"What are you doing for work now, anyways? It seems like something like this would require quite a bit of capital and time on your part." My mouth closed with a click, knuckles whitening on the wheel. Fucking wrong thing to say.

Business. It was the right thing to say for business. And if she didn't have the capital or time? All the better for me. Easier to say no. Which I was saying no matter what. And then I'd buy the property out from under her.

Pain lanced through my fingers, and I loosened my white-knuckle grip again. Watched her.

She hugged her arms to her chest, smaller, before arching an eyebrow and smiling bigger.

"Well, I landed a job at that boutique hotel we always used to walk by—"

"The historic one with the huge white columns and the badass bar?"

"Yeah." A small smile.

"Good for you, Em. I knew you could do it." She'd loved that place, talked my ear off about the architecture and history on more than one occasion. Pride, shocking and strong, surged through me.

"It was great." She beamed, even white teeth flashing in the dark. "I loved it. Loved meeting all the different people, being in the thick of downtown and managing the day to day, that place was like a piece of art." She paused, clicking the door lock into place. "But the owner sold. I've been at the restaurant, went home to help my parents after everything went south..." She trailed off, her forehead creasing. "How about you watch the road, seeing as how this place is full of suicidal deer." She nodded at the blur of four legged figures cropping grass on the side of the highway.

"Aw, look at Bambi." I snuck another glance at her. "And that's good. Good for you." She'd always tried to do right by her family and friends. That hadn't changed.

"Yeah. Good for me. Back at home, living with my parents. You're the one with the big-shot investment career, remember? Congrats on that, by the way. My ex was always begging me to hit you up with one of his latest business ideas." Bitterness laced her tone.

"Fuck him." The words came out stronger than I meant, and I rubbed at my mouth in surprise.

"Ha. Been there, done that." She shot me a sideways look, and I rubbed the stubble on my jawline. "And here I am, now, asking *you* for help."

She didn't have to even say it. I could hear it anyway. The silent *fuck you.* It was in the way her eyes narrowed, the drumming of her fingertips against her arm, the tightening of her jaw.

Why had I agreed to meet her?

This would be so much easier if she didn't know who would be buying out the property from under her. Although I hadn't known she'd be staying there until this morning. Didn't even know that was an option. My eyes wandered to my phone, to the texts she'd sent me. The owner had asked her to. I turned my attention back to the road, turning it over in my head, trees flying by as Alan Jackson crooned from the car speakers.

I'd agreed to meet her for the same reason I always did. Em called, and I came. I blew out a breath. Turned my head to glance at her.

And because intuition and experience told me that her staying at the old cabin was important to whomever held the deed. Probably had been in a family a long time, the seller probably wanted someone who would appreciate it. That would fit with what Robert told me. It wasn't unheard of.

Though much rarer these days.

The Bronco hit a pothole in the asphalt, and I flung an arm out to keep her from popping out of the seat.

Her skin was soft. My throat grew tight, and I grit my teeth.

Our eyes met. Hers were frustrated. Irritated. And so damn blue against the crimson fall of her wild curls.

I hoped mine didn't show what I was thinking. I'd gotten better at hiding, at lying, in the years we'd been apart. Maybe it would help me now.

Maybe I was screwed.

7

———

Night leeched the color from the tall pine trees around the cabin. I was here. Finally. A huge exhalation rocked my chest, and I hugged myself. This was it. My new beginning. If I closed one eye and tilted my head ever so slightly, the faint outline of the adorable cottage garden sort of slid into view. A mosquito buzzed, and I slapped my neck.

"Did you bring bug spray?" Jack carried my duffel on one shoulder, his own bag on his other shoulder.

Nope. Didn't want to tell him that, he'd just judge me for being unprepared.

"Let me carry that," I said instead. "You're not a pack mule." I motioned for the duffel, but he swatted my hand away.

"And let you sprain your bad ankle in the dark like you did senior year? No, thanks."

"Well, when you put it like that..." Hobbling around at graduation parties hadn't been a highlight of my high school experience.

"What's wrong?" The muscles of his back bunched as he turned to stare at my face.

"Nothing."

For a moment, Jack seemed like he might press the issue, his forehead furrowing in concern. But he didn't.

Hmmm.

A naked bulb swung from a four by four, the only light outside the cabin. Moths and insects swarmed it, casting weird shadows that stretched and shrank along the dirt path. Jack hustled out in front, making good time on his way to the cabin while I lagged behind. This place gave me the heebie-jeebies. It didn't look quite so creepy in all the pictures I'd spent so much time staring at.

"So excited for my long weekend alone at—" I glanced around. "—a murder cabin."

Crap. My excitement and sense of self-worth deflated faster than a day-old balloon. My hopes were all-in on this place, and it looked like the setting of a D-list horror film. At night. I swallowed again, my throat dry.

At least I wasn't blonde. Then I would definitely die. The blondes always were the first to go. I patted my hair, and Jack turned back to me.

"You sure about this? You could always see about booking a room at the B&B I'm at."

Yeah, and admit failure? Nope. This wouldn't be another dumb decision by Emma.

"I'm sure." Squaring my shoulders, I watched the bulb sway. Out by myself, middle of the woods, in a cabin of unknown origin. Oh, and without a car.

Impulsive, rash, stupid.

Check, check, checkity-check.

Wooden steps creaked under my feet, and I shivered as a cobweb brushed my cheeks. "Gross. If this place is nasty inside, maybe I *will* find a room with you."

And lose out on the potential discount the owner promised, but still. *Three nights, three days, sundown to sunup.* Hadn't seemed like much to ask at the time. Too good to be true. But now that I was here? It seemed a little weird. And a whole lot creepy.

"With me?" Jack asked.

"No, not *with you*, with you." *Ugh.* "Listen, the pictures online hadn't looked that bad..." But the quality of the photographer was more than questionable.

I swiped at my face, hoping I didn't now have a spider in residence in my hair. No way was I staying here if it resembled the inside of a dumpster. Or if there were knives as a main décor piece. Or a torture chamber. Or whatever.

"A torture chamber?"

I must've said the last part out loud. *Whoops.*

"It'll be fine. You said the owners left the keys under the flowerpot, right?" He foisted the bags off onto one of the rocking chairs dotting the oversize front porch. Bending over, he reached for a quaint little green frog with a red geranium growing out its back, lifting it up. How bad could it be, with a frog roomie?

Great, now I've jinxed myself.

"Yep, that's what she said." I laughed at my own joke, nearly choking on my spit as my eyes widened. His jeans showed off a newly sculpted butt. He'd always been fit, but this was next level. Near Jason Momoa Aquaman levels.

"Aha!" Triumphant, he dangled the keys in front of me.

I cut my eyes back to his face. Guilty.

"What's wrong?" He slid the keys into the lock, eyes on my face.

"Nothing." I patted my head innocently, making sure it was both web and spider free. *Nothing to see here. Not checking out your butt, why would I do that?*

"Really? Because it looked like you were staring at my... assets."

"You wish. I'm tired, and I'm hungry. I don't have the energy for this." My hands shot to my hips, and I stepped into the shadows, trying to hide the fact that my cheeks probably matched my hair.

"I don't keep snacks in there," he deadpanned, raising one eyebrow.

I snorted. I couldn't help it. Wait. *Was he flirting with me?*

The Jack I used to know would have been joking, making fun of me. But this Jack, this wasn't *my* Jack. No, this was corporate Jack, business dude on a day off.

"I cannot deal with you right now." Shaking my head, I pushed past him into the cabin. Fumbling in the darkness, my hand found the switch on the wall. I flipped it twice. Nothing. "Jaaaaack."

"What now?" He tugged the bags inside, depositing them on the hardwood floors.

"The lights aren't working."

His hand covered mine, and he jiggled the switch using my fingers. It was a simple movement, and yet—my stomach flipped. *Butterflies.*

Light flooded the room. Jesus, if I was blushing before... I cringed. I was probably ovulating or something. I'd have to check my period tracker.

That was the only reason I could think of that my body kept telling me to hop on top of Jack Colson and ride him into the sunset. Those treasonous reproductive urges, mmhmm.

"You look hangry, Em. I better get those snacks." His dimple flashed in his chin, and I tore my eyes from him. Snacks weren't gonna cut it. I had my mind on a whole damn meal.

"Wow. This place isn't half bad." The sad, deflated balloon in my chest took a hit of helium and soared back up.

A colorful geometric rug set off the light hardwood floors, a cognac leather couch flanked by two poofy white armchairs. A sleek fan whirred on the ceiling, providing a much welcome breeze.

"Yeah, it's not so 'murder cabin' in here, is it?" He squeezed my arm, then turned to head out the door. "Too bad there isn't a bar in town. We could go out, just like old times."

Like old times.

No. I had to cut that line of thinking out.

"Too bad your girlfriend couldn't make it. It's a great romantic weekend place, huh?" I slid my hand across the supple leather couch before plopping down on it.

He paused, a muscle in his back twitching through the thin v-neck tee he wore. "Yeah. Yeah. It is."

Guilt flooded over me, and I sprang up from the couch. He had a girlfriend. Sure, maybe there was chemistry between us, or at least, I thought he was hot, but he was taken.

The timing was wrong. As always. As it had been five years ago when I made an absolute ass of myself. I couldn't let my one-sided feelings get in the way of our friendship again. I'd missed him too much.

If having him as a friend meant dealing with the Kitty 7.0, then so be it. Jack was worth it.

Even if I did want to jump his bones.

"I'm gonna explore—"

"Be right back—"

We both laughed.

"Don't get lost, Em. There's two bedrooms, and I know how bad your sense of direction is."

"You know nothing, Jack Colson."

"Don't even get me started on *that* show." With a shake of his head, he stalked out the door, tension rife in his body.

Drifting into the small kitchen, I flipped another light switch. White cabinets, clean enough. An old turquoise fridge. I opened it, surprised to see it stocked.

"Not bad." Fresh deli meat, a few condiments, some fruit and juice. A bottle of cheap wine. She'd said the pantry would have some basics, but cooking wasn't exactly my thing. Like everything else my parents tried to teach me, I'd been shit at that too.

A folded note read "Enjoy your stay! Remember the discount!" complete with a poorly drawn smiley face. I squinted at it. Did it have horns? Was it a Pac-man ghost? Unclear.

Boxed wine didn't seem like a half bad idea. Rummaging around, I located two glasses and filled them to the brim.

"I see you found the good stuff." Jack leaned against the doorway, and I sipped off some excess before handing him a glass.

"Oh, yeah, nothing like a little Franzia to get turnt up."

"Did you just say what I think you said?" The corner of his mouth tugged up.

Butterflies. Every time he smiled.

"Turnt up on Franziaaaaaa!" I yelled, using my best WWE announcer voice.

"You are as ridiculous as always." He sipped his glass, screwing up his nose at the taste.

"And you're so fancy now you can't even drink the finest of all boxed wines?" I sniffed the glass, swirling the contents, "I detect notes of blackberry, finely macerated and mixed with wheat." I sniffed again. "A hint of gunpowder, old sweat, and stale socks."

Jack snorted. "Sounds about right." He raised his glass, and I clinked mine against his, preparing to down another gulp.

"I mean, it's no André Spumante, but it'll do the job."

He shot me a quizzical look, his handsome half smile lingering before he swallowed down more Franzia. He wiped the back of his hand over his mouth, and my knees went a bit weak.

"Okay, you ready to pitch me?"

My heart slammed into the wall of my chest. I plunked the wine down on the table, watching the burgundy contents wash across the inside of the glass. "Wait, now?"

"Are you *not* ready?"

I ran a hand over my mussed hair and took a deep breath. "I can be, but—" I gestured to the stale red wine. "—I wasn't planning to over wine. I wanted to do it right. Professional. Besides, you weren't even supposed to be here right now."

Jack snorted, swigging some more. "I'm kidding. We can do it tomorrow." *Do it?* Silence lengthened between us. I tried to look anywhere but at him.

"Your professional presentation, that is," he finally added, plucking the note off the counter. "What does this mean?"

I shrugged, nonchalant. Pretending my dreams didn't hinge on needing a massive discount to make them happen.

He raised an eyebrow.

"The owner said that she would be willing to, um, talk about a discount after I had an 'old fashioned' sit down and stayed three nights here." Gah. I *still* couldn't lie to him. I waved a hand at the living room. "Something about making sure I was the right buyer. Apparently, the place has been in her family for the last two centuries."

"Hmph." Ah, the good ole Jack grunt. And there was that look in his eye. Like a shark scenting blood in the water. I resisted a fist pump. He was interested? I *could* pull this off, convince him to invest, and spend our mutual money on refurbishing the hotel and make all my dreams come true and we would ride off into the sunset and—

"Wait." He pressed his fingers into my wrist, staying my hand. His voice was low, serious. "Do you hear something?"

A thrill of adrenaline raced through me, and I scooted closer. The weirdness of the gas station attendant hadn't worn off yet. Not to mention the suicidal deer before that. Definitely regular adrenaline, and not just my overactive sex drive.

"That's the sound of our livers slowly dying, thanks to this crap." He raised an eyebrow at me, and I rolled my eyes.

"Don't scare me like that." I raised my glass again, and he held up a hand, stopping me.

"A toast." He tilted his chin down at me. "A toast to old friends and new relationships."

My heart sank. That did it. He must be pretty serious about Kitty 7.0.

I raised my face to his, matching his grin with a fake one of my own.

"I'll drink to that."

And I did. I drained the whole glass.

8

———————

JACK

Em guzzled her wine, eyes closed, lips firmly around the rim. Her slender throat moved as she swallowed, and I pulled my eyes away before drinking more of mine. Toasting to new relationships was a mistake. Clearly, I'd rattled her.

Another sign she wasn't ready to tackle a project like this. Talking her out of taking on this property was already half in the bag. She'd do what she always did, knot the rope and then plop it around her neck with a devil-may-care-smile as her long fingers tightened it.

On the wall, a black and white cat clock ticked, its eyes and tail swinging in tandem. Right, left, right, left. The eyes stopped on my face for a beat before going back to swishing. My jaw dropped, hairs raising on the back of my neck.

What the fuck?

I scrubbed a hand over my face, feeling the beginnings of a headache. Must be more tired than I thought. Just in case, I held the glass up to the harsh fluorescent kitchen light and swirled the remnants of the wine.

"Oh, come on, Jack. It's not that bad." Em snorted, emptying more wine into her glass.

"No, it's not, I just thought I saw..." I shook my head. "Never mind."

"When do you need to check in to the other B&B?"

My eyebrow arched. The way she said *other*, like she had this whole thing in the bag and was only waiting on guests to book. She had the right attitude, at least.

"Latest I can check in is eight, I've got a couple hours at least." Wincing, I polished off the rest. Em settled back against the counter, her gaze steady on me. Wine. I tugged the black spout. Deep red liquid streamed into the glass.

"You still really into beer?" Em's hair streamed over one shoulder, soft and silky.

"You remember that, huh?"

"Hard not to, seeing as how you made me try every variety you came up with." She sipped her glass, the red staining her full mouth.

I tapped a finger on my jaw, as one corner of my mouth curled up into a half-smile. "I don't recall you lodging many complaints."

"They were good." She smiled up at me, hazel eyes wide, and my heart sped up. "Most of the time. I bet they're even better now."

Was that pride in her voice? I smoothed a hand across the countertops, relieved to find it clean. This cabin really wasn't a bad little set-up.

"I haven't had the time like I used to. Work keeps me busy." I tilted my head, looking out the window. Darkness stole across the landscape, the lingering fingers of light giving up their embrace. Late-season cicadas filled the evening air with their plaintive songs.

"But you loved that." Her shoulders lifted, and my mouth went dry. *Keep your eyes straight ahead. Don't look at her boobs.* They were great boobs. "I always thought you'd end up owning a huge brewing company. You know, make the most of your degree, but also do something that makes you happy. Isn't Aiden a head brewer now, somewhere in Deep Ellum?" Her nose crinkled as she pursed her lips, and I glanced back at the clock. Who was she, to sound disappointed in me? To judge?

It stung.

"Yeah, well, things like making a living and being successful must've gotten in the way. What are you up to, anyway? Living the dream?"

"*This* is my dream." She swallowed. Turning away from me, she refilled up her glass. "Things were hard after the economic crash. Theo, my boss—he sold to a big hotel chain. He fought for me, but they brought in one of their own, and I lost my job..." A freckled hand reached up to push hair from her face, her hazel eyes pinning me. "I've been helping my parents out at their restaurant, and saving money, waiting for this. For the time to be right." Defiant, she stuck one hand on her hip, as though daring me to say something about it.

At a loss, I sipped my wine. Her body nearly vibrated with defensiveness, a taut line stretching from her neck to the graceful slope of her shoulder. When Emma set her mind to something, she went in, guns blazing. The problem was her short attention span.

Still, if she was dead set on this, if I couldn't talk her out of the hotel—could I truly overbid her and buy this place?

For partner? Yes.

She cleared her throat, then arched away from the counter, piling her wild hair on top of her head and securing it with the ever-present rubber band she wore on her wrist. "Wanna make a bet?"

"Uh-oh. That depends." I dragged my eyes away from her

hourglass figure, focusing on the weird cat clock instead. I couldn't shake the feeling that it was watching more than the passage of time. *Probably needed batteries.*

"If I beat you at Scrabble, you have to buy dinner tomorrow. If I win, it's my treat."

"You brought Scrabble with you?"

"Like I'd come on a trip with you without it. Remember that time you literally ran laps around the table after you beat me and Lena?"

"Ha, yeah, and then you two threw conspired to throw your Sonic slushies at my face? Ruined my favorite shirt."

"Taught you a lesson, though." She sashayed from the kitchen, and it was all I could do not to stare at the curves under her jeans. Fuck. Who was I to think I could come out here with her, with my Emma, and not land right back under her spell?

"What, that you two are shit spellers and complete cheaters?" Grabbing my glass, I followed her to the living room, where she dug through her duffel before tugging out a rattling game board.

"Are you going to bitch and moan all night, or are you up to a challenge, Jack?"

Moan all night.

The words caught fire in my brain, and I sank onto the couch. Too much wine. I needed to slow down.

Too much wine, and too long had I wondered what it would be like to make Emma moan all night.

"Since it's age before beauty, I'll let you go first." She winked, crossing her legs and settling on the floor. In one hand, she shook the bag of letter tiles, in the other, red wine sloshed against the side of the glass, coating the sides like blood. She tossed the bag, and I caught it in one hand.

"Fine," I managed, my voice husky.

"Aha, so you *do* admit I'm the prettier one."

"You've always been the prettiest thing I've ever seen." My fingers tightened on the velvet pouch, and I withdrew the requisite seven tiles before tossing it back to her. "Is that a Crown Royal bag?"

"Desperate times." Em shrugged again, a frown flashing across her face.

I wanted to scrub that look from her face, wanted to bask in her chaotic sunshine until I was burned by it. My throat tightened, and I squeezed my eyes shut before I finally managed to focus on the letters I'd drawn.

C, A... I blinked. Had I *ever* felt like this around Caroline? We had five years of nothing gaping between us, and then here Em was, setting me on fire like always. And me, acting the fool over her again. Well, it would be different this time.

Because I planned to take her dream away. *Tit for tat.*

Across the table, she worried her lower lip, still stained crimson from the Franzia. Drawing attention to the perfect dip in it.

I drank again, deeply, trying not to imagine what it would be like to finally kiss them. To think, I imagined I would be awkwardly reliving some of the worst moments of my life, thanks to Em, when it was the same as always with her.

Familiar. Easy. *Perfect*.

"What, did you forget how to spell?" She arched an eyebrow and pointed to the sand running out. "Looks like you've got about a minute to figure it out, big boy."

"Big boy? That's the best trash talking you've got?" I snorted, shaken. I *couldn't* kiss her.

She swigged her drink, a thoughtful cast to her eyes. Sighing, I looked back to my board. I'd also picked out a J, I, and an L. Perfect. I mixed up the letters, added up the points and laid them on the board.

"If memory serves, first play gets double points, yeah?" I

grinned at her, then let out a laugh. "So that's twenty-two, suck it."

I swallowed. *Suck it* was a poor choice. It had me... imagining. The leather couch creaked as I shifted.

Her eyes widened as she took in my word. Her throat bobbed. "Is that supposed to be funny? 'Jail'?"

"What? Me kicking your ass? I mean, it's kind of funny." But she didn't seem mad... she seemed hurt, her forehead wrinkling slightly, lips pouting.

Realization dawned.

"Oh, shit, Em, I didn't mean anything by it. It's just a game. I'll play a different word."

"No, no, of course, I get it." She rocked backward. Putting distance between us. "You know what, I think I had too much wine. I'm going to turn in early. Be safe getting to the B&B, I'll lock up after you."

"Em—"

But she was already on her feet, draining the glass dry. God, I was an idiot. *Of course,* she'd reacted like that. Em never got over what she'd done our senior year, that stupid mistake that cost her college scholarship.

Because of a stupid dare from me. Breaking and entering into that old house was supposed to be a funny one-off, not end in a night in... jail. I winced. Not force her to stay back at home, going to community college on her parent's dime, doing hours of community service, before taking out student loans and coming to Austin. With me.

Disappointment warred with familiar shame, and I rubbed the stubble on my face. Quietly, I set my half empty cup on the coffee table, staring at the word spelled across the board. The sound of rushing water spilled out of the kitchen, before the faucet squeaked off.

Time to leave.

I pushed off the couch, moving on autopilot, letting the

door crash shut after me. A quick look at the jamb affirmed it needed to be re-hung. One more thing she'd have to fix, if she bought the place.

My hands fisted at my sides, and I cleared the front porch steps two at a time. Emma Cross wasn't going to fix up the place, because *she* wasn't buying the goddamn place. The deal would close after I undercut her bid, and then we'd raze the cozy little cabin to the ground. I would make partner, buy my shiny new sports car.

My stomach cramped. *Must be the wine.*

Or guilt. Who knew?

"Not me." The words tumbled out, surprising me. Shit. Maybe I shouldn't drive. It was dark as hell, and by the sound, the mosquitoes buzzing around my head must have been the size of Thanksgiving turkeys. The mosquitoes wanted me here, even if Emma didn't. She'd made that abundantly clear.

Another sound caught my attention, and I slowed, then stopped.

Skritch, skritch.

An inhalation caught in my chest, and somehow, I choked on spit. Coughing and sputtering, I beat a fist against my chest.

Lamp-like yellow eyes beamed from underneath the Bronco.

"*Son of a bitch.*"

Behind me, the door of the house slammed open. But I wasn't about to look away from the threat.

"You okay?" Emma's voice was rough. I didn't have to turn around to know she'd been crying, didn't have to recover the five lost years between us to know she was upset.

Then she sniffled. The glowing eyes turned towards the house.

"It's fine, everything's fine."

"Is that why you screamed?"

I kept my eyes on the threat, my body between it and

Emma. "It wasn't a scream. It was an exclamation." Soft footfalls sounded behind me, and I reached my arm out, motioning for her to go back inside. "Stop. There's something under the truck."

"Oooh," she breathed, crouching down, her head even with the side of my hips. A flashlight clicked on, and the high beam caught a flash of grey and black, before the fattest raccoon I'd ever seen jetted towards the woods. "Really scary."

"It surprised me."

"Don't worry, Jack, I'll keep watch, in case he comes back for more." Her hand patted my shoulder, the flashlight sweeping over the ground near my truck.

My name never sounded better than it did when it came from her lips.

Rolling my eyes, I fished the keys out of my pocket and climbed in.

"Want me to check the back for any stowaway forest creatures? I hear they like it when you sing to them, I could coax them out and make some new animal friends. Heeeere, roomy, roomy, roomies!"

"Is that right?" I muttered.

I turned the key. Nothing. Outside the car, Em started singing, presumably to lure more skulking vermin from their nighttime romps. I rolled my eyes, turned the key again.

Déjà vu.

I rested my head against the worn leather steering wheel. What were the odds of both of our cars shitting out on us in one day? Grimacing, I turned the key again. Nothing. "You've got to be kidding me. Come on, baby, I *just* took you to the shop."

Em stopped crooning. Too bad, she might have actually scared our nocturnal visitors away.

"What did you call me?"

Tension rocked my body. "Just talking to the car. It won't start."

New battery, fresh oil, nothing but normal maintenance on it. What the hell was going on with my truck?

"Fuck it." With one last sideways look at the ignition, I grabbed my suitcase from the back seat and hopped out. "Looks like I'll be staying tonight, Em. If it's all right with you, of course."

In the dark, I couldn't make out her response. A moment later, a quiet "okay" slipped from her lips.

"Hey, I'm sorry about…"

"No, don't apologize. Don't worry, I know better than everyone that I'm overly dramatic. You didn't mean anything by it. Come on, let's get inside before we get eaten alive by bugs."

"What are you talking about?" *She knew she could be dramatic? What asshole convinced her of that?* "You aren't *dramatic*. Most of the time. If anyone should know why you're sensitive about that, it's me, Em." Suddenly, nothing was more important than making her understand. "It's me."

She stepped closer, the flashlight bobbing across the ground.

I enveloped her in my arms, squeezing her to me, close enough to feel the ragged sob rip through her. "That was some bullshit. All of it. You know how I feel about it."

It was true. I might not be sure how I felt about Emma, especially not since we'd parted ways in a shitshow of such epic proportions, but I sure as hell knew she'd taken the fall for a lot of us that night.

9

EMMA

Everything about the bedroom was normal. Clean, comfortable, nothing fancy. White linens, white curtains, a couple odd pictures on the walls. Clean was all I cared about, at this point. My mouth already felt like sawdust, courtesy of the awful wine we'd both powered through. Raw, my eyelids were sandpaper on my face after my impromptu cry sesh on Jack's shoulder.

Yeah, not dramatic at all.

But the wine and cry and *another* glass of wine had done their job, and I sank into the bed with a solid buzz and a devil-may-care attitude. The room was dark, the fan was on, and I was half asleep as soon as my head hit the pillow.

Skritch, skritch, skritch.

I sat bolt upright, banging my forehead on the brass bedstead on the way up.

What the fuck was that?

I froze. Listening. Waiting. The uncanny feeling of being

watched slipped over my skin, making it crawl, my hair standing on end.

This shit always happened to me. It drove everyone crazy. Every little sound turned into a ridiculous capital-e Event. Poor Jack had seen more than his fair share of meltdowns in his time. A lovable quirk, he'd said, laughing so hard tears streamed down his cheek when he found out a malfunctioning alarm clock had scared me.

I'd sworn off watching horror movies in college. I was jumpy enough as it was. I didn't need to give my brain anymore nightmare fuel. I threw the covers over my head. My breath boomed out of me under the acoustic shelter of the quilt, my heart ratcheting up in my eardrums. Plus it was too dark, and completely stifling.

I peeked out.

Probably an animal, just hanging out in the murder cabin. Heck, I'd already serenaded a racoon, for crying out loud. A chill ran over me, and the hair on my arms stood up.

Shouldn't have thought about a murder cabin.

Skritch, skritch, skritch.

I slapped a hand over my mouth to keep from crying out. The sound wasn't coming from the yard. If it had been outside, I could've ignored it. Probably.

Whatever made the sound was *inside*.

I would *not* wake up Jack for this. I was a grown woman. I could handle my shit.

"I took a self-defense class in college," I told the noise. *Yeah!* "I'm not afraid to beat you to *death* and poke your eyeballs right out!"

Ew. Maybe a bit too far.

From under the warm nest of blankets, it was hard to tell if my very serious death threat had made an impact.

Skritch, skritch, skriiiiiitch.

My heart thudded in my chest, caged by bones that any self-respecting monster could snap in two with no more effort than it took me to swat a fly.

Then again, who said swatting flies was easy? Those assholes were fast.

I swallowed, tossing the blankets aside. A breeze from the fan swirling overhead cooled my exposed skin, sending fresh goosebumps down my arms.

"You better get ready," I muttered, eyeing the nightstand. "I was forced to play intramural softball at work one year. Everyone said I was a menace!" And I could definitely hit an object bigger than a softball, though I hadn't had much luck hitting those at all.

The lamp.

It would be a great weapon. One of those old school brass deals, a little too matchy-match with the bed for my tastes. Surely the owner wouldn't mind if it picked up a few dents in its newfound life as a brutal weapon. One tug and it was unplugged, a satisfying weight in my hands.

My feet slicked over the wooden floorboards, and I half-crouched, feeling my way along the wall in the dark.

The noise was louder now, frantic even.

Underfoot, a floorboard creaked.

The noise stopped.

I took another step, white knuckling the heavy lamp.

I swallowed again, though my mouth was ridiculously dry.

Another step.

The closet door loomed ahead, a creamy white barrier to whatever eldritch asshole was keeping me awake. Black tentacles filled my imagination, curling out of the door. Why, *why* did I think that?

I shook my head, like that would somehow reset it to pre-Cthulu fear levels.

Skriiiiiitch. Skritch-skritch.

My hand closed over the brass knob, cold and heavy under

my fingers. A loud exhalation ripped from my lips, and I clenched my teeth, raising the lamp overhead.

It was colder near the door, and a fresh chill washed over me.

No sooner than I turned the knob than the door swung open. Heart in my mouth, eyes wide, I jumped out of the way, bracing the lamp overhead and bringing it down with a resounding shatter. In the dark, all I could see was a small, pale moon of a face.

"Fuck you, fuck you very *much*," I screamed, raising the lamp again. Arching my back, I swung it overhead, but it stuck.

"What the hell, Em?" Jack's bleary voice cut through my adrenaline-fueled rage. Holding the lamp in one hand, he reached out with the other, flicking the light switch on. "What is going on?"

In front of me, something vaguely human-like lay across the floor, curly hair spilling out towards me.

Yelping, I pushed back into Jack. I did not want that hair on my toes or any other part of my body. His chest was warm and hard, and I pressed into it, letting the lamp go.

"I heard a noise." My voice was scratchy and raw, and I cleared my throat, trying to swallow the lump in it.

"Of course, you heard a noise, Em, we're out in the woods. What does that have to do with this?" He gestured to the shape on the floor, one eyebrow practically disappearing into his hairline.

Placing the lamp on the bed, he stepped out from around me, crouching and picking up the object on the floor.

"It's a doll." He gripped its neck with one hand, showing me the perfect porcelain face, fake eyelids blinking with each movement.

"It was making a noise—in the closet—I swear." The doll's head bobbed as he picked it up. One eyelid closed slowly, then reopened. "It just winked at me."

Jack just stared. "Did you have more wine when I wasn't looking?"

And I'd smashed its head. I knew I had. "I heard it shatter."

Jack's gaze slid back to me. "You broke the bulb in the lamp. See?"

Tiny shards of glass glittered on the wood floor.

"Oh."

"We're in a cabin way out in the middle of nowhere, and if you didn't notice, there's a huge crawl space under here. It's not built on concrete like the houses you're used to. All kinds of creatures can get under the floor and hang out and make babies."

"It wasn't something making *babies*, Jack." I gestured to the doll, its deep pink lips parted in a rosebud smile. "I heard *that*. And the closet door opened on its own."

Jack sighed, putting on his patented '*I'm listening but I don't believe you*' face.

"Em, I know you're tired. I know you're stressed. And *trust* me, I know how easy you scare. But there's a reason for this." He shifted on his feet, eyebrows arched, as the floor creaked beneath him. "It's an old house. It's gonna have quirks. I bet you stepped in just the right spot to loosen the latch. Come on, it's late."

In his hand, the doll's eyes blinked again, her glassy stare frozen on my face.

"Put Lucy on the bed."

"Lucy?" Jack scratched the back of his neck. I must've woken him up with my screeching, he hadn't even thrown on a t-shirt. Just boxers. Green and black plaid boxers, to be specific. I tried to keep my gaze on his eyes. Firmly north of the six-pack south. Danger lay down south, that's for sure.

"Earth to Em," Jack said slowly, waving a hand in front of my face.

"Lucy." Yep, nothing to see here. *I wasn't just checking out your hot bod.* "Yeah. She needs a name. Put her on the bed."

Shaking his head, Jack put the doll on the bed, where she lay, still and inanimate. Most definitely inanimate. Not creepy at all.

Four-foot lifelike dolls with blinking eyelids were absolutely not creepy and totally normal. Totally a cool thing to have your kid play with, every girl and boy should have a demon doll of their own.

"Now what?" Jack stared at me, hands on his hips, lips pursed. Irritated.

"I'm not sleeping in here." It burst out of me before I had time to think about it. "It's Lucy's room, she can keep it."

"Fine." Jack shrugged, a bemused smile on his face. I tried to focus on the smile and not on the interesting things his pecs did when he shrugged. On the bed, Lucy just stared. A silky curl slipped over her cheek. "I'll sleep on the couch."

I swallowed again. My throat was going to crack if I kept trying to do that. My fingers and toes tingled, the after-effects of adrenaline still working through my system.

"Come on, let's get some sleep." His fingers clasped around my wrist, and he tugged me out of the room.

Lucy didn't even blink, staring at the ceiling, silent and still, hair splayed around her as the door closed.

"Did I hear you tell that doll you'd beat it to death and that you'd taken self-defense?" He bit his cheeks, his nostrils flaring as he bit back a laugh.

"Shut *up*." My cheeks burned.

He mimed zipping his lips, throwing the key away, but his dimple gave him away. I sighed, leaning into him slightly.

"Sorry. I didn't mean to wake you."

"Hey, what kind of friend would I be if I let you beat down an unidentified doll threat by yourself?"

A *friend*. A friend I had no business looking at like he was a hunk of man meat ready to be jumped. I inhaled, closing my eyes.

My former best friend. Potential business partner. Someone else's boyfriend.

Taken, taken, taken.

10

JACK

The door to the bedroom—the bedroom I no longer would be occupying—closed behind me. Em's bedroom now. She was probably half asleep already, all soft skin and bare legs tangling in the sheets of the bed I'd already warmed.

I closed my eyes, inhaling deeply. Pushing the thought of her *now* back, swallowing it.

Demon doll.

A laugh threatened to careen from my throat, and I stifled it, nearly shaking with laughter. Sure, the doll was weird as hell, but certainly not possessed. There was a perfectly logical explanation for the noises she heard, and it wasn't from some random, antique doll.

I'd missed it at first, the remnants of alcohol still clouding my brain. Yeah, that was it. The alcohol. Definitely not thoughts of Em in bed.

Skritch, skritch, skriiiitch.

Hair on the back of my neck stood up, and then I shook

myself. No reason to let Em's paranoia get the better of me too. Or her drunkenness.

Skritch. Skritch-skritch.

I paused. Definitely an animal of some kind, probably trapped under the old crawl space of the house. Or like I'd told Em, getting busy, making babies.

At least *something* was getting busy. I cast another look at Em's closed door.

Fuck it. I was awake anyway. At this rate, I wasn't going to get any sleep until the noise stopped. The floorboards of the old house creaked under my feet. My shoes were by the front door where I'd left them. The flashlight the old man at the run-down gas station forced on us sat heavy on the kitchen counter, glossy finish gleaming in the dull light. Compared to the rest of the house, the kitchen was downright freezing, cold spots all over the place.

I shook my head, squinting at the vent on the ceiling. Someone spent some time refurbishing the place, but the damn AC still didn't work quite right. I wouldn't want to be here in the dead heat of a Texas summer or the middle of winter, that was for damn sure.

Skriiiiiitch.

I squared my shoulders.

What's the worst that could happen?

The little logical voice that came in so handy during my day to day of deal-making enumerated several points:

1. It's dark as hell outside.
2. You could fall and hurt yourself; see point 1.
3. If it is an animal, it could be rabid.
4. If Em is right, and it's not an animal, a heavy flashlight and your ego aren't going to do much against it.
5. It's most likely an animal.

Skritch-skritch-skritch.

"That's fucking *it*," I muttered, throwing open the front door. The absolute last thing I wanted was for Em to wake up again, she clearly needed some sleep. After working like crazy for her cuckoo parents and walking in on her boyfriend screwing some other girl... ex-boyfriend. *That asshole.* She spilled the reason behind their split after another glass of wine on the couch, before we both decided we needed sleep.

My hands clenched, the steel flashlight a comforting weight in one, the other balled into a fist. I stepped outside, letting my eyes adjust to the pitch black before flicking the flashlight on. The night air was remarkably cool, proving being out of the city did, indeed, have its benefits. Along with the vermin active under the house, that was.

Not under the house for long.

I depressed the button and swept the high beam of the flashlight across the latticed crawl space, white paint flaking in places, mildewed green where it met the dirt and mulch.

Shoulda put on jeans. Too late now.

I stepped around the corner of the house, to the window that faced out from Em's original bedroom, now inhabited by the porcelain doll. I shivered. Bizarrely cold outside, even for a September night. Especially for September in Texas, where it wouldn't normally turn wintry until the last week of December, and even then it would be a plaintive sigh, the sun finally unclenching its grip on the state. Mulch crunched underfoot.

At least I'd been smart enough to put shoes on.

"Aha." There it was, the small hinged section that would allow me access to see what the hell was under the house.

Skritch, skritch, skriiiiitch.

"All right, furry dudes, it's time to haul off for the night and go curl up in a tree or something," I coaxed, opening the small gate and dropping to hands and knees, then stomach. The bright beam of the flashlight illuminated an amalgamation of garbage and dead leaves, a few random shiny things reflecting. I crawled forward as far as the small opening would allow. Which meant only my flashlight arm and my head was under the house. I squinted, finally sighting ratty, chewed up cardboard. A nest.

A familiar pair of glowing eyes winked to life.

"Son of a bitch." My head smashed into the top of the crawlspace.

The eyes moved, blinking open again less than a foot in front of my idiotic face. The raccoon hissed, baring small yellow-white teeth, then chittered, clearing cussing me out in trash panda.

My ass couldn't haul out fast enough. The ragged edge of the crap lattice work caught the edge of my t-shirt, ripping it as I squeezed back out, covered in dirt and moldy leaves and probably animal shit.

Thank God Em wasn't here to see this.

Demon doll murder cabin my butt, rabid raccoon was the clear culprit. Solved it. The Hardy Boys didn't have shit on me.

Maybe shit on me wasn't the right term, considering I was probably covered in raccoon scat now. I sat back on my calves, brushing my hands off on my pants, flashlight abandoned on the ground, generally congratulating myself on a job half done when the damned animal rushed me, snarling and hissing.

I leaped. Michael Jordan would be jealous of the vertical I achieved.

"Fucking *hell!*"

Crossfit be damned, raccoon Olympics sent me higher than I thought possible. The animal chittered, weird tiny hands clasped together as it watched, a happy little bandit.

I stepped back, and the raccoon went to all fours, bunching its body like a cat.

Could raccoons jump?

I didn't want to find out.

"Yeah, and stop making that racket," I told it, backing away slowly.

It huffed, tail twitching, and hissed one last time, clearly unperturbed, before waddling its furry ass back into the crawl space.

"Well, that went well," I said to the night air.

Skritch, skritch.

I knew what I was doing tomorrow. And this time, I'd wear jeans.

11

———

Had I eaten garbage the night before? It certainly tasted like it. I licked my dry, cracked lips.

Not garbage. Cheez-its and Franzia, my brain reminded me.

A strand of hair glued itself to my cheek, and I peeled it off, failing in my attempt to smooth it back. Golden yellow sunshine dripped through the blinds, coloring the room in the soft light of morning. I smoothed my hand over the cotton quilt, its deep reds and royal blues oddly comforting.

Unlike last night. I closed my eyes again. Maybe if I squeezed them hard enough, last night would be erased. I opened my eyes.

Nope. Still there.

I *had* heard something. It *had* been colder towards the closet door, and I may not watch horror movies anymore, but I'd seen enough to know that meant one thing. *Ghosts.* The door swung open, and I bolted upright, heart hammering.

Jack.

My back sagged against the headboard, and I rubbed the bridge of my nose.

He was still clad in only boxer shorts, another quilt wrapped around his chest.

"Good morning, doll killer."

"Ugh."

"I started coffee."

I perked up, inhaling. Ahhhh, yes, the indisputable aroma of coffee drifted towards me.

"My hero."

Jack rubbed the back of his neck, rewarding me with a small smile. And a muscular bicep.

"I'm thirsty," I blurted. *What the fuck?* I hadn't meant to say that.

"I bet, after drinking like a freshman rushing a frat." He stood there, staring at me, and heat rose across my chest.

I stared back. The morning light glanced off the sliver of exposed abs, the boxers showing off thighs well-muscled from years of playing soccer. Soccer games I'd gone to without fail, rain, snow, or shine. He was *my* best friend. Mine.

Regardless of how much I'd messed up, and he'd messed up, and the timing had been wrong, and all the crap that nearly broke us four years ago—

I wanted him. Not just his body, though I wanted that, for sure. The sooner the better. But no. I wanted *him*.

It was a revelation. It hit me like a ton of bricks, falling straight out of the sky and onto my inordinately thick skull. *Screw Kitty 7.0.* My eyes were wide open, and a blush crept into my cheeks. I chewed my lip. What was I supposed to do with this?

Ruin another relationship of his?

Again?

Jack stood there, crossing his arms across his chest.

Watching me. Waiting. Waiting for me. He'd always been waiting for me.

"Are you waiting for me?" It slipped out. I hadn't meant to say it, and yet, I couldn't look away.

He cocked his head at me. "Well, yeah. I need to get dressed."

"Oh, oh. Of course. Uh..." I shucked the covers off, sliding out of bed. "Yeah, me, too."

"Em!" Jack's jaw dropped, and I stopped. He sucked in a breath, eyes raking over me, before turning around.

I glanced down. I must've taken my shorts off in the night. From the waist up, I was fine. Old raggedy t-shirt, slipping off one shoulder. A long t-shirt. Not long enough. It stopped right at my ass.

"What, Jack? I have underwear on. I'm more covered than a swimsuit."

"Out." His back tensed. It wasn't a bad look. Very 'Fireman of the Week' calendar.

I shrugged, and the shirt slipped further off my shoulder. Not that he could see it, with his broad back to me. "Sorry, I didn't realize..."

He was with someone else. *Again.*

"Meet you in the kitchen, fully clothed. For coffee." I slipped past him, so close I could feel the heat emanating from his body, smell the faint scent of his body wash. My stomach grumbled. "And then we're going into town to get groceries."

"Deal." His voice sounded strained. I resisted the urge to sneak a peek at him, instead, I placed one foot in front of the other until they took me to the bedroom I'd started the night in. Jack's door shut behind me, and I slumped forward, leaning my head against the wall.

What the heck was I going to do?

I opened my eyes, taking in the sight of my bare legs. At least I'd shaved recently.

Well whatever I was going to do, I needed to put pants on.

Unless we did *it*. But *it* wasn't gonna happen.

I opened the door, refusing to let the possessed doll scare me in the light of morning.

"Hi, Lucy. Hey, girl, don't mind me. Just need to get some pants on." I forced myself to make eye contact with the porcelain doll reclining on the rumpled bed. Her eyelashes fluttered, and I nearly wet myself.

The fan.

They were moving because of the fan. Not because she was a demon doll out to butcher us in our sleep. Obviously.

That would just be silly.

"Anyway, hope you slept good," I prattled, my voice high-pitched and squeaky. I needed to get a grip. Get a grip. *Uh-huh.* My navy duffle sat right where I'd dumped it last night, carefully folded contents on full display.

"I'm uh, gonna change somewhere else. Give you some privacy. Bye now." I tugged the duffle, a blast of cold air buffeting my hair back. I backed out the still open door, keeping my eyes on the still doll on the bed.

And ran ass-first into Jack.

"Come on, Emma. Put some damn pants on," his voice rasped out, and he coughed twice, as though trying to clear it.

"I can't change in there, she's still sleeping. I don't wanna piss her off." I held the duffel over my lower parts, and the bedroom door slammed shut behind me.

"Her?" He stared at me, confused. "Are you talking about the doll?"

"Um..."

Jack laughed, a burst of noise that had me smiling at the warmth of it. "That's a little weird, even for you. But whatever floats your boat."

Even for me? I shrugged, walking sideways into the tiny,

shared bathroom. That hurt. Reminded me of Dan. *Always a bit much*. But Jack wasn't Dan.

"*You're* the one being weird. You've seen me *sans* pants before." A wicked part of me wondered what he'd do if I dropped the duffel and flashed him.

His nostrils flared again, then he threw up his hands and stormed off, floor creaking underfoot.

"By the way," I called after him, unable to resist firing a parting shot, "I'm fresh out of scuba suits if you're wanting to go swimming later. You'll have to figure out how to deal with my bare legs sooner or later."

The only answer was the sound of irritated rummaging from the kitchen.

The white door snicked shut behind me, the itsy-bitsy bathroom as bare bones as they came. White and black penny round tiles set off a brand-new toilet, a sticker still on the tank. The sink looked to be built for visiting gnomes, so small there was barely room for the faucet and handles.

Certainly not room for my makeup and all the other crap I'd lugged with me. Why'd I bring the damn makeup anyway?

There wasn't any reason to *wear* makeup all the way out here.

My stomach roiled, and I gripped the edge of the white porcelain sink, staring at my reflection in the mirror. Some subconscious part of me must have known. Known I'd been hiding my feelings for him, and yet, here they were, all the feelings ready to explode out of me in a torrent of self-sabotaging sexy times.

What the hell was I doing?

I should've learned my lesson five years ago.

I blinked at my reflection, the freckles from a long Texas summer showing stark against my skin. Cover 'em up, my mom had always said. Better to hide the imperfect puzzle pieces that made me who I was. The strap of the tank I wore slipped over a shoulder, and my hair slipped across my face as I hung my head.

So I wanted Jack. Was exploding with feelings for him. Had brought makeup to look nice for him. Nothing new there. Story of my entire life. Maybe... maybe I could *seduce* him into business with me. That was possible. But wrong. I shook my head, sending water flying.

No. I wasn't taking Door Number One. That was the coward's way.

Behind Door Number Two? *Fucking commit.* Convince him my plan for this rickety old place was the best possible investment he could make. Be brave, and in the words of celebrity design guru and my dream life coach Tim Gunn, *make it work.*

Door Number Three held no mystery; no, it would be an absolute shit show of me running back to the apartment above my parent's garage and settling in with my waitress apron for the long haul.

My knuckles whitened on the sink, until I dropped my hands, and grabbed my paisley blue toiletry bag, rescuing a beat-up brush from its depths. I flicked a piece of broken eyeshadow off the handle, leaving a smear of shimmer in its wake.

I'd faced a demon doll last night. With nothing but a heavy lamp and my conviction that I could take whatever asshole was scratching around the guest room.

Sure, it was *just* a doll, a weird-ass creepy one, but I'd been brave in that moment.

I ran a brush through my auburn tangles. I could be brave again. I closed my eyes. I would rebuild that old hotel from the ground up and make it mine. I was willing to tear myself down to the studs to make it happen.

I would be brave for myself.

I STEPPED out of the shower, narrowly missing stepping into the toilet. My foot slid across the steamy tiles, sweating from the heat of the water. The shower must've taken less than five minutes, but I'd gone through about fifty changes of heart while I scrubbed my skin.

My conviction to stick to the plan seemed to run along the same lines as the loves-me loves-me-not game I played with daisies and sunflowers and whatever unsuspecting weed I could sacrifice as I walked to school.

I had to convince Jack I'd be the best business investment his company could possibly make. I knew I could be. Could feel it down into my bones. Right now, I was in go mode. I did a little headbob, slapping my wet arms against my legs.

Get hype.

Operation: Weekend Getaway was officially underway. Phase one consisted of hygiene. I smelled better, now it was time to get pretty. Studies show people tend to give more attractive people what they wanted. First things first, the BO had to go-go.

Baby steps.

Phase two would consist of absolutely nailing my pitch, showing him I wasn't a flake, that I was committed and would follow through.

Shit.

I'd already screwed the pooch after Lucy the demon doll from hell made her ill-timed appearance. Fucking Lucy.

Worst case, he would politely listen to my pitch before driving away and leaving me all alone in the murder cabin. Well, if his car worked.

Muhahaha.

Wait. We were both stuck here. I frowned. If this *were* a horror movie...

"Don't fucking go there," I admonished myself.

The AC kicked on overhead, a fan in the ceiling whirring to

life. I clasped a hand to my chest, heart jumping at the noise. My head snapped up, looking for the source. The mirror had fogged completely. Moisture ran down the side, a steady drip pooling in the basin of the sink.

Probably triggered by the steam in the small room. No biggie.

I ducked my head, searching for a hand towel to rub it dry. Nope. No hand towel. Not a surprise, considering how they'd fit a three-piece bathroom into the square footage of a postage stamp.

Clutching the towel I'd wrapped around my body, I raised my hand to wipe a corner of it across the surface of the mirror.

I froze.

The mirror was no longer fully fogged. Instead, a phrase scrawled across it, sinister in beaded moisture.

You're not alone.

"Fuck me!" I backed away, my pulse racing. Another step, and I caught my heel on the side of the bathtub, tumbling ass over teakettle back into the tub. The shower curtain rod popped off the wall, beaning me square in the forehead before crashing to the tile floor.

The doorknob turned, and Jack's head appeared in the crack in the door. His eyes went wide as he took in the scene. Okay, me. Took in me, wet as a drowned rat, naked save for a wet towel and a shower curtain, legs up in the tub.

"Are you okay?"

"No! I mean, yes, I'm not hurt, but look at the mirror!" I pointed with one hand, trying to cover my goodies up at the same time.

He opened the door wider, letting a rush of cooled air into the sticky bathroom. "You're not alone?" His eyebrows rose. "What's that supposed to mean? Listen, Em, you don't have to leave me messages on the mirror..."

"Will you just shut up?" I interrupted, gesticulating wildly.

"I didn't write it, Jack! I got out of the shower and there it was." I kicked a foot, trying to dislodge myself from the bathtub. I only succeeded in slamming my toes into his calf. "Jesus, Jack, that's like hitting a brick wall, what the hell have you been doing?"

"Working out." His lip curled into a smile. "And Em, come on. This is weird, for sure, but it's probably some kid who stayed here last drew it on and it didn't come off when they Windexed it. Besides, it could mean like, 'you're not alone' in the inspirational sense. Not 'you're not alone' in the I'm gonna come murder you in your sleep sense." He rubbed the back of his neck, staring at the message in the mirror.

"Oh yeah, that's real helpful." I squinted at him. He seemed a little more apprehensive, at least. I wasn't sure it made me feel any better.

"Where did you say you heard about this place?"

Squirming, I tried to get to my feet. "I... I did my research." Real convincing, exactly what I'd want to tell a potential business partner, for sure. "I've been watching this property for almost a year, been watching the comps and waiting for the price to drop after the bubble... but you know what? I do *not* scare easy. That's freaky. You have to admit it." My hand slipped on the edge of the tub, and I thudded back in.

"Here, lemme help." He snorted, reaching out to take my forearm in his hand. I grasped his, and he pulled, bracing against the doorway. Between the two of us, it was too much force. My feet slid across the wet tiles, scrabbling for purchase, and I practically vaulted into his arms.

Wet, naked, and completely flustered, the only thing separating our skin white terry cloth and his thin t-shirt.

"Uh, okay, thanks." I pushed against the hard plane of his chest, trying to back away from him without ending up straight back in the tub. The bathroom was downright claustrophobic with him in it too. I couldn't get away from him. I didn't want to.

Our eyes caught. His pupils dilated, black lashes setting off the effect. Setting me on fire.

My heart rate spiked again, and it wasn't from fear.

His lips parted, and I could've sworn he leaned closer. I blinked. Broke eye contact.

"I'm gonna get clothes on. Sorry you had to see me like this. I didn't mean to upset you earlier, I'm sorry. Thanks, I mean. For your help."

Jack nodded once and angled sideways out the door. He didn't look at me once.

Damn it.

So much for bravery. Ha. I was about as brave as the raccoon under Jack's Bronco.

On the mirror, the words dripped, and I scowled at my reflection in the letters before wiping them away.

You're not alone.

I was going to die alone unless I figured my shit out. And the deed would probably in this dumb cabin.

12

EMMA

J ack held his phone up, not taking his eyes from his coffee cup. "I had your car towed. Mechanic said it's gonna take him a few days to get parts, thanks to the holiday weekend. So until then, we're stuck together. And here, unless I can fix the Bronco."

Stuck together. The two words knifed through my brain.

"Is it so bad—to be *stuck* with me?" I settled on one of the rickety bar stools at the kitchen counter.

His head drooped between his hunched shoulders, steam curling around his chin. Dark stubble traced his jawline. How would it feel, to touch it? Would it be soft or prickly?

My hand reached out, as possessed as the stupid doll in the guest room, before I caught myself, snatching it back to my lap.

His head tipped up, eyes on the ceiling, and he sighed. "Of course not, Em."

"Listen, Jack. I'm sorry. I shouldn't have made you uncomfortable earlier. I didn't think it was a big deal, but it was, obviously and—"

"It's not that." He shook his head, his mouth screwing up to the side. "Things are just, you know, I thought we could try to keep it somewhat professional."

"Of course. I apologize." My stomach churned, and I hugged my arms to myself. "Of course. Maybe we should talk about everything that happened, you know, clear the air. What do you think?"

I let the question dangle between us, tracing a stain on the Formica countertop with an index finger. It hung there, heavy, ponderous, and I wondered if he'd swipe at it, bringing the ceiling of our friendship down.

Our past.

"What's there to talk about? What's done is done."

I'd been staring at him, the way the muscle in his temple twitched. My gaze skittered away as he turned his towards me. I could never stand it when he was upset with me.

I would be brave.

"No, Jack. We should talk about it. I messed up. We *both* messed up." My palms were sweaty now, and I rubbed them along my cut-off shorts.

Jack half-rose from his barstool. "I came for you, you know. To your apartment. When Beth called it off."

Her name danced around the room, a not-forgotten specter haunting us both. Beth (Kitty 6.0) had been perfect for Jack. So sweet, so smart, and dependable, utterly loyal. It made no sense that she broke his heart right before he proposed.

"Oh." My stomach hollowed. What had I been doing in the immediate aftermath of finding out he was about to pop the question to Beth? I hung my head, and a red curl escaped, tickling my eyebrow. Shame followed, an electric spike that tingled into my palms. It was a question of *who*, not what.

I lied. I couldn't do this right now. I couldn't wade through the muck of our past. Everything in me screamed at me to run, or to fight.

But that was *old* Em. The new and improved *me* was focused on the future. Focused on getting shit done. I was going to be the spreadsheet I wanted to see in the world. I was going to make the Microsoft paperclip my bitch.

I'm coming for you, Clippy.

I took a deep breath, met his eyes. "Okay, then. Should we get down to business?"

"Business?" he echoed.

"Yeah. You know, the reason we're both here?" It came out harsh, cold. That was fine by me. Who would've thought spreadsheets would be my new safe space? Not me. Certainly not Jack, who stared at me, flummoxed.

I rummaged through the small bag I'd left on the floor last night and pulled out my laptop, wincing a little at the definitely unprofessional stickers littered all over it. I'd have to scrape those off. Eventually.

"You want to do this now, huh?" His eyes tracked my every move.

"If you want to." *No, not really.*

"I'm ready when you are, Emma Cross." The way he said my name, like he savored the taste of the syllables on his tongue, sent a thrill through me. "But this is—this conversation is far from over."

Deep breaths.

I needed to forget, for one moment in time, our shared history, all the unspoken awfulness between us, the regret, and the shame. Jack had been my best friend for most of my life. And now, maybe I could convince him to be my business partner.

A second thrill shot through me as the screen loaded an image of the outside of the cabin with the sunflowers and salvia before it, still one of the most picturesque places I'd ever seen. And I was here, making a play for the future I dreamt about for a year straight.

With or without Jack. I slid a glance to him, heartened by his expectant look, the way he pursed his lips in contemplation.

My heart rate sped up. This was it. This was my chance. *Don't blow it.* Fingers hovering over the trackpad, and I closed my eyes before clicking the icon that would launch my presentation. A killer presentation in the murder cabin.

"You really did this right, huh?"

My stomach flipped at his incredulous tone. Why was it so hard to believe that I would do it right? Squaring my shoulders, I squeezed my eyes shut.

Yeah. Like eyelids were enough to block out the memory of Jack's face the night I blasted to his apartment, telling him how I felt. Telling him that I loved him, before he proposed to Beth, and then, when he rejected me, hooked up with the first cute guy to buy me a drink on Sixth Street.

Be the spreadsheet. Taking a deep breath, I cued the presentation to begin.

"Mr. Colson—" I lavished a dazzling smile on him. "—I realize that my attire and our locale are unorthodox, but far be it for me to provide with you anything less than the most professional presentation I am capable of."

A small grin flashed across his face, before he schooled his expression, sitting up straight in his chair.

Ha! Point for me.

"Continue." He nodded, all business. Except that spark in his eye. The one that said he might start laughing at me at any minute, if I decided to put on a comedy show instead of a business proposal.

"As you know, I've worked in the hospitality industry for the better part of a decade, after receiving my degree from a prestigious university, one I believe is also your alma mater." I clicked the first slide. An animated projection of my plan for the hotel illuminated the screen. Thanks to all my good tippers, I'd managed to scrape together enough money to get a professional artist, who turned my ideas into an amazing mockup. The image blossomed from the scary picture I snagged directly from the real estate site into my dream. A bustling hotel boasting a rustic glam meets southern gothic aesthetic. In softly twinkling lights, the name I'd settled on winked above the column flanked door.

And just like that, our shitty past, the tension between us, and even the dated kitchen... disappeared. *Real estate nirvana.* My shoulders relaxed, and I tossed my damp hair over one shoulder.

"The target market for The Inn at Piney Woods is anyone who's looking for an escape from their daily life. Whether it's a middle class family of four looking for a weekend getaway full of adventure—" I pressed the slide, leading to a second visualization of a ropes course and canoe launch site. "—or adventurous singles looking for a break from the doldrums of city life —" Click, and the tiny house rental neighborhood filled the screen with an estimated completion date three years out. "—or a romantic getaway." An image of a couple dining outdoors, laughing in a clearing festooned with fairy lights. "The Inn at Piney Woods caters to all these guests and more."

Jack's eyebrows raised, and I let myself have a little mental fist pump, as a treat. The online graphic design class I'd shoveled into my brain after moving in with my parents was paying off. No more than three fonts, same color scheme throughout, pleasing ratio of text to image. And the coup de grâce, of course, the beautiful illustrations I'd managed to animate. Barely managed, smoothed along by copious amounts of diner coffee. And advice from the artist, who'd been more than happy to help, glad to have work after the damned pandemic.

I clicked the presentation again. The corners of my lips curved as his eyes widened.

"The Inn at Piney Woods will also be uniquely positioned to cater to corporate retreats, and I've created both an a la carte style approach for companies to pick and choose what events and courses they think best, as well as several packages at varying price points."

"What are the price points?"

I smirked. Anticipating the question, the next slide answered it like a motherfucking boss. The graphs responded as I tapped the mouse, changing based on the package inclusions. The next slide displayed the add-on options for a retreat, including horseback riding, the ropes course, use of a classroom, a wine tasting hosted by a nearby winery, ideas for local speakers and their pricing...

In other words, it was pitch-perfect. Heh. I paused, waiting for questions.

Jack simply nodded. His face gave away nothing. I worried my lower lip, clearing my throat before continuing.

"This beautiful tree-lined property stretches for the next forty acres, some of which is prime waterfront real estate." The slide on the screen featured the waterfront image from the google search. "While the small town is less than booming, I believe, if marketed correctly, we could turn this place into an idealized country retreat for those world-weary of the pace of life in nearby Dallas and Houston. An easy day trip to take it easy." I clicked the slide, and a stock photo of smiling men and women around a stone campfire filled the screen, along with the logo I'd agonized over, likely driving the poor artist crazy.

I clicked again, sliding my eyes to his slightly raised eyebrows.

"According to the current owner, the old hotel property is in serious need of renovations. We would require seed money to oversee an entire overhaul, but it should qualify as a historic building. I've been in touch with Travel & Leisure magazine, and they expressed interest in running a 'fixer upper' style feature on it." Translation: I'd had a Twitter exchange with Travel & Leisure, which made it not *quite* a lie.

"I've secured a lawyer and financial advisor to help guide me through the licensing and tax side, and here..." The screen changed to a financial breakdown, showing the cost for filing each separate government required credential. "...you can see where we've decided a plan of action for securing each, as well as approximate cost and timelines."

The last slide featured the high points of my resume. I spent hours debating whether to include it. Watching Jack's reaction was torture, but I waited the minute I'd rehearsed for him to read it.

Squinting, I wondered how I looked in black and white to him. Was I more than the sum total of parts? I'd worked my ass off for those promotions. Sure, it hadn't been the most sparkling of jobs, but I'd been at that boutique hotel a long time. Long enough to know what the hell I was doing, anyway. And then was laid off, along with the rest of the support staff.

No reason to add the year or so I'd spent working for my parents as waitress, lifter of heavy things, and de facto social media manager and marketing coordinator.

The slide changed on its own, the cheery face of my former employer. He excitedly agreed to contribute a video endorsement. For some reason, the enthusiasm that made me tear up when I first watched it now made me feel a bit queasy. "We don't have to watch this."

"What is it?"

"A video recommendation letter. My old boss jumped at the chance to help out."

"Ah."

Nothing else. He just... sat there. Fingers laced together. Looking bored?

I cleared my throat again, then fiddled with the coffee mug still steaming on the table. "We bring it back to life, market the hell out of it, and I know we could have something really special. I already have staff hires in mind, as well as salaries plotted out for each. Oh, and the artist who helped me put this together shared a few branding ideas for the Inn's website."

Jack made a noise low in his throat. What was that grunt supposed to mean? Was I now a grunt translator? I shifted, narrowing my eyes at him. The cat clock on the wall ticked and tocked, counting the seconds until I ruined this shot. *Time of death? 9:23 a.m.*

"If I know you, you're less interested in the grand plan, and more interested in the numbers. So here."

Now *this* was the part that took me near 24 hours, a phone-a-friend lifeline, and a constant diet of caffeine. Blood, sweat, and Starbucks. And tears. I clicked the slide.

"Potential profit and loss, plotted out for the next decade." On the screen, the visualization software bloomed to life, showing a flat line deep in the red, and then epic rise into green as time lapsed. I snuck a look at Jack, his eyebrows raised slightly, lips slightly parted. *Not bored anymore, big guy?*

"Even without the mystery discount the owner is hinting at, our break-even point is anywhere from three to four years out. This time lapse accounts for marketing, renovations, insurance, and staff. I plan to live here, work a barebones staff. I've already paid for design services and I'm prepared to run the desk and marketing myself."

Silence. I twined my fingers together.

"I was thinking we could head up to the hotel on Saturday, maybe take a picnic lunch, see what we're working with. You know, decide if it needs Chip and Joanna Gaines or if it's a complete teardown." I tried to keep my voice from breaking. Had I ever wanted anything so badly? "I can do this. All I need is a partner."

"I'm impressed. The visuals are a nice touch." His voice was bland. Unimpressed, despite what he said. My eyes narrowed. Jack swigged his coffee, eyes never leaving the screen. On the wall, the cat clock ticked and tocked, eyes flipping from left to middle to right. The graphics reset, looping. I could feel the next word deep in my bones before he said it.

"But I'm not sure this is the right move for my company."

"Oh." It blew out of my mouth, and I sank back into one of the wooden kitchen chairs. Disappointment rocked me.

"However, why don't we take a look around town, see how deep the seller is willing to discount for you, and I'll send your presentation up to one of the partners. See if they bite. And a picnic up there sounds... nice."

"So you're saying there's a chance?" I went for broke, busting out my best *Dumb & Dumber* impression. *Jim Carrey, eat your heart out.*

Jack made an amused grunt. Grunt translator extraordinaire, that was me.

"Maybe not the best movie pairing to reference, considering you're trying to sell me on this." He steepled his fingers, eyes tracking my leg jangling against the linoleum floor.

"It's always worked before. You used to think I was funny." And why did I have to say that? This could be a fresh start for us. As friends and partners. The blue and red graphics reset again, caught in a loop they couldn't abandon. Just like Jack and me.

Swallowing, I closed the presentation software.

"I'll email it to you." It took no time, the email already prepared and ready to go. Unlike the actual plan, which swung in the balance between us.

"I'll let you know what the partners want to do." Jack rubbed his hands over the yellowed wood chair.

And that was that. No compliments, no questions, no nothing. I'd blown it. He dismissed the idea completely. What happened to him, that he could laugh and joke with me one minute, then turn to ice the next instant? This wasn't the man I knew five years ago.

Faced with his silence, this lingering expectation of never

meeting *anyone's* expectations, unable to say anything, unable to do this by myself... The silence stretched and stretched, laden with expectation. Until it snapped.

"You'll let me know what the partners want? Do you always do what your company wants? Or do you ever do what *you* want?" No. *No, I did not just say that.* My hand rose to my mouth, my breath warm on my palm.

"Do you ever think about what *anyone* else wants?" He threw his hands wide and stared at a spot on the ceiling. "You always knew just what to say to hurt me."

Sticks and stones could break my bones, but words... His were a knife, plunging straight into my heart. Apparently one I wielded just as well.

"I never set out to hurt you. Never."

On the wall, a black and white cat continued to tick, counting the seconds since I'd ruined my pitch. Chances at reviving the dead, cold corpse of our friendship? Slim to none. I blew out a breath. Couldn't bring myself to meet his eyes.

"What happened that night, that really hurt, Em. It fucked me up. For a long time." He swept a hand behind him, rubbing the nape of his neck.

"Jack, please, I didn't know. I didn't know Beth was there when I went over. I'm sorry."

The cat clock's eyes darted back and forth, the plastic smile meaningless and empty as my too-late apology.

"Let's not do this right now." Jack pinched the bridge of his nose with a thumb and forefinger. For a dude over six foot, he seemed... small. *My fault.*

"Tell me about this new girlfriend." *Ah, fuck.* Yeah, that was the way to get him to realize I was stable, the Inn at Piney Woods a great investment. Change the subject. Brilliant plan, Emma.

His gaze darted behind me, to the frill-covered window and

his truck beyond. His lips pursed. "Let's go see about getting the truck started and getting you some groceries."

"Mmhmm." Something was up. If I knew Jack, I knew that face. And it didn't take a genius to see he was changing the conversation, too. Which was good, because I was clearly no genius at relationships, especially where Jack was concerned. Before I could process what exactly he was avoiding, he was up and storming through the front door.

Slowly, my feet followed him, and the quicksand masquerading as my brain took in the remnants of the Scrabble board from the night before. My nose crinkled. I felt raw, sunburnt all over. I'd been a fool to think we could move on from our past.

A blast of cold hit the back of my neck, and I shivered. I'd have to fix the AC in this place if I was going to live here. The game looked different. I paused, staring at it. Instead of jail, the board now spelled out a phrase.

Play with me.

I tilted my head. Jack wanted a rematch? A redo? I sucked in a breath. It wasn't over between us, not yet. I caught the screen before it clanged shut, and I scampered out behind him, not bothering to lock the cabin door.

He hadn't *said* no. If he wanted a rematch, a do-over, hell, I'd give it to him.

13

JACK

The sun dealt the promise of heat, even at midmorning. But the sweat wetting my armpits wasn't from that. I was an asshole. Midges swarmed around the Bronco, and I waved them away. As far as business proposals went, it wasn't half bad. Good, maybe even great. Which made me feel even worse. Em clearly sunk hard-earned money into it, the animated projections were top notch. And her plan was solid.

Problem was, I would never be interested in going into business with her.

The odds of me helping her at *that* level were slim, something she should know, since she saw what owning a business did to my parent's relationship. It nagged at them, tore at them, made them so worried and upset that when the business went under, all they had left of their marriage was resentment. *And it was supremely shitty of me to lead her on.* So why didn't I just tell her the truth?

I frowned, rubbing at the nape of my neck. My shoulders

ached. Should've just bunked in the bed with Em last night.

On autopilot, I climbed into the Bronco and turned the key, before remembering the engine was dead.

Except, the old truck started.

"That's my girl!"

She'd settled in her passenger seat like she owned the place. Hair fell in unruly waves around her face, the phone in her hand casting a blue glow on her luminous skin. Even the Bronco seemed like a time machine, and I could almost see the ghostly outline of her teenage self there, knees hugged into her chest as she laughed and joked. When had things changed between us? When had she become more than that?

"It's like no time has passed."

She flinched back, blinking rapidly. I swallowed. Of course, time had passed. She'd broken my heart, led me on, and now here we were. Trying to pretend like nothing like that had ever happened.

"Remember the time we went tubing in high school?"

"And I forgot sunscreen and torched my skin?"

The corner of my mouth slid up. We'd floated the river all day, with our rag tag group of friends, and that night I'd—

"Did I ever thank you for the aloe vera application?"

I kept my eyes on the road, my smile disappearing. She remembered it, too. How we'd stayed at the house, the rest of our group hitting the town while I constantly applied lotion to her poor, red shoulders. Her neck. Her back.

That's the night things had changed. For me, at least.

"I'll take your silence as a no."

My gaze skipped back to her. Her full attention was on me, her eyes narrowed and lips pursed.

"I remember." I'd never forget.

There was a whole lot more I wish I could forget. Wishing, however, never got me anywhere. Honesty had.

I blew out a breath, my knuckles whitening on the steering wheel.

"My firm doesn't normally fund hotel ventures." Out of the corner of my eye, I saw her turn slowly toward me, her phone forgotten.

"What?"

"We do mostly upscale shopping developments, and we're the middle-men, the scouts. We don't see the completion of a project. I want to be honest with you." Except I was *still* lying.

"What? Why didn't you tell me that to begin with?" Her fingertips left white indentations on her thighs.

I knew that tone, it was the one that meant she was close to losing her shit. My throat was thick with lies.

"Because you asked me to. Because I could help, if your plan made sense... from a business perspective. Maybe the partners will decide to roll the dice on your venture." Doubtful, since I'd never send it to them. Since I was going to undercut her bid and buy the property out from under her.

I was going straight to hell.

There was silence as she chewed it over. Dark evergreens flew past the window, and I took the exit into the quaint, small downtown area. The need to explain, to make her smile, grew. I coughed, as though that would dislodge some honesty.

"This town has potential," I hazarded. A fact. "Your plan does, too. But Em... it's been years since we've even been friends. Could you be friends? With me?"

My heart sped up, a fine line of sweat beading on my upper lip. I didn't want a goddamn friendship. I wanted Emma Cross, all of her, in a way I always hoped for but had never even really tried to get. God, if I could go back in time.

"Friends," Em echoed.

I rolled my shoulders back, trying to ease the tension settling between them. I needed a workout. Or a run. No, that wasn't right. What I needed? It was *more* than a workout. I cleared my throat, focusing on the GPS directions to the local feed store. Right turn ahead.

"I'm interested in investing." *Fuck me.* Why did I say that? Was I? I spun the wheel, and the Bronco bounced as I hit a pothole, the words flying out of me. "I have my own funds, and I can help secure any additional resources we might need. We would have to negotiate terms, and if I agreed to it, I would want everything in writing." My stomach sank. This was promising something I could never deliver, not if I wanted to make partner. Which I would need to, to keep cash flow for the amount of renovations necessary. I rubbed a hand over my face, darting a glance to Em.

She sat, silent. Her rosy lips were an angry slash of color across milk white skin and a constellation of freckles. I pumped the brakes, slowing down, and her head jerked towards the window. Avoiding my gaze. Not answering.

I slid into the asphalt parking lot, put the truck into park, and slammed my foot down on the parking brake. As if *that* would put me back in control. But I wasn't. I was desperate, desperate to have Emma Cross back in my life, with her flaming red hair and her adventures and I would take her anyway I could, friends or more.

What was it about her? Losing control was only ever a problem with Emma. Part of me wondered what Caroline would think.

"Why do you think I wouldn't be able to get my own additional resources? Someone besides you?" Her eyes iced over. Skewered me.

I rubbed my chin, flummoxed.

"Because you called *me.*"

"I called you." Her tone was flat, and she stared out the windshield. "I did call you. Because I thought you... I thought your company was one of the best."

I squinted at her. There was something she was trying to tell me. I was no fucking good at this. "What are you trying to say?"

She continued to stare. We were going to have to talk about it. And soon. If we were going to do this together, we needed to put all our cards on the table.

"Em." *In for a penny, in for a pound.* "Your pitch was good. No, you know what? It was great. I think this has potential. I believe in it, and I believe in you. I also know how fast a business relationship can turn to shit."

"Because of your parents."

"Because of my parents," I agreed.

"We're not your parents. We'll talk, and for one thing, *we're* not married. We're barely even friends, at this point." She unclicked the seat belt, then clicked it back in place before unfastening it again.

"That's true." Fuck me sideways, it *was* true. A pang rippled through my chest. I inhaled. "You know what? Let's just get it all out there." The words rushed out of me in a tangle of syllables.

"What is it you want to say to me?" She crossed her arms over the seatbelt, then wriggled against the strap on her collarbone.

"What happened..."

"We fucked up," she finished. "Both of us."

I made myself meet her eyes. Forced her to look. I deserved it. Deserved the regret I wallowed in since that night.

"And this isn't a grocery store," Em observed. Changing the topic. "Unless you're on a rabbit food diet." Her eyes scoured my body, dipping down my chest, lower. I shifted. If she kept staring, things were going to get uncomfortable. I could wrap her in my arms, press her lips to mine, finally know what she tasted like. Finally live out my fantasy of making out with her in the back of my truck.

"What's wrong? You're looking at me weird." She flipped open the vanity mirror. "Do I have something on my face?"

I grunted.

"Fine. You want to do this now, get it all out?"

I wanted to do something now, that much was true.

"Like ripping off a band-aid," I said.

She nodded, squaring her shoulders, her expression hard.

"Let's see how it's healed, then."

Mine never had.

14

———

"**Y**ou didn't wait. What was I supposed to do? I wasn't going to beg. You either wanted to be with me, or you didn't." He didn't sound angry. It would've been easier if he'd raged. "But you came to my apartment, said you loved me, that you'd broken up with that asshole Chris for me."

"I didn't know Beth was there." One of our friends filled me in on that sordid detail. It still kept me up at night. "I had no idea she was listening." Should have, from how he came outside, didn't invite me in, from the crazed look in his eye.

"Jesus, Em." He shook his head, olive skin reddening as a deep blush of embarrassment spread across his face. "It wasn't just her. Her whole family was there. I'd just asked her dad for permission to marry her."

"Oh." A small word. Inadequate. "Jack, I'm sorry. I'm so sorry."

He scrunched his eyes closed, forehead furrowing.

"Don't be sorry." His body tensed, and then he straightened, letting out a long sigh. "It's over. It's been over for a long time.

Beth and I weren't going to work. She never trusted me enough to know I would never cheat on anyone. She always thought you and I..." He trailed off, and I swallowed. The look he gave me sliced through my chest.

"I thought you chose her, Jack. You said no!" Tears welled, and I blinked furiously. "You can't be mad at me for hooking up with that guy. I thought you were going to *marry* her. I didn't know." It sounded lame. I didn't even buy my own bullshit. Frustrated, I raked a hand through my hair, only succeeding it making it even wilder. *Well, this wasn't going the way I'd wanted it to at all.*

"That's the thing, Em. You didn't know. But your timing really fucking sucked."

I blinked at the harsh words, but he wasn't done.

"You ran away, then found the first guy who wasn't *me* to shack up with. When I saw you outside your apartment, kissing him..." He rubbed the stubble on his face.

Out the window, a guy in canvas overalls trekked into the feed store.

Jack tilted his head, his eyes on fire as he met mine. Unshed tears threatened. I blinked. I didn't want to cry. Not over this, not again. This was *our* do-over.

"If we're going to go into business together, I need to know I can trust you. As a business partner. As a friend. And that means that you don't just run off and hide from me when things go wrong. Because they will." A short, husky laugh punctuated his words. "That means we keep this relationship open, and friendly, and we don't—" His huge shoulders heaved as he let out a long sigh. "We don't lie to each other. And if you want to be business partners, we can *only* be friends."

"Uh-huh." He thought I was a liar? Jack was taken. So in his mind, I was also a homewrecker?

I guess that's what history said I was.

"You're in a happy relationship. Why would I jeopardize my dream to be with a guy who loves someone else?"

He grunted, unfastening his seatbelt, face stoic. "I'll be right back, and then we'll go get food."

And that wasn't weird at all. I should have been happy. Finally had it all out in the open. Should have been relieved, at the very least. I leaned my forehead against the passenger side window. The door clicked close after him, leaving me alone in the car with nothing but my regret.

THE PIPED in music and orange on burnt orange color scheme seared my senses, leaving me blinking in the cool fluorescent light. Especially after the quiet ride. Silent except for the rattle of the two humane raccoon traps Jack stowed in the back of the truck. The grocery store was a seventies flashback. Whatever corporate entity owned the place hadn't bothered to update it in decades.

"This place doesn't inspire confidence," I muttered. More like ptomaine poisoning. Could I really give up Whole Foods and Trader Joe's to live out here on my own? I glanced at Jack. He'd be here often enough, as a partner. The thought warmed me.

Even without Jack, the answer would still be yes. I couldn't wait to get out of my parent's house. I *needed* this. My nose wrinkled. But I'd miss my prepped meals.

Jack prowled ahead, scanning the scant shelves with the practiced air of an artist surveying a blank canvas. Thank god he could cook.

I should've felt better, the truth finally out in the open. A path forward for our friendship.

All I felt was empty. And tired.

"How's your mom?" The woman was a legend in our neighborhood growing up. We'd race past our house on our way home from the park, and the aromas swirling outside would draw us up short. She'd done her best to teach Jack everything she knew about food and cooking, and the end result was decidedly in my favor. Something he used to love showing off, had probably influenced his love of brewing beer. Well, former love.

"She's good. Refuses to talk to my dad. The divorce got really nasty, really fast."

"I'm sorry."

No wonder he didn't want anything besides business professional between us.

He plucked a half dozen mangoes from the black plastic crate, sniffing them before settling them in the cart. Fresh strawberries followed, tomatoes and cilantro crowding in. Cooking was his thing.

Eating was mine. We made the perfect pair. I sighed.

"Remember that time you made that chocolate soufflé?"

Jack reached for a bundle of herbs, stopping short of the cart as he half-turned toward me.

"The one that turned into a burnt black puddle on the bottom of my oven? Gee, thanks for the confidence booster." He shook his head before turning back to the greens displayed.

I picked up a bunch of silvery herbs, sniffing their fuzzy leaves before he took them out of my hand.

"Sage. Good choice." He plopped it in the cart, next to bright yellow lemons I hadn't seen him grab.

"What's sage do?" I trailed behind him, shivering in the over-refrigerated meat department.

He stopped again, pivoting towards me with a pained expression. "You seriously haven't changed a bit, have you?"

My chest constricted. Hadn't changed a bit. Was still the selfish, cowardly asshole that had ruined everything for him. I bit my bottom lip, nudging my shoe along the yellowed linoleum.

A warm hand cupped my chin, and I stared up at Jack from beneath my lashes.

"Hey." His brow furrowed. "Don't look like that. You know what? I'll teach you to cook this weekend. Deal?"

I nodded, mute. I pressed the tears that threatened to escape back, swallowing against the tightness in my throat. I couldn't think of anything to say. My face was in his hand. All rational parts of my brain shut down. And then it was gone again. I gripped the plastic handlebar of the shopping cart to steady myself.

Breathe in, breathe out.

The smiley face logo on the handle grinned at me, and I noted all the ways children were not allowed to hang on the cart. Wonder if Jack would let me sit inside and push me around? I had a vision of us, him handing me ingredients, me screaming WHEE as we raced around the store like teenagers playing supermarket sweep on acid.

Then his words caught up to me.

"Wait, you'll cook for *me* this weekend? What about the B&B you're booked at? Don't you have your *own* property to see?"

His dark eyes widened slightly before his gaze slid sideways. "I'll still find time to see it. And I canceled the B&B this morning."

"What? Why?"

He faced me fully, his eyes glinting. "Because the owner left a long, rambling message on my phone last night, about how I was still expected to pay the full price for the weekend but he'd give the room away."

My jaw dropped. "That's awful customer service."

"No kidding."

"How much money are you out?"

"It's a business expense, and my company won't even realize I'm staying with you. It'll be fine."

He seemed so nonchalant about it. Staying with me. "That guy sounds like a jerk."

"Oh, I agree with you there. Seems like the Inn at Piney Woods could easily corner the market here." He winked, and hope welled inside me.

A brown package landed in the cart, followed by a whole chicken and steak of some kind. I raised an eyebrow. This was going to be an expensive trip. The brown butcher paper was waxy against my palm, and I scanned the black and white label.

"Jack, these are expensive." Yeah, that's it. Concentrate on nit-picking his grocery shopping.

"Because they're delicious. And fresh. Relax. We'll split the bill. Business partners, right? Still cheaper than eating out."

I harrumphed, placing the trout he'd selected back in the cart. If I hadn't had a hissy fit last night, I would've won Scrabble and he'd be paying for the whole thing, which reminded me...

"So you want a rematch? I saw what you spelled out." I trailed a finger across the grocery label.

"Huh?" Jack turned the full force of his concentration on me, and I faltered.

"The message on the game board?" *Play with me.*

His lips curled to the side in confusion, blinking rapidly. "I'd love a rematch, but I don't know what you're talking about."

"Jack, shut up. Don't mess with me." I shook my head and laughed, punching his shoulder. "The words on the board were pretty hard to miss. Play with me?"

"I honestly don't know what you're talking about." His attention was back on groceries.

Mine was not. The hair on the back of my neck stood at attention. "You're being serious."

"Em, you ok? Your face is pale."

"Ha." I forced a laugh. "It's always pale." If he was playing a joke on me, payback was going to be a bitch. I'd have to come up with something good. Still, the eerie sense that something was *wrong* wouldn't leave me alone.

"Wine?" He tugged the cart behind him.

Trailing in his wake, I gripped the handle. "We have some at home. At the house, I mean." Home. It was not home. Not yet. And just because Jack felt like home didn't mean he was. I swallowed again, my palms sweaty.

"I'm not even going to dignify that with a response. Boxed wine is fine, but if we're gonna cook, we need something better."

"If we're going to cook with it, why does it matter what kind it is?"

"Because it flavors the whole thing. Just trust me. Don't you trust me?" He peeked over his shoulder at me, and I nodded. I did. God help me, I did trust him. It was *me* I didn't trust.

We rounded the corner, heading down an aisle filled with bottles and beer.

"You two must be the fine couple renting the old cabin. Charlotte told us all about you."

Startled, I gasped, my hands fluttering to my chest. Jack covered a laugh with his hand, shooting me an amused glance. *Scaredy cat.*

An older woman held a magnum of wine in her hands, the giant bottle dwarfing her torso. Her steel grey hair was piled on top of her head in a strict bun, rhinestone glasses perched on the bridge of her nose.

"She did?" Jack asked.

"We're not a couple," I said at the same time. Jack rolled his shoulders, angling his body towards me.

"Who is Charlotte?" He crossed his arms over his chest, shooting me a look.

"The property owner." I scrunched my nose. At least, I was pretty sure I'd been dealing with her representative.

"Oh, yes, my dears, Charlotte is just wonderful, isn't she? I picked out what's in your fridge for you and delivered it just like she asked, I hope it's all right." The old woman hobbled towards the cart, examining the contents with interest. "Oh, boy, you two must be having such a romantic time. I hope the old place isn't giving you any trouble."

"No, it's very nice. Needs a few upgrades, but nothing huge." Back in autopilot response mode, Jack's finger dipped along the wine labels.

I bit my lip. *Giving us any trouble?* The game board flashed before my eyes.

"What kind of trouble would it give us?" The words tumbled out of my mouth. Demon doll trouble? Haunted board games? Who the fuck knew what else?

She blinked, owlish behind her spectacles. "Whatever do you mean?"

"The cabin, you said it might give us trouble." I traced my finger along the smiley face on the cart.

"Yes, dear, of course. All that old plumbing." She stepped towards me, her lavender and baby powder scent making my nose scrunch up. "So much history up there. Charlotte just can't stand to let the place go. Especially not to her old competitor's family." She tsked. "Haven't been many offers other than that old bastard. Pardon my French. I'm Katherine, by the way."

At that admission, Jack stopped, eyes narrowed at Katherine, his expression cagey.

I stared at her, the torrent of words eddying around me before I remembered my manners. "Nice to meet you, Katherine. I'm—"

"I know who you two are." Katherine gave Jack an appreciative once-over, before winking theatrically at me, her wrinkled face exaggerated.

Jack placed two bottles of white in the cart, followed by a bottle of sangria.

Her wrinkled face brightened. "Are you two having a party? Goodness!"

"Just us. Old friends, lots to catch up on." It *was* a lot of wine. Maybe he had a lot of liquid business lunches.

"Hmmph." She cast an appraising look at Jack's backside, a tiny smile tugging the corner of her wrinkled face up. "Well, I'll leave you two to it. Charlotte and I are just so glad someone besides that ill-mannered old man is interested in the property. We know he'd just ruin it. Just like he has everything but that store he owns." She leaned closer, and I caught a whiff of her floral perfume. "Between you and me, the only reason that store doesn't go under is because it's the only place you can buy a hammer and nails in a ten-mile radius. Oh look, here's my St. Genevieve." Katherine bestowed a brilliant smile on me, her eyes crinkling up at the corners. She cradled the big bottle of wine in her arms and began shuffling towards the meat counter.

Jack raised his eyebrows at me, and I shrugged my shoulders in response.

"Oh, and dears?" The woman turned back towards us. "Do be careful not to venture too far into the woods. There was an awful accident there years ago. Charlotte will be most put out if anything were to happen again." She crooked her fingers at us in a tiny wave, clutching the bottle of wine.

"Nice to meet you," I called out, before her words landed. *An accident?* I whirled around. "Jack, this whole—" I gestured wildly, attempting to encompass the entire planet but mostly succeeding at pointing to Shiraz. "—*thing* is creeping me out."

"It's just wine."

I scowled and crossed my arms.

"Accidents happen, Em." His eyes narrowed, looking after the old woman.

"You can't tell me this isn't weird."

"She just wants us to be careful. The weirdest thing here is that their beer selection is terrible."

"Do *not* tell me I have an overactive imagination." I squinted at the beer. He had a point. "You should've brought some good craft beer up. This place could use more than this." I gestured wildly.

"That would've been smart. Aiden had a new cider he wanted me to try, I should have gone to see him and gotten us a growler." He wrapped a hand around the front of the cart, pulling it behind him. "And I didn't say that. I think you have a perfectly active imagination."

"Okay, but seriously, Jack, first the doll, then the mirror, then this *accident*?" And the scrabble tiles spelling out 'play with me.' I shivered.

"You forgot the weird gas station guy already?"

I threw my hands up in the air. "See? You *do* think this is spooky."

He clucked his tongue against the roof of his mouth. "No, I think we're in a town so small there's not even a bar, with a bunch of friendly old ladies that like to gossip and a cabin that has a raccoon problem. Besides, we haven't seen each other in years, and we have... unfinished business to hash out, and I'm gonna teach you how to cook. Once and for all."

I slanted my head at him. The way he said unfinished did not make me think of the boardroom. More like the bedroom. A new emotion replaced the creepy feeling. Confusion.

"You aren't creeped out?" I managed.

"Nope." He turned, watching my face, an unreadable expression on his. "She was a nice old lady, probably knits afghans for her grandchildren, just lonely and trying to chat. Now if you meant about teaching you to boil water, hmmm, that might scare me a little."

I ignored the barb and the devilishly handsome smile that

went with it. "She might make afghans out of human hair and necklaces out of teeth she's collected, too. How do you know what an afghan is, anyway?"

"I know things."

I harrumphed, pulling at a yellow pricing sticker.

"Em, If you're really not comfortable, we'll leave." He grinned at me, the smile sending heat spiking through me. *Down girl.* "Besides, who's gonna mess with us when they'd have to get through me first?" He flexed his muscles, planting a kiss on his own bicep.

"You're out of control." I rolled my eyes. Mostly to keep from panting in the beer and wine aisle. He had nice arms. Hell, he had nice *everything*. "Fine. Nothing's weird, everything has a rational explanation."

"Yep. Raccoons and questionable plumbing."

And mysterious accidents. And strange old ladies. And possible arts and crafts using human teeth and hair.

And wine, lots and lots of wine.

15

———

Unloading groceries was infinitely easier when another person insisted on carrying all ten sacks inside at once. *Show off.* I needed to look away from the tight ass and rippling shoulders.

But I didn't.

"You sure you don't need help?"

"Just open the door." His arms bulged, and I raced past him on the porch stairs, and stopped dead in my tracks.

"Uh."

"What?"

"It's already open."

"Did you lock it?" Jack paused at the threshold before barging in, groceries bags swinging from his arms.

I racked my brain. "I don't remember?"

He set the groceries on the floor, eyes glancing around the living room. "Stay here."

He picked a wine bottle out of the sacks, still wrapped in a brown paper bag, before stalking into the kitchen, sidling in like he was in a movie. The house stayed quiet, not giving up its secrets. The only sound the quiet ticking of the kitschy cat clock on the kitchen wall.

I clamped down on the inside of my cheeks to keep from laughing. "Are you going to get whatever opened the door drunk?"

He didn't turn around, but I knew my joke hit when his shoulders tensed. "It's a weapon."

"Why are you whispering?"

The look he gave me was long-suffering and nearly sent me over the edge into hysterical giggles. I knew if I started laughing now, I wouldn't be able to stop. Also, it was kind of hot. That he wanted to run in and brain whatever or whoever had opened the door to the cabin.

He squared his shoulders, heading for the hallway and two bedrooms. I eyed the groceries at my feet. There were two bottles of wine left. The sangria looked to be the largest. Hefting it over my shoulder, I followed Jack into the hallway, still stifling a laugh.

Jack burst through the bathroom door. "Clear," he pronounced.

"Did you check the bathtub?" Jack's paranoia was rubbing off on me. Or maybe mine was rubbing off on him?

He jumped, nearly crashing into me. "I told you to stay at the door." That tiny bathroom was going to be the death of us.

"I thought you might need back up." I winked and swung the sangria like a baseball bat, clicking my tongue as though I'd knocked a ball out of the park.

He rolled his eyes, staring at the popcorn ceiling as though it would back him up.

"Lemme get this straight—you're ready to believe this house is haunted, and then when there is a very real proba-bility of an actual human being in here, you're fine?"

I opened my mouth but couldn't think of a good response. He had me there.

A muscle in his temple twitched as he shook his head, angling for the closed bedroom door. He opened it with a rush, and my heart skipped a beat. What if there *was* someone hiding in there?

"Clear." He strode into the room, opening the closet door with extreme force, leaving it swinging in the hinges.

I stuffed a hand over my mouth to keep from laughing, scared hysterical laughter threatening to burst forth.

He shook his head, rolling his eyes in clear disgust at my lack of survivor instinct, shouldering past me and into the second bedroom, where I was treated to a repeat performance.

"Anything?" I asked, as he leaned against the doorframe, a slightly manic expression in his eyes.

He shook his head, and I released a whoosh of air. A laugh bubbled out. It built, and suddenly I was gasping for breath, my eyes tearing up. "Clear," I managed, doubling over, the sangria pressed to my diaphragm.

Jack snorted, then began to chuckle with me.

Behind me, the guest room door was still open, and I had a straight shot of the empty bed.

Empty.

"Jack." I straightened slowly, fear trickling down my spine.

Instantly, his relaxed posture changed, and he gripped the neck of the bottle with both hands.

"What." The single word slammed into me. He was freaked out, too.

I swallowed, my skin crawling.

"The bed is empty."

He looked between me and the bed, not understanding.

"The doll. Lucy was on the bed when we left."

Goosebumps prickled my arms and legs, and my stomach churned.

The demon doll was gone.

❧

THE CLOSET DOOR rattled against the wall, swinging wide as Jack flung it open.

"This isn't funny, Em."

My laughter mutated into a high-pitched giggle, wild and uncontrollable. Eerie. He shot a look at me over his shoulder as he tore through the closet. A red and black fleece blanket landed on the floor, followed by a baseball bat and a hand crank storm radio. A heavy black flashlight crashed on the ground.

A gasping breath knocked me to my senses, and my weak legs gave out, jelly underneath me. The wood floor was cool on the hot skin of my legs. "I know it's not."

The white linen bed skirt moved in the artificial breeze of the fan.

"Did you check under the bed?"

"You're sitting by it, why don't you look?"

Why didn't I look? Why didn't *I look*? I mimicked the words at his impassive back as he continued his futile search for a porcelain doll that was most certainly not hiding in the closet.

"I saw that."

"Saw what?"

"Just put your tongue back in your mouth."

Punchy on adrenaline, my mouth opened before I could stop it. "I bet none of the girls tell you that."

The rummaging stopped. I gulped against my suddenly dry throat. His weight shifted, and I knew he was going to turn around and stare at me. I did not mean to make that joke, I did not need to see that face. I did not need to admit anything at all.

Looking under the bed seemed like the safest choice.

Wood squeaked against my bare legs as I scooched closer to

the frame. The linen was soft and thin in my hand, and I snatched at it.

My hand fell. The air near the floor was cool. Much cooler than the rest of the room. I swallowed again. No time like the present.

No time at all.

Three, two, one. I snatched the flimsy layer up, holding my breath.

No doll.

I noodled to the floor like overcooked pasta. Breathe gushed out of me like a living beast, ready to run as fast as it could. My heart hammered against my ribs like it, too, was trying to get the fuck out.

I didn't blame it.

"Anything?" Jack's approaching footsteps shook the floor. I coughed, sending the ruffle and a family of dust bunnies into the wind. I lifted it again, one eye closed, just to make extra sure.

"Lucy isn't home." I scooted closer. A box, more square than shoebox, lay underneath the bed, coated in a thin layer of dust, clinging to it like a frothy negligee. "There is something."

I stretched my fingers out, the tips of my middle and index finger making contact with it, then slipping off. I grunted, rolling to my stomach and angling my shoulder underneath the brass frame.

"What is it?" Jack's feet were by my hip, and he crouched down to sneak a look.

"A box." I wanted to know what was in the box. I was dying to know what was in the box.

The bottom of the box springs rasped against my hair, and I held my breath in an unsuccessful attempt to keep my lungs dust free.

My fingers stretched out again.

There. I had it.

As soon as it was mine, an evil thought crossed my mind.

A scream tore from my mouth, echoing under the brass bed. The dust bunnies fled in terror. I screamed again, clutching the box.

"It's got me! There's something!" I barked the words out, punctuating each with a brisk intake of air.

"What the fuck, Em?" Jack's strong hands wrapped around my waist, tugging me out and back onto the floor.

Wide-eyed, I sucked back a laugh as he rolled me onto my back. He hovered over me, halfway into a pushup, corded muscle standing on end as he peered under the bed.

Too close.

I squeezed my eyes shut, but no matter how hard I pressed my lids together, I couldn't escape the familiar smell of his cologne, the heat of his body.

Danger of a different sort.

The tightening in my abdomen had nothing to do with pretending to be afraid, and everything to do with the absolute hunk of a man practically on top of me.

His breath ruffled a loose hair on my temple. I'd let the box go in my attempt to be ridiculous, and now Jack bent lower, his chest brushing against my breasts as he reached for it.

Manic laughter bubbled up, and it took me a moment to realize it was coming from me.

"Well, well, well, isn't this kinky? What, was the bed too far to go?"

My laughter died out. Our heads swiveled towards the door, fast enough to make any horny owl jealous. Er, horned owl.

Lena.

Breath whooshed out of me in an explosion, and I pressed my palms against Jack's chest in an effort to get clear of him.

"You invited *her*?" I wiped my damp hands against my legs, trying to make them forget the hard plane of his chest. Like swabbing my palms would make me forget. Like even *Lena* appearing would make me forget.

"Shut up, sis." She smiled, but her eyes were still narrowed, flitting back and forth between Jack and I. If I got any hotter I would explode into flames on the spot. "Jack said he needed back-up." An arched eyebrow punctuated the statement.

"Don't," I said automatically, watching Jack get to his feet with all the grace of a wild jaguar. *Rawr*. I tore my eyes away, focusing on Lena. Chestnut curls trailed over her shoulder, her freckles standing out like constellations across her skin. Hazel eyes ringed in dark liner peered up at me, and her shirt told us the future was female.

My lips stretched out in an answering smile as disbelief and irritation at Jack faded away into pure glee. I was so freaking glad to see her. Except for the part where she definitely didn't think Jack and I should be rolling around together.

"You needed back-up, huh?" I cut my eyes to Jack. He shrugged, rubbing a hand across the back of his neck. But Lena grinned and drew me into a hug.

"He called the best," she said as we drew apart, "and I'm ready to help however I can, since I know how much this place means to you." Flipping her hair over a shoulder, she gave him a quick hug. "It's been too long, Jack."

A muscle in my forehead twitched. Of fucking course Jack thought my big sister would be a calming influence on me. Everybody did. Like I was some out of control toddler who needed her holding my hand at every moment. She side-eyed me as she stepped away, her patented *'what the fuck are you doing, Em'* look written all over her face.

Damn it.

Lena was a good sister. A great sister, even. But if anyone knew just how deep my bullshit river ran, it was her. She was my genetic bullshit monitor. I couldn't so much as lie about having a good day without her breathing down my neck.

Keeping this attraction to Jack under wraps? Next to impossible with her around.

"So, uh, I wasn't interrupting anything, was I?" She twirled a curl around her finger.

I put my hands at my hips, jutting one leg out.

"No. I mean, we ah..." My hands dangled at my sides again, and I shifted my weight, causing the floorboards to creak.

What do I do with my hands?

"Yes, we were just—" Jack started.

"No, I was looking for—" I said at the same time. I crossed my arms across my chest, rocking back onto my heels. Too aggressive. I dropped my hands, clutching one wrist with my hand.

Lena's eyed darted between our faces as though it were a particularly interesting tennis match.

"There's a ghost," he said. I tried to compose my face as though his admission didn't surprise me.

"Do possessed dolls mean anything to you?" I added.

She held her hands up, closing her eyes and shaking with repressed laughter.

"Listen, you two are adults. If you're boning, good. *Finally.* Whatever. I don't care."

I ran a hand through my frizz of hair, sending a dustball floating to the floor.

"We're not having sex, Lena. Jesus *Christ.*" Jack threw his head back, huffing out a breath of irritation. "This is strictly a business arrangement."

Okay. Disappointment, unbidden and unwanted, pushed through me.

Lena's eyebrows shot up, and I schooled my features into place.

"He's got a girlfriend. Kitty 7.0." Oops. Hadn't meant to say that.

Jack threw the black box onto the quilt covered bed, causing the ancient springs to squawk.

"Sorry, her name's Caroline," I corrected.

Lena looked between us as though we were playing tennis at Wimbledon.

Jack sighed and pinched the bridge of his nose. I scratched at one of the mosquito bites I'd earned the night before.

"Well, if you are so serious with her, why is my little sister here and this *Caroline* isn't?" Lena tapped her toe against the wood floor, lips pursed.

A choking sound of disgust rumbled from his throat, and my eyes slid back to the black box. A simple noise shouldn't have unraveled me. And yet, my stomach had been replaced with a cement block. I'd have a hard time eating all the food we'd just bought with a cement stomach. Maybe I could shove it all in a smoothie and drink it through a straw.

Trout smoothie. Yum.

"Earth to Em, anybody home?" Lena sighed, sharing a long-suffering look with Jack, who didn't seem as irritated as the cement-inducing noise led me to believe.

"This cabin is haunted. It's as simple as that." I flung out a hand, gesturing to the box, black and unassuming and in no way absorbing the light of the room or doing anything haunted at all. Couldn't it at least act spooky?

What a disappointment. My life was just full of them. I sighed.

"Okay... we were talking about Caroline," Lena said, and Jack shook his head in disbelief. Well, that was on him. He'd known me long enough to know I was the GOAT at changing subjects.

"Good for you, but she's not here, and you are now, and this place has a fucking ghost." I pointed at the box on the bed.

"A *fucking* ghost, huh?" She waggled her eyebrows at Jack. "So that's why you two were tangled up on the floor? The mattress is haunted? Though, I have to say, Em, this is nicer than the pictures you forced me to stare at for the past twelve months."

Frustration leaked out of me. What was it with sisters? They knew just what buttons to push, and when they pushed them, it was always ten times more obnoxious than anyone else.

"Fine. Maybe I *should* stay in here. You know, enjoy the ghost. Maybe I'll get lucky and it will be a *fucking* ghost. Better ghost dick than cheating dick, am I right?"

Lena's mouth dropped open. Jack looked like he wished he could disappear.

I didn't care.

With that, I squared my shoulders and stormed out of the room, floating on righteous indignation and the knowledge I'd had the stupidest last word known to mankind. Or ghostkind.

16

JACK

"Thanks for coming, Lena."

"How could I resist? Long weekend in paradise, hanging out with my baby sister and you like nothing's changed." She took a deep breath, straightening the quilt on the bed. "Jack, are y'all all right? Is Emma?" Lena's mouth was pinched in worry.

I blew out a deep breath, raising both palms up. "She's changed. We've both changed." Still a hellcat, for sure. Still brilliant as a lingering summer sunset, all fire and glory. But different. Tempered. Not brittle, though.

And me? I was a cold, lying bastard, through and through.

"You're worried about her." Lena frowned at the box on the bed.

"No." I wasn't. Worried about doing business with her, maybe. Worried that I'd seriously miscalculated insinuating I was still with Caroline. Worried that there was no way I could do business with someone I cared about so deeply.

That was the problem. I cared. Too much. This shit would end badly.

But didn't I have to give it a chance.

"Then what the heck is wrong with you?"

"She wants to go into business with me." My stomach churned. "I think we should convince her not to waste her money on this place." *So I could buy it for my company, clean conscience.* I fisted my hands at my side.

Lena sighed, closing her eyes and sinking onto the squeaking bed. "Oh, Emma. You selfish girl."

"She's not selfish." It sounded like a growl.

She squinted up at me. "What about asking you to 'go fund her' isn't selfish? She knows how bad it got for your parents. And for you."

I tilted my head, considering. Em did know.

"Your parents were at each other's throat for years over their business," Lena plowed on. "It *was* selfish of her to ask you. We all knew it, hell, the whole neighborhood could hear them fighting with each other. Besides, no way she's ready for a financial commitment like this."

"Enough." It slid out of my lips, icy. "I remember better than anyone how loud they could be." No matter how far I turned up my music, how many pillows I put over my head at night, I could still hear them. Would never forget my mother telling me to never, ever, go into business with a friend or partner unless you were ready to cut ties with them at a moment's notice.

How trust was a commodity for the gullible.

Somewhat chastised, Lena picked up the box. A noise came from inside it, like something heavy slid around.

Skritch, skritch, skritch.

The hair on the back of my neck rose.

Lena jumped off the bed so fast she practically levitated, throwing the black box onto the floor. The lid separated from the top of the box, revealing the contents.

"What is that? Were you guys being serious about a ghost? Because honestly that's not funny and I signed up for moral support, not being dragged to hell." Her voice had increased an octave in pitch, and her eyes were as large as saucers.

I bit back a laugh. "You know, you used to make fun of Em constantly for being easy to scare, but you're just as bad."

She put her hands on her hips and stomped. "It's not funny, Jack."

I snorted. "It is, and no, it's not a ghost. It's a raccoon."

"Raccoons are nocturnal," Lena said automatically. "What's in the box?"

Hmmm.

Stooping over, I scooped the box from the floor. A key lay inside.

I pulled it out, the black velvet ribbon smooth against my fingers.

"What's it go to?" Lena peered over my elbow.

"No idea." I held it up, looking at the door handle. "It's too old to go to anything in here."

Skritch-skritch skriiiiitch.

Lena jumped, air whooshing out of her.

"Don't worry. I've got a plan for that raccoon." And it was in the back of the Bronco, ready for deployment. But that didn't seem as important now.

Now I wanted to figure out what the key in my palm unlocked.

17

EMMA

The sun beat down across the raggedy grass and dirt lawn. White cotton wisps of clouds did nothing but provide the briefest hint of shade, only to be sucked across the sky too fast to help. September in Texas. Hot enough to be July anywhere else.

Emerald green trees around the cabin cast long shadows, and my flip flops slapped across the wooden patio. The screen door slammed behind me, and I squinted against the bright afternoon light.

A dull ache in my chest tightened, contracting with every whoosh of my heart.

What was I doing?

Lena called it like she'd seen it. Guilt washed over me. Jack was taken. Taken, taken. Off limits, off the market, undateable. And she'd seen right through me.

And I *had* been flirting. Couldn't even lie to myself about that.

The wooden rocking chair creaked in protest as I sank into

it. I drew my knees into my chest, hugging them to me as I buried my face between them.

What the fuck was I doing?

Jack didn't want me. Maybe once, a long time ago—but I'd ruined any chance at that happiness. At him. At us.

Ripped up into a million pieces and flushed down the drain.

"Hey."

My back stiffened, and I tilted my head, peeking out at the newest murder cabin guest. "She brought you with her, huh?"

"We're a package deal now, you know." Lena's fiancée, Jen, shifted the brown paper grocery bags she carried. "Don't move to open the door for me, or anything. Wouldn't want to inconvenience you."

I smiled through clenched teeth, when the door banged open. Jack walked through, his hair mussed, a dust bunny clinging for dear dirty life to his fitted t-shirt. It had been silkier than it looked, the perfect accompaniment to the hard flesh underneath.

"Saved by Jack yet again, Em." Jen flashed a grin at me, and I returned it, despite the tightness in my throat. I swallowed, willing the cement block Jack had lodged in my body to dissipate. Jen's offhand remark hit home.

"I didn't know you were coming." Jack held the door for her.

Jen blew a breath out, shuffling sideways through the door to fit by Jack's huge frame. "I'd leave, but there aren't many options around here, I can tell when I'm not wanted. We called the other B&B, but the guy who answered was a real asshole. Besides, he said they didn't have any vacancies. Guess it's in here with you... or in the car."

I didn't want to hear any of this. I didn't need any of Jen's woe-is-me bullshit right now. I had my own woe-is-me bullshit to sort through.

There are only so many tons of bullshit one person can sort

through. It's science. Laws of diminishing bullshit returns. It is known.

"It's not that. There are only two rooms... I just figured Lena and Em could share, is all."

Jen peeked her head in, and I sat my cheek against my knee, watching her. She was gorgeous and tough all at once, put-together but never fussy. She always seemed immaculate, even now in her polo and chambray shorts. In pristine New Balance. Preppy to a popped-collar tee. Next to Jack, she reminded me of a greyhound, all lithe energy and intelligence next to Jack's solid muscle.

"Oh, look, there's a couch, Em can sleep there. Or you can." Her shoulders lifted. "Or you two can share a room." She winked, and I clamped my mouth shut in a thin line.

A beetle clicked along the porch banister. Iridescent wings folded into a neat round body. I watched it so that I wouldn't have to watch Jack watch me.

I could feel his eyes on me, his irritation at Jen's couch assumptions rolling off him.

Solidly irritated. Everything about Jack was solid. Personality, brains, body. Solid. Nothing wiggly about him.

I tore my eyes away from the bug as the door slammed behind Jen, pressing my forehead back into my knees, feet flat on the seat of the chair.

The slatted patio floorboards creaked, and the rocker gently moved.

"Hey."

"What?" My voice was muffled against my legs, my cheeks heating the skin on my thighs.

"Lena was just teasing you. That's what you two have always done. Still do, I guess."

I peeked out from under my hair. Jack squatted beside the chair, somehow managing to look both adorable and ferocious as he balanced on the balls of his feet. Only Jack. I closed my eyes, shutting him out. He wasn't wrong. Lena and I could be jerks extraordinaire to each other. Always had been. It's our love language. Still, this was supposed to be my happy place. I was here, in the cottage, flowers all around me, bees bumbling and buzzing merrily from bloom to bloom.... Tears pricked my eyes.

"Hey. Come on, Em, how is this any different than usual?" His hand was on my shoulder, his muscled forearm barely registering in my periphery.

Because it's about you, idiot. Because she knows *I've always loved you.*

I sucked in a breath, shock rendering me limp. *Love.* It was that simple. And that difficult. My brain reeled, and I focused with laser like clarity on one thought above all else.

Jack was taken.

If I truly loved him, if I cared for him at all, I couldn't stand in his way. I had to let him go. Wasn't that what the old song said? Or saying? If you love somebody, set them free?

Definitely a Sting song.

Humming a little, I straightened in the chair, tucking my legs in crosswise underneath me. Nearby, a cicada began singing, and the green beetle took wing across the thick summer air.

"I'm just grumpy. I didn't get much sleep. Probably hangry, too. And it's hot. Too hot out here." *Babbling, Em, straight babbling.*

Jack cocked his head at me, lips pursed. He knew I was lying. But he also knew I got hangry.

"Lunch and a swim."

"Lunch and a swim," I echoed, keeping my face blank as he rose to his feet, beaming down at me. Then my brain fired. Jack in swim trunks. Water sluicing down his shoulders, his six pack. I swallowed.

"I don't know."

Jack rolled his eyes. "Fine. Stay here and stay hot." His gaze met mine, and something sparked between us. *Stay hot.*

And then Jack crushed that spark, closing his mouth with a click and put a hand on the door, headed inside.

Stay hot.

I lurched up, the chair rocking me forward and slightly off balance as I slammed onto my feet. My brain scrambled for something to say. Anything. I couldn't go back to how things had been between us. I couldn't lose him. I'd support his relationship. I could be a great friend. I could do now what I'd failed to do with Beth.

I could push all that heat down deep inside, until it froze over.

"What was in the box?" It exploded out of me. I closed the distance between us, and his eyes narrowed. As if he knew what I was thinking.

"A key. An old one. Antique." If he had an inkling of how my brain was operating, a search and destroy mission dead set on rooting out all romantic thoughts, he didn't show it. His shoulders were firm, the perfect picture of a linebacker on the opposition team. Broad. Strong. Dangerous.

Get it together, Em.

Well, nobody said it would be easy to just turn off my emotions. I wasn't a fictitious hundred-year-old vampire creeping on a high school kid.

"You have the oddest look on your face." He tilted his chin.

I scrubbed my palm over my eyes, as though it would wipe my traitorous thoughts away.

"A key?"

He took his hand from the door, leaning against it, capable hands hidden in his pockets.

"Old. Too old to be anything in this place." Jack jerked his head towards the cabin. "I mean, maybe the original cabin, but

I checked—the locks here are new. No." He shook his head, lush lips quirking to the side. "It's something else."

Curiosity bloomed in my chest. And I welcomed it, relieved. Better curiosity than the lust that raged there previously.

A mystery. My eyes widened, and my lips curved into a broad grin.

Jack pinched the bridge of his nose. "God, Em. I know *that* look."

"What look?" My eyelashes batted of their own accord.

He groaned, choking back a laugh. "That's the exact same face you made junior year."

"Listen, the mascot had it coming."

"He did *not* have it coming."

"No one *made* you prop the closet door open." My eyebrow twitched, but a laugh threatened to escape.

"The way I remember it, you threatened to replace my shampoo with superglue if I didn't aid and abet your criminal activity."

I huffed. "It was hardly criminal. Youthful prank, sure."

He arched an eyebrow, one hand leaving his pocket to poke me on the shoulder. I'd stepped closer at some point in our conversation, closing the gap between us. Drawn into his orbit, the gravitational pull of his bulk more than I could resist.

Can't deny physics.

"And it's the same look you had when we got caught digging in the graveyard."

"You always make that sound so much worse than it was. I wanted those tulip bulbs, okay? They were the perfect Mother's Day present and you *know* it."

He snorted, his meltingly brown eyes never leaving mine.

"They looked good in the front yard, admit it." I squinted up at him. The tulips bloomed bright pink and orange the following spring.

A smile graced his lips, wrinkling the corners of his lips, and my breath caught. I pivoted, coughing into my hand.

Resist. Resist.

A deep, throaty sigh sounded from where Jack still stood, leaning against the front door of the murder cabin. I didn't have to turn to know just how his chest looked as it rose and fell. To know that he was close to capitulating.

"I tell you what, Em. I saw a hardware store back in town. Maybe they can tell us what kind of lock the key belongs to. We'll grab a sandwich, eat on the way, come back and swim." Jack's voice dripped with reluctance.

I peeked at him over my shoulder. He still wore that small smile.

Despite convincing him to go along with me again, I couldn't gloat. I might have won the battle, but I'd surrender before the war.

I wouldn't hurt him again.

"All right, Scooby. Should we tell the whole gang before we get in the mystery machine?"

His jaw dropped in mock indignation. "You and I both know I'm Fred."

"Hmmmm. I don't know. *Fred* doesn't love sandwiches as much as you do."

"Fine. Fine!" He threw his hands up. "Get in the car. We'll eat later."

I bounded a few steps forward, the patio creaking underfoot, before pulling up short as I remembered we were missing an integral part of the plan.

"Umph." Jack's upper body slammed into my back, and the kinetic energy provided by his forward motion propelled me off my feet. Objects in motion, or whatever.

And I was airborne.

My breath whooshed out of me in a strangled noise. Is this what it was like to sky-dive? Time slowed as I fell, face forward, sure to end up with a mouth full of East Texas dirt. I scrambled to catch myself, hands reaching out. Though the purple and red firecracker salvia *was* especially gorgeous from a mid-flight angle. A fat bumblebee collecting nectar paused, as though to say, *hey lady, flight isn't anatomically possible for you.*

Glass houses, bumblebee.

Then Jack's muscled arm wrapped around my chest, stopping my fall. Pulling me close. My back snug against the hard plane of his pecs, my butt up against.... My eyes widened and the clean scent of him washed over me, holding me as tight as the arm keeping me from falling.

"Em—" His breath was torment against my ear, the sensitive skin of my neck.

I couldn't handle the closeness. My hormones started rampaging, adrenaline and endorphins and estrogen King-Konging their way straight to my ovaries.

"We need the key!" The words screamed out of me, and King-Kong paused his downward path, my ticking hormonal clock clenched in his hand.

As for Jack's hand, it was on my boob. Under his grip, the friction of his palm, my nipple got hard.

With one headlight...

Terrible songs notwithstanding, I needed to move. Distraction! Distraction.

"Show me the key." I whipped out of his grip, pretending not to pant, hugging my arms around myself. If he so much as mentioned touching my boobs, I'd either choke him or jump his bones.

With one headlight...

The more I thought about not singing that damn song, the more it threatened to come out of my mouth.

Jack's face was blank, confused, maybe. He pulled a key from his back pocket.

And just like that, my hormones quit. King-Kong shut his

stupid gorilla face and jumped off my fallopian tubes. I stepped forward, the hairs on the back of my neck now at attention.

A skeleton key. Pitch black. An aged satin ribbon hung from the end.

"Oh, that's definitely a cursed object." I dragged my gaze back to his face.

Jack stared up at the porch ceiling, as though the lazily spinning fan shared his irritation with me. I looked up, in case there was a dangerous bug he watched instead.

"Do you want to go, or not?" He finally asked, after finishing communing with the ceiling fan.

I rolled my eyes and started towards his Bronco. Jack stood, still shaking his head in annoyance or laughter, I couldn't tell.

"Get in loser, we're going shopping for cursed objects," I yelled back at him, jerking open the Bronco's door open and hopping in.

18

———————

EMMA

The Bronco squealed, moaning in slight distress as Jack threw the wheel to the left. I didn't blame it. The tension between us was thick enough to cut with a knife. The air rife with unsaid things, my skin electrified from the memory of his arm around me.

I ignored it. So what if the skin was the human body's biggest organ?

It wasn't the organ I was most concerned with.

Jack cleared his throat, and I jumped. He gave me a look. The one that clearly asked, *what the hell is wrong with you?*

Oh, nothing, Jack, just thinking about licking you. Nothing to see here.

"You sure you can handle this?"

I opened my mouth to object, but he held up a hand. "I know, I know. You're super tough when it comes to pulling a prank, but we both know that you had nightmares for months after we went to the drive-in theater to see *Scream*."

"I'm a grown-up." It didn't answer the question, and he and I both knew it.

But he only shrugged, reaching for the door handle.

It was just a key. That's all.

No way was the cabin *actually* a murder cabin. There was a reasonable explanation for the fog in the mirror of the bathroom and the possessed demon doll and for the fact that the entire freaking house gave me a serious case of the 'get me the hell out of heres.'

If it hadn't been for Jack, I woulda been the hell out of there. He stood at the entrance to the hardware store, eyebrows disappearing into his hairline.

Oh. I unbuckled the seat belt and jumped out after him.

THE STORE WAS a throwback to decades past, evidenced by the thin layer of dust accumulated across every surface. Texas themed knick-knacks competed for space with hammers and wrenches and the usual odds and ends at a hardware store. Distorted country music jangled through the air, slightly slow and off pitch and altogether awful. I winced.

"What's wrong with the stereo?" I nudged Jack, my elbow grazing his torso. He glanced down at me, the first eye contact we'd made since the historic boob graze. Still electric. *Too soon.*

For me, anyway.

"Haunted speakers." His gaze skittered away and he picked up an armadillo statuette with an incredulous look. The little armored rodent basked in a field of bluebonnets and sported a crown of yellow roses. "Look at this beauty."

"I'd rather not. And haunted speakers? That's not a thing."

Jack's expression turned serious, his playful smile vanishing. "What, you think speakers can't be haunted? Anything can be haunted. Take this beautiful piece of artwork, for example. Definitely possessed by the spirits of roadkill past."

"I hate you," I muttered, examining a jar of questionable salsa that appeared older than I was.

"You love me." His dimple flashed, and I caught myself on a shelving unit before I swooned. "What's wrong, did you twist your ankle earlier?"

"Yes, uh-huh. I did." I didn't.

"Welcome in, y'all. What can I help you two fine folks with today?" An older gentleman appeared behind the back counter, watching us with narrowed eyes. "You plan on buying that armadillo, or you just taking it on a walk?"

Jack set the statue down, and we exchanged a look.

"Any idea what kind of lock this key goes to?" Jack's voice was lower, gruffer than usual. He produced the black key, and a nervous fluttery feeling bloomed in my stomach as I watched him hand it over.

"See here, this is a skeleton key. That's the beauty of old things like this, they can open nearly anything." The old man's jowls quivered as he smacked his lips, taking the key and turning it in his hands. Then something flit across his face, a tightening across his eyes, a slight flaring of the nostrils. Before I could place it, his expression returned to one of nonchalance. "Not that your generation would know much about quality, but they don't make 'em like this anymore."

I mentally crossed that phrase off my baby boomer bingo card. Four more and I might screech into the abyss, maybe startle some dust off the shelves. B-I-N-G-O.

"It was in a cabin we're staying at for the weekend," Jack explained, avoiding my attempt at eye contact, though I detected a slight twitch in his jaw.

Found it up at the murder cabin, know anything about doll possession?

"Aw, y'all must be the sweet little honeymooners everyone's

been talking about. Heard you might be in the market for that ol' run-down place. Real money pit, if you ask me."

"All it needs is some TLC and *someone* with a vision." And a shit ton of money, and time, and literally no other life prospects. Kept you focused. "And we're not together." No reason to pretend. Or make Jack any more uncomfortable around me. Not when I was *this* close to getting him to invest on my dream with me. I glanced at him, gauging his reaction.

Oh. Oh, no.

The corners of Jack's mouth turned down. The warmth went out of his eyes.

Ugh. Now he was probably thinking about how much it was going to cost to make my vision come to life. How it *was* a bad investment. I toed the scuffed-up floorboards, staring at the chipped pedicure on my feet.

How I was a bad investment.

"Hmmph. You kids better use protection up there."

"Excuse me?" My jaw dropped, and I mentally blacked out another bingo square for use of 'you kids.' And a third for being an old, interfering coot.

"Ya know, DEET? For the bugs?" The man rummaged around beneath the register, producing two dark green cans of bug spray. "Ticks, mosquitoes, you name it, it'll bite. Better safe than sorry."

Jack's jaw twitched again. I cleared the 'old coot recommends saving it for marriage' square on my imaginary bingo card but was ready to fill it back in at a moment's notice.

I eyeballed the nametag on the man's taupe utilitarian button down. Earl. Of course his name was Earl. "So, the key? Any idea why it would be in our cabin?" I prompted.

"Of course," Earl continued, white and hoary eyebrow raised, "if y'all need another type of protection, the pharmacy has plenty."

That was it. I slammed my hand down on the counter. "Earl!"

Earl held up his hands in the universal mea culpa sign. "I don't sell sunscreen here, miss. Just trying to help."

Sunscreen. I couldn't even look at Jack. Sunscreen. I filled the 'old coot' bingo square back in out of spite. He *knew* what he was doing.

Probably.

"This here key." Earl dangled the key by the aging ribbon, and I stopped myself from snatching it out of his hands. "I don't need to tell you what kind of lock it matches. I can tell you exactly what it belongs to."

He leaned closer, a conspiratorial narrowing to his eyes.

"The old Gertrude Akins Hotel. Used to be the glory of this town. Couples, families, you name it." His eyes closed briefly, a small smile on his face. "Operated close to a hundred years before it closed. Good thing we've got an even better bed and breakfast in town now."

Fumbling around, he produced a brochure with a picture of a bona fide Hansel & Gretel style Victorian house. Ick. So not my thing.

"Is this where you were supposed to stay?" I asked Jack.

"Looks like it." He shrugged, but his eyes were mischievous. "I bet you'd look great in a floral bed surrounded by matching floral wallpaper."

"Now see here, you two, there's no reason to go knocking a small business owner's pride in joy. No respect anymore." Earl swiped the brochure off the counter.

"Sorry," I squeaked out. Damn small towns! Earl was probably BFF with whomever ran the place. I grimaced. *Not a good way to fit in with the locals, Emma.*

"As far as your key and that hotel..." He shook his head, the irritation replaced by an even sterner look. "I would steer clear of there if I were you."

I leaned in, my voice low, a near whisper. "Why not?"

"Because it ain't safe, missy. Nope. It's been condemned. Only functioning part of that old place is the owner's cabin, where you two are staying now." He opened his mouth like he wanted to say more, then closed it again, running a hand through his hair. What was left of it, at least.

"Because it's abandoned," Jack said. It wasn't a question. He gave me a meaningful look, as if to say 'I told you so.'

Earl leaned back, gripping the edge of the weathered Formica counter. "That's certainly part of it. Never safe to go poking around an old, rotting house, is it?" He raised an eyebrow, and I scooched closer. "But that's not the whole story. Nope."

"What's the whole story?" I couldn't keep the dread out of my voice. Next to me, Jack shifted, his elbow nearly rubbing against my shoulder. I failed in ignoring it.

"Things go wrong up there. Ever since Miss Gertrude Charlotte Akins passed. There was that drowning, and then that fire." Earl dropped his forearms to the counter, so close now I could see a slight mustard stain on the corner of his mouth. "Don't go in there because it's not safe, sure. But one of the reasons it ain't safe is because it's haunted."

"Haunted," I breathed, rapt.

"Haunted," Jack repeated. Glass half-empty-of-ghosts mindset, that one.

"Believe what you want to believe." Earl shrugged, pushing the bug spray at us. "Just don't come runnin' to me with your tail between your legs when you find somethin' you can't explain."

I startled as a whoosh of indignant air burst forth from Jack. "You expect us to believe that?"

Earl narrowed his eyes, his paunch pressing into the countertop. "I don't *expect* you to do anything. Just tryin' to give you a friendly warning, is all. In fact, if you folks wanna stay out here for the weekend, I just had a room open up at my bed and breakfast."

"Your bed and breakfast?" Jack stepped closer. "Is that right?" There was no mistaking the menace in his voice. Damn. Our boy Earl must've gone and pissed him off on the phone. I stifled a giggle.

"Best one round these parts, and always will be. Stay out there if you ain't interested, don't bother me one bit." The glower he leveled at Jack belied his nonchalance. "Don't go lookin' for trouble and you won't find it. Simple as that. Bug spray comes to $12.79."

I scrounged up a twenty-dollar bill and tapped my toes on the floor while Earl huffed and puffed and nearly blew the register down as he counted out change. The blackened cast iron key sat on the countertop, and I picked it up.

It was heavy in my hand. Surprisingly warm to the touch, though that made sense, seeing as how Jack carried it in his back pocket. I grew less jealous of the key when I remembered how Earl held it, too.

Earl stuck out a fist full of coins and bills, jaw thrust forward.

He looked pissed, dumping the coins into my cupped hand without meeting my eyes.

"You really believe there is a ghost?"

Pursing his lips, Earl drew his eyes up and away from the key.

"I believe this world is right full of things we don't understand. I believe I've seen things at that house ain't nobody can explain. Y'all should get out of town while you still can," he paused, tapping his temple, "I *believe* y'all shouldn't go messin' with things that don't wanna be messed with. Not like that girlie down the road with her Tarot and her tea leaves and coffee."

"What girl?" I asked.

"One that makes them pastries, kolaches. Real good. Too bad it comes with a side of the devil."

I bit my tongue, tempted to ask him just how she served the devil: Sautéed? Fried? With okra? But decided better of it. Like a damn adult. I mentally patted myself on the back.

Jack rolled his eyes so hard I could've sworn I heard them rocketing around his eye sockets. With one last long look, Earl bustled away from the register off to restock his bug-spray or inventory screws, who knew.

"We're getting kolaches."

"And a psychic advice?"

"It's called tarot, smart ass," I said, committing to the idea. "Although, if she has a psychic device, who am I to argue?" All I knew was that I wanted to wipe the know-it-all smirk off Jack's face, prove there was a ghost/demon doll, but also never *see* said ghost or demon doll.

Oh, and that I had no business even imagining screws. Period.

"We can go there only if you tell me what you're thinking about," Jack said.

I gave him my most pissed-off bitch face. "I'd rather walk."

19

———

EMMA

Tarot, Kolache, and Coffee was an eclectic mashup that landed somewhere between swanky café and dark arts and crafts. A massive display filled with multicolored crystals and packs of gorgeously illustrated tarot cards. A spellbook. Candles, candles, and more candles. A few crystal balls, covered in crushed velvet and accompanied by signs proclaiming that if we broke it, we bought it. And to leave them covered.

Which, naturally, made me want to pull their plush little blankets right on off.

"I don't even have to ask what you're thinking."

"What?" I said innocently.

"You want to yank off the covers."

I fingered the corner of a particularly tempting cloth. "Maybe."

"Don't." Chimes filled the air, and a dark-haired woman moved towards us from the depths of the shop. "Don't take the covers off."

I smiled, dropping my hand. "Why? Will bad spirits take over them?" I wiggled my fingers a bit.

The woman was about my age, late twenties, raven black hair and full red lips, a bit shorter than me, great figure. Jack's type. I tried not to scowl.

"That's possible, I suppose. But more likely? They could cause a fire." She pointed to the open window and sunny skies. "They amplify the sun." She frowned at my disbelieving expression. "It's physics, not metaphysics. It's like when a kid roasts an ant with a magnifying glass."

"Charming," I said.

She smiled, white teeth flashing. "Isn't it? What can I do for you?"

I cleared my throat, trying to decide how to proceed. Trying to decide if I really wanted to go there. To contact the spirits. Or whatever.

She tapped a long, black nail against her cheek. "Why don't we start with coffee and see how you feel?"

I bit my cheek and glanced at Jack, who shrugged. I rolled my eyes. Great help, he was.

"We have a ghost problem." I sighed, following her, trying not to notice how she wiggled her hips. Hoping Jack didn't notice at all.

When I looked back at him, he was studiously observing all the tchotchkes for sale.

It made me happier than it should have.

"Ghost problem, huh?" She didn't sound alarmed. Or surprised. "Y'all must be the people staying up at the old cabin on that hotel property. That place is downright good for business." A slight Texas accent threaded through her speech. "Kolaches?"

The yeasty, delicious smell of pastries wafted through the air, and I took a deep breath. Jack blinked like he'd awoken from a dream, inhaling deeply, eyes widening with fresh interest.

"I'll take that as a yes. I'm Tara. Y'all are a little late, but I still have a few from this morning. Half price, since I don't expect another rush at this hour." She winked and bustled behind a heavy wood counter I hadn't noticed before, pulling out several fruit-filled pastries and the unmistakable shape of sausage filled kolaches. Two cups followed, and she fussed over arranging everything on a floral tray before filling a gorgeous silver carafe with coffee and setting the whole ensemble on the table.

"Sugar? Cream?"

"No, thanks."

"So now that you have carbs, tell me all about your ghost infestation."

Jack and I filled her in between bites of delicious pastry. My role was the explainer: lay out in logical detail all the things the ghost(s) had done. Poor pitiful possessed porcelain Lucy, creepy cold spots the steamy message in the mirror, the sad entreaty in scrabble tiles, the Bronco not working, then working (at which Jack let out a big sigh and even bigger eye roll) and finally, the cursed key.

Jack's role was to consume inordinate amounts of kolaches and punctuate my narrative with disbelieving grunts.

Tara listened, asking questions and smiling or frowning as she paced the room, her long glossy black hair swinging. Black polished nails skated over the surface of her displays, slender fingers tugging out books until she had a rather large pile.

I grimaced. "How bad is it?"

"Well, your spirits don't sound unfriendly." She stretched the word out, lips twisted to the side as she thought. "But I don't like the doll possession. That's decidedly bizarre."

"Decidedly," I agreed. Tara was clearly good people.

Jack shook his head and opened his mouth. I shoved a kolache in it before he could argue.

"So do you think I should—"

"Tch tch tch!" She held up one finger, and I snapped my mouth shut. Jack shot me an aggravated frown as Tara flipped through the trinkets and books she'd piled. A minute passed. Two. Kolaches occupied some of my time, as did the coffee.

Finally, she thrust a small book onto the table.

"Here. There might be something in there to help you."

"Might be?" I asked.

Jack canted his head skeptically, his eyes narrowed. The bit of cherry filling left on his lip really ruined the effect.

It made me want to kiss it off of him, for one thing.

Nope. Bad idea. Bad.

"We'll take it," I nearly shouted.

Tara clapped her hands, her bracelets jangling on her arms. "Perfect. You'll know what you want to use when you thumb through it."

Jack looked between us, incredulous. "You've got to be kidding me. This is your advice? No wonder you said that property is good for business."

My eyes narrowed in irritation. But then the red cherry filling called to me, a matador's flag to a bull. Right above the bow on his upper lip, that cute little speck needed to be wiped away. Just one liiiiiittle touch would do it. Or a nice loooong lick.

I cleared my throat. I needed to get out of there before I did something stupid. Stupid and regrettable.

"How much for the coffee and food and the ... spell book?" My fingers grazed over the rough black fabric cover, tracing the silver embossed swirls and whirls.

"Fifty dollars." Her smile dimpled. "I take cash or card. No checks." She pointed to a sign next to an iPad register.

Highway robbery.

I glanced back at Jack, who was licking his lips.

I ground my teeth and produced the card.

20

JACK

Lena peered around the corner of the kitchen as Hurricane Emma swept through the living room, trying to catch my eye.

I ignored her. At this rate, I wasn't going to have to do anything to convince her this place was a bad investment. She was doing it all herself.

So why did that make my chest ache?

"We should do a séance," Em pronounced, rummaging through the coat closet.

Lena's eyebrows nearly shot past her hairline.

"What? How do you go from telling me we should leave immediately to wanting to make contact."

"Maybe it's a friendly ghost?"

"What are you even looking for, Em?" Lena's eyes were narrowed in concern.

"Candles." She held out a bag full of tealights.

Jen appeared in the hallway, disbelief etched on her face. "Candles?"

"She wants to hold a séance." Lena shot her a knowing look.

I ran a hand through my hair. "The guy at the hardware store said there was a ghost. Now she has a spell book and she wants to make friends with it."

"Good idea," Em muttered, still elbows deep in the closet.

"It's not a ghost."

"Fine." She spun toward me, a ferocious curl to her lip. Attack dogs were less terrifying. "Then what's your big explanation, Jack?"

I loved her like this. All fire.

"I told you. Raccoons. And probably mice. We don't have a ghost problem. We have a vermin problem."

"Maybe that can be part of our business plan." Her blue-gray eyes glittered dangerously. "We can specialize in eradicating pests from all planes, earthly and astral." She stalked towards me.

"See! Even you know this is ridiculous."

"What's *ridiculous* is that you don't take me seriously. Ever."

She was so close now I could graze her flushed cheeks with a finger, if I only reached out to touch her. My heart sped up. My brain scrambled to come up with a response.

"I do take you seriously. I think you are stressed out, I think noises kept you up all night—" *Stop there, stop there, don't...* "—and I think you're spiraling after being used by that asshole you threw to the curb, and you're coming up with any excuse to backpedal from your grand idea to buy this place, same as always." It floated out of my mouth before I had time to shut it.

Em's eyes went wide with shock. And hurt. My ears rang in the sudden silence.

"I didn't mean that."

"Yes, you did." She bit her lip. "Fine. Fine. I'm a flake, whatever."

"I'm sorry, Em. I was out of line." I couldn't lose her again. Not after all this time apart.

She crossed her arms, steely blue gaze pinning me. "It's not okay. But maybe you're right." Deflated, she collapsed onto the couch, fluffing a pillow dazedly.

"No, Em. I was wrong. You can do this." I sat next to her. I was such an asshole. "You can do anything."

She looked up at me, tears brimming along her eyelashes. Sniffling, she wiped her thumb across her eyes. I half-reached out to help before anchoring my arm in my lap.

"This doesn't mean there isn't a ghost." Her chin jutted out.

"You're right. It *is* possible. And I'm sorry. Really. You didn't deserve that."

A slight smile dazzled me. One inch more and I could take her hand in mine. I kept the thought that there was, indeed, a raccoon, and I had, indeed, met said raccoon, to myself.

Time to initiate plan: Humane Raccoon Capture.

Impulsively, I reached out and squeezed her hand, losing a second to marvel at how soft it was, how it fit in mine. The flush on her cheeks deepened. We were so close I could count all the freckles across her nose. Smell the citrus and spice scent of her skin.

I could kiss her.

And ruin any hope of working with her. Which would be the last nail in the coffin of our friendship. Her lips parted, and I sprang to my feet.

"I'll, uh." I scratched my stubble. "Go see about eliminating any chance of the noise being raccoon related." Set up the traps. Humane, of course.

"I'll come with you." Jen reappeared, hair pulled back in a tight ponytail. I was so wrapped up in Emma I hadn't even noticed she'd left. Lena leaned against the wall separating the kitchen and living area, exasperated.

"Sure, okay."

21

———

EMMA

The bread squished under my fingers as I tore a piece off the artisan-level sandwich. Particular didn't even begin to describe it when it came to Jack's level of weirdness preparing food. Sweet and savory caramelized onion. Crisp fried bacon, just on the edge of burnt. Crunchy verdant romaine, paper thin mesquite roasted turkey.

Shoulder-to-shoulder, he'd forced me to stand near him and watch. Explaining in low tones how the onions should look as their sugars broke down, turning them golden brown. He watched the bacon like a hawk, lips pursing as it fried in the cast iron pan he dug out of one of the cabinets.

How could anyone not fall in love with him? The way he attacked the simple process of putting together a sandwich—it was art. His single-mindedness and obsession with making a masterpiece out of the most mundane ingredients.

And it paid off.

"Good?" His eyes were on me as my teeth sank into the

sandwich, one leg tucked underneath me. My skin thrummed at the attention.

Friends, friends, friends, friends.

I chanted to myself, an internal mantra. If only I believed it.

"You don't like it?" He angled his head, chewing slowly. Thoughtfully. The way he was with everything. "You've got the oddest look on your face."

I swallowed the lump of food stuck in my throat. "You're delicious."

Fuck.

"Your cooking. The food. The food is delicious."

Jack snorted, and I suppressed the urge to dive beneath the table, choosing instead to take an even larger bite. Yes. Because that was all I needed to do, choke and then force him to wrap those ridiculously buff arms around me and...

This was ridiculous. I stood up, so abrupt I knocked the chair over behind me.

"Em..." Jack stared at me, open-mouthed.

"I'm going to check out the lake. Take a swim. I don't feel like eating."

What I wanted my lips on *wasn't* a sandwich.

I pivoted away, running from the kitchen. Jen and Lena were already down at the lake, splashing and being annoyingly in love, but whatever. I didn't have to be near them. In the room where they'd stashed our stuff, I tore off my clothes at record speed, tugging the suit on and fastening the top as quick as I could.

In the cool dark of the room, it was obvious when the phone screen lit up. Jack's phone. On the charger. My eyes darted to it, because, well, it was bright and shiny and I was standing right there.

A text. From Caroline.

I mean, it was right *there*. He didn't have his screen locked. I could just peek. I shouldn't.

So that meant I absolutely would.

Caro: @ your house now. Thanks for packing up my stuff. I really do wish the best for you. Sorry it ended like this

The phone slid from my fingers. What the actual fuck? What the *fuck*? My head spun, vision blurring.

He'd packed up her stuff? Why would he pack up her stuff? Why wasn't she on her goddamn business trip? My stomach turned, nausea rolling over me in a wave. The room shrank, disappearing until it was just me and the light from Jack's phone screen.

Jack *lied* to me. He told me they were together. Wait. *Had* he told me she was his girlfriend? Not exactly. So why didn't he tell me they'd broken up? I was a split second from staring at the ceiling and screaming the word at the fan.

The answer was simple: because he didn't want me.

He'd never want me. Not again. He lied (okay, by omission) about Caroline because he *knew*. My pulse throbbed in my temples, heat rising across my chest and neck and face. *Shame.* Jack *knew* I wanted to jump his bones in a repeated, heated, super-hot fashion and was keeping me at arm's length when I'd rather be at dick's length.

Fuuuuuuck this.

The house blurred by me. I slid on my shoes, ignoring the hulking hot mess of a man who definitely looked like a total asshole with a cute kitchen towel draped over one shoulder as he deposited my mostly uneaten sandwich into a plastic bag.

I heard him call my name. It made me angrier. The sweltering heat of the September afternoon hit me full force and I blinked against the sudden assault of sunshine.

How dare it be sunny in a moment like this? How dare it?

Dust curled up around my feet as I stomped through the trail.

What had he said to me? 'Would it kill me if I acted like I cared about his happiness for once?'

"Well, fuck you very much, Liar McLiarson." My angry muttering startled a rabbit, who tucked tail and ran into the underbrush. Hide while you can, Thumper. Bambi's mom gets killed, spoiler alert.

The wooded trail was denser than I expected. The already narrow path grew narrower, blackberry brambles brushing up against the bare skin of my legs. I slapped a hand down, squashing a bloodthirsty mosquito. Great. Now I'd be covered in more attractive bites and probably get chiggers or ticks or both.

Not the love nibbles I had in mind.

I'd been fooling myself. As usual, the hot mess express (it me) left all rational thought of *actually* doing something to move forward, and instead I'd thrown all those dreams away for a shot with Jack Colson.

"Would it kill him to be honest with me for once?" I shouted, raking a hand through my hair. I tilted my chin up. A flock of grackles took wing from a nearby tree, sending a cascade of pine needles to the forest floor. Tears threatened, and I blinked rapidly, surprised by how quickly the trees all but eclipsed my view of the blue sky.

Irritated by my stupid watering eyeballs, I continued down the trail. My sandals slapped across the path, which, now that I looked at it, seemed a lot less like a path and a hell of a lot more like forest. Maybe what used to be a path. Another mosquito droned by my ear, and I slapped at my face. Damn. I should've grabbed the bug spray.

I stopped, peering around. The only sounds were the constant drone of cicadas, the odd rustling of undergrowth as small creatures darted out of my way. The caw of a crow.

Uneasy, my fingernails scraped across a new bug bite. *Sexy.*

How long had I been walking, anyway? Shouldn't I be at the lake by now?

Whatever.

I'd already gone this far, I wasn't about to turn around and get Jack. Nope.

I squared my shoulders, continuing down the overgrown path. The cabin must not have had many visitors lately, that was for sure. How much further I could go before I'd need a machete was debatable. A few hundred yards later, I stopped again. Looked around.

My neck prickled, and the unmistakable feeling of being watched triggered that weird animal part of my brain. The one that sat up and shook me and screamed, *'Danger, you absolute fucking moron!'*

I'd somehow dropped into a half crouch, looking back over my shoulder. Despite the heavy forest cover, I felt incredibly exposed. Probably because I was wearing the tiniest scraps of clothing I owned and had neglected to put on a cover up in my haste to get the hell away from Jack.

Stop thinking about hell, stop thinking about hell, stop thinking about...

The unmistakable sound of a large animal traipsing through undergrowth sent the hair on the arms straight up. Probably a deer.

Maybe an axe murderer.

Potato, po-tah-to.

I wheeled back around, determined to make it through the thicket and to the lake before my impending doom. At least then maybe Lena and Jen could find my body more easily. Should I leave behind bits of DNA evidence? Too bad I couldn't just leave behind scraps of clothes, seeing as how I was only wearing a bikini. I twisted the stretchy strand hanging from my neck.

I'd definitely dressed the part. Prime murder victim clothes.

I quickened my pace into an awkward walk-jog, hampered by the thin soles of my flip-flops slapping against the soles of my feet. And the thickening underbrush.

This was not the way to the lake. Clearly, this path hadn't been used in weeks, if not months. The sound drew closer, and I sucked in a breath, choking on it and making an odd sobbing noise.

I didn't want to die. Not in my bikini. Almost any other outfit I'd be okay with. Something cute, not overstated, but that spoke to my wittiness and potential. Something the detectives would look at and say, "Poor girl, stricken down in the prime of her life, right when she was starting to get it all together. And look how nice her shoes are. Such a put together outfit."

In the criminal justice system, fashion-based offenses are considered especially heinous.

I whacked another massive mosquito from my stomach. Well, if I died soon, at least these damn bug bites wouldn't itch anymore.

And it wouldn't matter that Jack hated me so much that he had to lie to me about dating Caroline/Kitty 7.0.

I'd never get to tell Jack how I felt. Or have sex with him.

That did it. Now I was pissed, fear melting into anger and absurdity.

I walk-jogged a few more yards, and suddenly the thick woods opened up into a clearing. The blue sky peeked out from behind a massive grey-black thunderhead.

Fuck.

No one was going to find my body if there was a storm.

No sooner had the thought crossed my mind than a loud peal of thunder cracked across the sky. A gust of air whooshed around the clearing, sending leaves swirling. Leaf-mold and the metallic scent of storm washed over me.

Something clacked, sending my adrenaline skyrocketing through my veins.

I turned, slowly, tracking the noise. To my left, flanked by two massive oak trees, stood an old, decrepit house. As the wind from the oncoming storm picked up, a loose shutter swung, flinging across a broken window.

The door hung open, the iron chains on the handles rendered useless by the fact the hinges on one side had come completely undone.

It must have been gorgeous, once, but now? The house was nearly entirely grey, the wood weathered and cracked beyond repair. A front porch wrapped around it, and a rocking chair similar to the one back at the cabin swayed in the wind from the storm.

And it wasn't the only thing moving.

A sign hanging from a beam in front of the door wavered in the wind. And above it, the motion that caught my eye. Something white, diaphanous, moved against the cracked window pane on the second floor. Shielding my eyes, I squinted at it. But nothing but darkness was there now.

Definitely not a ghost. A curtain. *For sure.*

This was *the* hotel. The damned haunted hotel.

Well, hopefully not a *damned* one.

Overhead, another thunderous crack sounded, rattling the sky. I winced, ducking on instinct. I shot a glance at the growling sky, then surveyed the building again.

No time like the present to check out my potential investment.

22

───────

JACK

The door slammed behind her, leaving me with a mouth hanging wide enough to catch flies. It snapped shut, and the sound of my teeth grinding against each other echoed in my ears.

Why?

Em stormed out like she caught fire, without a single glance or word in my direction. Then she stomped out to the woods. Wearing only a bikini. Looking... looking damn delicious.

But angry as a hornet. And headed in the absolute opposite direction of the lake.

Where the hell did she think she was going?

"Dammit, Em." My lips moved of their own accord, and I launched into action. Maybe she encountered Lucy the possessed doll again. Or saw a ghost. Or heard our masked trash panda friend.

I did *not* need Rocky the Rabid Raccoon taking out my oldest friend in the middle of the woods.

Oldest friend. The words stuck, thick and taffy-like, stretching themselves across my synapses. No.

More than that.

She would never be just a friend, never had been. I heaved a sigh. I never should've agreed to hear her pitch, never should've tried to make a play for the property once I knew she wanted it. I should've come clean from the beginning. I could never be a business partner to her—the brutal demise of my parent's marriage, the constant fighting, then the icy silence, the way they used me and my brother as pawns—but maybe I could be something else.

Maybe I could be *hers.*

Yeah, maybe if I didn't have to buy the property out from underneath her. Squash her dreams, convince her this property was a bad investment. Her laptop still sat on the kitchen counter, hilarious stickers crowding the cover for space.

This place probably wasn't a great investment; not for a first-time business owner.

Maybe I could help her find a better place. *Yeah, until she finds out my company screwed her out of her dream.*

Besides, I couldn't do it. I couldn't go into business with a friend. Not after my parents showed me just how badly it could end. And *badly* didn't even begin to describe it.

My mouth went dry, and outside, a tree limb waved in the wind. Beckoning.

Which left me with only one option.

Well, a series of choices, really.

On autopilot, I pulled my shoes on, lacing the shoes and shoving the near uneaten food in a bag. First, I'd go after her. Obviously, I wasn't going to let her wander around in the woods by herself.

Second, we'd have a picnic. *Romantic.*

Something in my chest constricted at the word. Was this what I really wanted? Once I jumped into the deep end with

Em, we would never go back. If it failed, *we* failed, we could never just be friends. We would either burn long and hot, or short and fast.

There were never in-betweens with Em. She didn't believe in gray areas. The world was black and white, or at least it used to be.

Romantic. Desire shot through me. Electric. The thought of my hands in her wild hair, her lips on mine...

Except she seemed mad as hell. But... *Em never could stay mad at me.*

I stuffed some paper towels in the bag, my fingers closing over a bottle of wine and adding it for good measure, too. Why not?

If we were going to—I rubbed a hand over my face. She said she wanted a picnic. I would give her the damn picnic. If *I* was going to try this, then I'd pull out all the stops.

Oh. That's what I was forgetting. I opened a door, located a corkscrew, and added it to the picnic.

Voila.

My fingers splayed on the counter, the bank of cabinets creaking against the sudden pressure. I couldn't go back. Em and I would never be the same.

And I wouldn't work with her, not like that. Not like my parents.

My head felt light, and I shook it, slowly. I was doing this. She wouldn't buy this cabin, this acreage, the raccoon infestation...

But *we* would do something else.

We could try to be together.

I could try that.

23

EMMA

The breeze kicked up a notch, sending shivers down my spine, the contrast between the heat of the day and the sudden chill of the September storm amplified by lack of clothing.

And Texas storms didn't play around. Nope. They were acts of god.

Lightning arced across the sky, punctuating the thought. I hugged my arms across my chest, cold. My breath came in ragged spurts, and I took stock of the speckles of dirt and scratches across my legs. Behind me, the wanna-be path most likely concealing a serial killer.

Before me, the hotel everyone in this damn town seemed to think was haunted.

And above me, the sure threat of a vicious fall storm. Clouds purpled the greenish tinged sky, and thunder cracked again, so loud I winced.

Fuck.

Haunted hotel versus axe murderer and death storm.

Fat droplets of rain splashed across my face. A pebble pinged off my head. Not a pebble.

Hail.

That solved that. Unless the hotel had a poltergeist, I was definitely going to be safer inside. Probably. Most likely. My sandals slapped against the rickety steps to the front porch, the sound of hail zinging across the dilapidated structure.

The door was going to be a problem. They must have been gorgeous in their heyday, curvy art deco glass now cracked. The left door sagged into the right, and I gingerly stepped over it.

The storm picked up. Wind gusted across my back, pushing me into the house and causing me to lose my balance. My hands spread across the filthy wood floors, and I sneezed, sending a cloud of dust into the air.

I added skinned knees to my collection of wounds. Still, better than a hail-induced concussion. Or an axe murderer.

I leaned back, sitting on my heels, letting my eyes adjust to the dim. Around me the hotel groaned against the onslaught of the storm. Or maybe it was the moans of tortured souls, who knew. Tortured souls might be good for business. Maybe I could market this fucking disaster child of a project as a haunted, lead themed excursions and go big on Halloweens.

I sat in a large, cleared space, a balcony with ornate wood fretwork separating what appeared to be rooms on the second floor. A bookcase lined the walls, a large built-in counter directly in front of me.

"Checking in?"

"I will KILL you!" I screeched, scooting back with a speed my middle school track coach would never have thought I was capable of.

Jack peered over the door. "That seems unnecessary."

I clutched at my heart, tears squeezing out. "What are *you* doing here?"

He was the *last* person I wanted to see.

He was the only person I wanted to see.

He stepped over the sagging door, wincing as he rubbed his arm. Jack managed it a lot more gracefully than I had, that show-off, especially considering he carried a large bag.

"Hmmm. Let me think about it." He cocked an eyebrow at me, his eyes trailing over my bare skin. Electricity followed his gaze, sending a fresh wave of goosebumps through me that had nothing to do with the storm and potential ghosts...

And everything to do with Jack.

He held up a finger, chocolate brown eyes finding my own, tear-filled ones. "One, you left the house in a rage. Two, you went traipsing off into the woods wearing nothing but a flimsy bikini and stupid shoes."

"My shoes aren't stupid." *For lying next to the pool.*

"Three," he continued, ignoring my rebuttal, "I'd really hate it if something happened to you."

"Were you behind me the whole time? Why didn't you say something? I thought you were an axe murderer." I shrieked the last part, irritated and raw and unwilling to recognize what he'd said.

But it lingered there, echoing in my ears, loud despite the caterwauling thunderstorm.

He'd hate it if something happened to me.

"Well, I'm not an axe murderer, but go ahead, be mad." He clucked his tongue and set the bag down on the dust and leaf-covered floor.

"You could have said, 'Hey, wait up!'" I mimed holding a hand up, feeling more idiotic by the second.

He crouched next to me. "I could tell I'd done something to make you pissed off. I don't know what it is." He reached out a hand, and I stilled, tensing against his touch.

He pulled a leaf out of my hair.

A leaf.

Ugh. Could I be more of a mess? Could *we*?

A sigh gusted out of me, lost in the noise of the gale force winds outside.

"Why are you mad at me?"

"Why do you think I don't care about your happiness?" I blurted. His eyes widened, and he sat down next to me. The floor creaked.

Outside, a tree branch flew across the clearing. White ice littered the ground, mud covered and filthy. Rain blew sideways, the dark sky lit by random flashes of lightning, followed by booms of thunder.

"Is that what this is about?" Jack gestured at the abandoned hotel, my bikini. "Here." He reached in the bag and pulled out a towel, wrapping it around me. His face was so close to mine, I would barely have to move to reach out and kiss him.

And I would have, if I hadn't known that he hated me. If I hadn't known he'd lied to me, that he didn't wouldn't me, and never would. It was all on the tip of my tongue, and then I swallowed it.

"It's not about *anything*. I wanted to go swimming and I went the wrong way. And now we're stuck in a haunted hotel while it rains hell outside."

"Oh." Jack looked around as though he hadn't realized where we were. "It's *the* hotel, huh?"

"Nah, it's another haunted hotel. Yes, Jack, of course it's *the* hotel. There's only one on the property, last time I checked. The good ole Gertrude Akins, AKA my Piney Woods Inn."

"Huh." He ducked his head, dark hair falling over his eyes as he fished around the bag. "I brought the key." He waved it around. "Looks like we didn't need it. Excuse me, valet, some help with our bags?" Jack mimed handing over suitcases. "No, no, no need to see the concierge, we already have our keys."

I couldn't muster a smile at his ridiculousness. I wanted to tell him. I wanted to ask him why he hadn't told me. But... I didn't want to know.

Not good enough for him.

I'd only ever hurt him. That's why he didn't tell me Caroline wasn't in the picture.

"What do you think it goes to?" Jack's voice broke through my sulking.

"No," I said. "I am not traipsing around and waking the spirits of the damned or whatever lives here."

"You really believe it's haunted?"

"I know things have been *off* since we got to this town. My car's not starting." I gestured around, the eerie moaning resuming. Jesus, it would take a fortune to restore this place. "The weird ass doll. All the people in town knowing something is fucked about this place. I know there are things I can't explain." *Like why you didn't tell me you weren't with Caroline anymore.*

He let me rant, waiting me out. How did he still know me so well? It made my heart ache.

"Maybe this is a terrible investment. Maybe it's less pie in the sky, and more six feet underground." I sniffled.

Jack snorted.

"It isn't funny."

A sigh. "You're right. It isn't funny, but you are. You always try to make people laugh, even when you're about to cry."

Another sniffle. "I'm not about to cry." I was. Just not for the reasons he thought I was.

"Okay, well you can sit here and sulk, and I'll go look to see what the key goes to." Jack stood up in one fluid motion.

"No!" I shot to my feet, clutching the towel around my shoulders. No way in hell was he going to leave me here. "That's scary movie rule number one. You don't split up to explore the haunted house."

"Then I guess you're coming with me." He set off, using the flashlight from his cellphone to light a path in the darkened interior.

"I'm so mad at you," I muttered, following him into the creaking hotel, siding vocally protesting against the storm.

Jack let out a low whistle. Bright light from his phone illuminated a grand staircase. The second-floor balcony yawned into stairs, splitting into two and flanking a large stone fireplace stretching from floor to ceiling. Weird wood carvings danced across the mantel. Nymphs and satyrs, vines and animals competed for space. Jack blew out a breath, sending white-grey dust flying into the dark.

"This place is amazing." He shined the light up the stairs. Outside, a peal of thunder shook the foundation of the hotel.

The newel posts were carved in the same fashion, writhing figures in either ecstasy or pain twined around the eight by eight slabs of wood.

"It's something," I said. That *something* being creepy as fuck. I really thought I could restore this place? That *I* could take on a project like this? This... this was more than a Joanna Gaines special, this was a money pit. My heart sank.

My hesitation must have shown in my voice. Jack tucked me under his arm, pulling me close. "Come on, Em, don't be scared."

I opened my mouth to object, to say I wasn't scared. But I was. And now I couldn't think straight, as all rational thought—POOF—disappeared due to the knowledge that the only thing separating Jack and I from being skin on skin were a few layers of fabric. Too bad he was a hateful liar. I pulled back, shrugging off his arm.

His eyes darted down. The light from the flashlight swung across my face, temporarily blinding me. Great. I blinked against it, frowning up at him.

Then that tingly sense returned. Someone, or some*thing*, was watching us. The hairs on the back of my neck stood up.

They were really getting a workout today.

Jack ran his fingers across the fireplace, tracing the lithe limbs until he exhaled in triumph.

I knew that sound. I did not like that sound.

"I knew it." His voice was low, a near whisper. I pulled the towel closer around me. The feeling of being watched multiplied. Maybe it was all the carved eyes boring into me. Maybe it was something else.

I didn't want to know *what* he knew.

And then he pulled the key from his pocket, inserting it into the fireplace. With a careful twist, the skeleton key audibly clicked, a lull in the fierce storm outside amplifying the noise. Dust billowed from the mouth of the fireplace.

A chill ran through me. The mouth of the fireplace. That's exactly what it was, and now the back stone panel coughed open, hinging backward and gaping into a black pit beyond. The creepy-crawly feeling of being watched intensified. My mouth went dry.

"I'm not going in there."

"Okay, stay out here." Jack shrugged, crouching down to fit his line-backer's body through the fireplace.

"No fucking way, and for the record, if you thought I was mad at you before, now I'm furious at you," I whispered, my furiousness diminished by the fact I was too afraid to scream at him.

"I'll protect you." Jack grabbed my dangling hand. God, it felt so good. Warm and strong and rough and so, so right. "And let the record show you've now admitted you were mad at me."

"It does not show that. It does not show that at all! I said if you *thought*, which is by no means an admission of guilt." I slipped into the fireplace, the dust and smell of fires long burnt out tickling my nose and throat. Coughing, I stepped into the room beyond. One small, cracked window provided evidence that the storm still raged outside. As if the sound alone wasn't enough proof.

"That's my girl." He pulled me closer, slightly behind him. "That's the spirit."

That asshole. He knew bickering with me would take my mind off the fact that we were definitely doing every damn dumb thing a couple would do right before they were murdered. And he also must be somewhat freaked out, if he was going to go all protective mode and smush me behind him.

Light splashed across the room. More bookcases, moldering and damp, still full of cloth bound tomes, the remnants of gilded lettering catching the light and glittering before falling silent again. A desk, scattered with leaves and odd debris blown across the house.

The light caught another reflective surface, and I choked on a scream.

The fucking demon doll.

"Is that—" Jack started to ask, and I pressed into him, hiding behind his back, as though shielding my eyes would make this mad shit stop.

A slamming noise echoed from behind us.

And that's when I lost my shit completely, jumping on Jack's back like a monkey and burying my face in the back of his neck.

The fireplace door was shut.

24

"Fuck, fuck, fuck, fuck, fuck." The words were muffled by Jack's soft, yummy smelling skin. My legs tightened around his waist, my arms wrapped under his chest.

I raised my head an inch to look over his shoulder. My hair swept over his shoulder, partially blocking my view. It was clear enough, though. We were trapped in this hidden library.

"I told you we shouldn't have come in here." My voice wheezed out, an odd cross between pissed off and scared out of my mind. I squeezed his waist with my legs, trying to hook my ankles together for added stability.

Jack reached an arm behind him, and his hand landed squarely on my butt. I stopped wriggling, all too aware of the fact I was nearly naked. My towel had been lost in the shuffle, now collecting dirt on the floor. He pressed up on my butt, and I scooted further up, rehooking my arms around his neck. Heat spread through my core and pooled between my legs, and I kept my head lifted, worried he'd feel the warmth of my blush if I put my head back on his shoulders.

I wanted him. He didn't want me, had lied to me to keep me away, and here I was, still lusting after him. Literally clinging to him.

Well, that part was for survival.

"We can get out that window. It's ok." He used the hushed tones one might with a wounded animal. I didn't blame him one bit. I was ready to fight or flight or both.

"Why is that doll back in here? Why?"

"I have no idea, babe. It's gonna be okay."

He was freaked out, too! For all the solid, gorgeous muscle I'd hopped on, Jack looked... *scared*. Tendons stood in stark relief against his neck, his pulse visibly throbbing against the chiseled line of jaw.

The realization didn't help. I swallowed against the lump in my throat, my skin prickling with goosebumps all over.

"Why did the door shut?"

"It's old. The storm's putting pressure on the house. Could be anything, could be everything." I felt him shrug. I mean, I felt *everything*. I was straddling the man's back. The pressure from his lungs taking air between my legs was keeping my brain incredibly confused about whether I wanted to have sex or freak out.

Who knew lust could distract me from inevitable death? Honestly, it was amazing that the human race had survived this long.

"So you're saying it *could* be a ghost?"

He sighed, and I fidgeted against him, then stopped. Friction was the enemy. Friction was my *best* friend.

"Don't scare yourself more." He turned, facing away from the fireplace. "Look." He shone the light on the top of the desk, and stepped towards it.

I started to slide off him, embarrassment winning out as the adrenaline faded. That and if I didn't get off him, I was afraid I might get off in another way.

Do it, do it, do it.

Jack stilled as I unraveled my legs. "You can stay there, if you're scared." His voice was a whisper, and I froze, halfway off, my swimsuit bottom wedged between my butt.

Didn't he know what he was saying to me? Isn't that why he'd lied about Caroline?

My body screamed yes, my brain screamed no, and my adrenal glands wept.

I hopped off him. Cold seeped through me, replacing the warmth of his body beneath mine.

Great. Now I had a better idea of what it would feel like to jump his bones. Now I had an even better idea of what I was missing.

Jack stepped towards the desk, the floor creaking under his feet. God, I hoped it didn't break. The last thing I needed was for us to fall into the subfloor along with all the ghosts. Or was that more likely for vampires? Whatever. I didn't think I could haul him out if he hurt himself. He was a big guy.

I wanted to know how big he was.

Across the room, the demon doll judged my horniness. I could tell. I stuck my tongue out at her, recoiling when her little false eyelids moved slightly.

Do not provoke the demon doll.

"Look, it's a guest book and journal."

I edged closer to the desk, keeping one eye on the glossy curls and porcelain face.

"It's a clue, Scooby!" I snickered, trying to allay my fear into humor. It would've been more convincing if I had choked on another sob.

"I told you, I'm Fred." Jack said absently, flicking through the yellowed pages, phone held aloft. "You're Daphne."

"Is that the one with the glasses?"

"No. The other girl. The one with the great—"

"Great what? Weren't Daphne and Fred like, an item?"

He stopped rummaging. "She was the one with the great *detective* skills. And who knows." But his body was tense. Did he think I was his Daphne?

No, definitely not. If he wanted me, he would've said something by now. Done *something,* like telling me he didn't have a girlfriend, for starters.

I shivered, hugging my arms across my chest. "It's freezing in here." Had it been this cold the entire time?

Jack turned the light on me, avoiding blinding me this time. "The storm must've brought a front behind it. It is nearly fall, after all."

"I want out of here." The primate part of my brain was screaming again. I didn't like this. I wanted to press back against Jack, I wanted him to carry me out of here, I wanted a lot of things that weren't about to happen. He didn't want them to happen.

The flashlight beam swung back to the window. It lightened outside, the wrath of the storm exhausted. Now, a steady lashing of rain replaced the hail and thunder. We were on the tail end of it.

"Take the book." Jack pushed it at me.

"Why?"

"Because there has to be a rational explanation to this. And I want to know what it is."

With that, he grabbed the towel off the floor and wrapped it around his fist.

"Jack, don't..."

He ignored me, smashing through the remnants of glass in the window. Rain pattered against the floorboards. I cringed. All these books were going to be ruined. Well, judging by the smell, they were already ruined, but still.

"Ladies first." He bowed, gesturing towards the now glass

free window. I eyed the glass, grateful for the sun now peeking out behind the clouds. That was Texas for you. Raining while the sun was shining.

I eyed the window with trepidation. I did not want a glass shard in my hoo-ha.

"Here." Jack had dropped the towel and grabbed my waist. I yelped, tucking into a ball as he lifted me through the window, depositing me on the wet and filthy porch. I hugged the book to my chest. God, if Jack's appearance was any indication, I was a disgusting mess. I inspected my bare skin as he stepped through the window, landing next to me with a little hop.

Blood trickled down my side. I bit my lip. When had I cut myself?

I hadn't.

"You're hurt, you big idiot."

Jack shrugged, and seeing his powerful shoulders nearly undid me. Especially since I knew exactly what it felt like to have him do that while I...

Enough of that.

"Let me see it."

My tone brooked no argument, and he held his hand out. A two-inch cut oozed blood, not thick, not too deep, but enough to be painful.

"Take off your shirt."

In one fluid motion, he shrugged out of it.

Damn.

Chiseled was a word I'd heard used to describe bodies, but it always seemed ridiculous. Until now. I counted six abs and two pecs and those amazing muscles that guided your line of sight right down to the main event.

I set the book down on the ground. Swallowing, I dropped my eyes to the shirt he held out. Using my teeth, I started a small tear, ripping the fabric apart by hand. Careful to put the clean side against his skin, I wrapped his hand, covering the cut on his palm.

"There." We inspected my handiwork, and a slow smile crept across his face.

"You're the best."

The words zinged straight to my heart, making my head spin. There was no reason for it, it was just a phrase, just something people said instead of thank you.

I wished he'd said thank you. Hope was starting to chafe.

I bent down, the book's leather cover slick with moisture and grime.

"Which way did we come in?" The rain had mostly stopped, just a thin lazy drizzle.

Jack stepped towards me, then stopped as I shifted away from him.

"I'll show you." He brushed past me, and I scurried behind him.

It hurt. It hurt, knowing he couldn't just tell me. Couldn't trust me to be an adult, to be mature around him. But wasn't that just what I always was to everybody?

Take care of Em. Em is wishy-washy. Emma isn't good at anything, can't settle down long enough to do anything right. To see anything through.

To be good enough to love.

Once Jack pointed out the trail, it was easy enough to follow his lead. I kept my head down, nasty, waspish thoughts barbed and stinging across my mind.

He sighed once or twice, holding his hand to his chest, half-turning to check on me. I didn't want to make eye contact. I didn't want to know what I'd see there.

So when he stopped cold in front of me, a serious look on his face, I almost walked right past him.

"Emma."

My name on his lips was a drug. Warmth blossomed across my chest, through my bloodstream. God, it hurt to hope.

This wanting, this ache.

"What?" I went for snappish and missed. It came out soft. Small.

I looked up at him. His head tilted toward mine, and he stepped towards me, closing the emptiness between us. His lashes were so thick and so close I could nearly count them, his brown eyes melting me into a goopy mess.

My heart stuttered. Time stopped.

He took the book from my hands.

Oh. He just wanted to look at the book. Not me. *Not me.*

I'd have to shove this down or leave. I couldn't keep pining over him—

The book thudded against the dirt, and Jack's arms crushed me to him. The hard planes of his chest met mine, and I breathed him in, shock and lust and that fickle hope, trickling back to life as though he'd shoved a hand in my heart before I slammed the door shut.

"Em."

His breath was warm on the top of my head, and I tilted my chin up.

"What's this—"

And then his lips were on mine, drowning the question. I had my answer, anyway. His hands kneaded the small of my back, and I lifted up onto the balls of my feet. More. More.

My tongue, greedy and quick, darted across his lips, and the kiss deepened. He moaned into my mouth, or maybe we both did. In an instant, he gripped my ass and lifted me up. I wrapped my legs around him. They felt so right there, so right.

Heat flooded me, and he tightened his hands on my back, on my butt, massaging my sensitive skin.

His hand. I broke the kiss off. "You're hurt, we should get back and get it cleaned up."

He groaned again, nuzzling against my neck. I arched into him, my eyes closing.

"If you think I'm worried about that scratch when you're right here, like this, then you have no idea how long I've wanted to do this." His hand stroked my chest, a feather light touch down my ribcage, and I shivered.

"But you're cold. And we're both dirty."

Disappointment swelled, hollow and empty in my chest.

"Hey, Em. Look at me."

I met his eyes, so full of warmth, and kindness, and something else. I recognized it. Lust.

"We aren't done." He placed a gentle forefinger against the dip between my collarbones. "We're going to finish what we started." A wicked grin curved his face and need knifed through me. "We're both going to finish this."

Good lord. We couldn't get back fast enough.

25

JACK

Everything disappeared but Emma. Her coppery hair in my hands and soft, bare skin pressed against me. The clean smell of soap and the citrus shampoo.

The world condensed to pure need. She fit into my arms perfectly, and I wanted to run my hands all over her curves, lay her down and explore what made her moan, what made her beg.

I needed my pants off, and we were still deep in the forest. I wanted to be deep in something else. Her tongue licked the inside of my mouth, her hand featherlight on my back, and I groaned. Her skin was cold underneath my fingers.

Damn it. I was an asshole. She must be freezing still.

"House. Now."

"What? Why?" Her eyes were heavy lidded, her lips swollen and rose-red from our makeout session. "Did I..." The sex-addled expression on her face changed to confusion.

"You're perfect. This is perfect. But you're freezing. Look at your skin." I pointed to the goosebumps running across her arms. She shrugged, then shivered. I pulled her close, savoring the way her breasts felt smushed against my chest. I wanted to see them. I wanted to get her naked and just stare at her.

"Come here." I grabbed her waist and lifted her up. "Hop on."

"You can't be serious." Em squealed, then locked her legs around my waist, hanging onto my shoulders like a monkey.

"Hey, body heat's important." My brain was hardly functioning, I was so focused on how she felt against my back, the fact her legs were open and on me.

My body seemed to scream at me that she was FACING THE WRONG WAY and I gritted my teeth, trying to ignore my raging hard-on.

"Hang on, little spider monkey." Of all the stupid things to say.

"Did you just quote... Did you really just say that?" Em's musical laugh rang out, her warm breath tickling the sensitive skin beneath my ear as she hugged herself closer to me. "Last time I checked, you hated Twilight."

"Watching movies with you was always the highlight of my weekend. Even if I didn't pick them." I shook my head, rueful. I'd never hear the end of it.

I couldn't wait.

Why had I waited so long to do this? Why had we waited? So many years, completely wasted. This felt so right. Like everything else—hell, everybody else—I had been preparing. I hustled down the path back to the cabin, and Em's breath made soft whooshing noises as she bounced up and down on my back.

When she started kissing my neck, I nearly lost control.

"Do you want me to throw you down right here?" I demanded.

"Oooh, you like that, huh?" She blew cold on the spot she'd been kissing, and it was my turn to get goosebumps.

"What I like is you. Anything you do, I'll like."

"I have some ideas about what you'll like."

My dick strained against my pants, and I briefly squeezed my eyes shut as I double-timed it through the woods. "What's that?" I ground out.

"I think you'll like the way I taste. And I think you'll like it when I take you in my mouth."

"Em." I could hardly walk straight as it was. And it had less to do with her on my back and more to do with the fact all the blood was rushing somewhere besides my head. Well, to a different head.

A wicked laugh curled past my ear, and she squeezed my torso with her thighs.

Something pale flickered on my periphery. The cold breeze licked up my ankles and shins. I paused, my breath coming in quick huffs. There. Movement caught my attention again, and I pivoted, trying to figure out what it was.

"What's wrong?" Em's body went rigid on my back. "What is it?"

Her voice, hushed and hot on my neck, reminded me of what was at stake.

"I thought I... I saw a deer, I think. That's all." Still, my spine prickled, and a new desire to get to the cabin quickly reared its head.

Emma. I wanted to kiss Emma. Emma, who I had just lied to. Again.

There was no way it had been a deer.

Deer didn't stand on two feet.

26

———————

Lena and Jen were still gone. Their car was missing, they must've gone into town.

Good. *Great.*

"Hey, are you okay?" I asked. Since we stopped in the woods, he'd seemed intent on racing back as fast as he could.

After throwing the locks on the door, Jack tossed the book on the floor, where it slid across and stopped as it hit the couch. He fell on me in an instant, picking me back up. We were out of breath, scratched up and dirty and neither of us cared. My back hit the wall, my legs wrapped around him.

"I take that as a yes," I squeaked out.

"It's a *hell* yes." His eyes were fixed on me, intense. Long lashes couldn't hide the desire there.

I couldn't get any hotter.

He traced the line of my jaw, nipping at my lower lip. One hand ran down my ribcage, and he slipped it under the side of my bathing suit bottom. Everything condensed to the building pressure between us. In me. His hand wrapped around my neck, his thumb rubbing across my throat as his fingers scraped against my hairline, his lips sealed over mine, cutting off all rational thought. Need. Pure need.

His mouth left mine. I wanted it back.

I tilted my head into his palm, and I let out a low moan, writhing against his bare chest.

"Do you think we can both fit in that shower?"

"There's only one thing I care about fitting right now." I clamped my mouth shut, my eyes flying open.

Jack let out a laugh, his head thrown back. "If you think I'm going to waste this…" He ran his fingers down my side, and I shivered. "With a quickie, then you don't know me at all."

I pressed my mouth against his, shutting him up. I didn't care how long it lasted. I didn't care at all. I wanted him, and I wanted him *now*.

His abs were smooth and hard between my thighs. Jack kissed the same way he did everything else. With a ferocity and single-mindedness that made me weak. And wet. He took a few steps backward, walking us across the house. He turned, kicking the bathroom door open and depositing me in the tub. Shutting the door, he flipped the lock.

My body ached for him. But my reflection told the story of where we'd been. My lips were full and raspberry red from being kissed, but my face was smudged with dirt, and grime trailed all over my body. A quick look down at my legs confirmed they were still an absolute mess, dried blood and dirt and a few bruises.

Then a cold torrent hit my back. I squealed, and Jack cut off the sound with another kiss, his lips a search and destroy mission.

I hoped he wouldn't destroy my heart.

I pulled him close, and his hot body cut out some of the chill as the shower caught up and turned hot. My hands couldn't get enough of his body, running up and down his chest. It was like one of those renaissance sculptures I'd studied in college when I thought I wanted to be an art major.

Unbelievable. Too good to be true. And yet, here he was, naked and wet and under my fingertips, his tongue in my mouth, his lashes dripping with moisture as he kissed me.

I closed my eyes, and he snapped the shower curtain shut behind him. My head bounced into the wall, and I laughed into his mouth. He drew back, gaze heavy lidded, promising fireworks and ecstasy.

He stared at me for a moment. "So beautiful."

I felt a blush creep across my chest and up my throat. Jack grabbed the soap and squirted some on my shoulders.

"And so dirty." He worked a lather up, washing the dirt off my shoulders. My breath grew rapid, as his careful hands stopped just short of my breasts.

He cleared his throat. "Can I..." Jack bit his lower lip, and if I'd had any defenses left, that would have crumbled them.

The knot on my bikini untied, and I threw the scrap of fabric onto the bathroom floor. Jack stared. Blinking, he looked up, his gaze dark and steady.

Heat pooled between my thighs, and Jack ran soapy hands down my chest, pausing to lightly caress my nipples. I leaned into him, my knees wobbly and unsteady, as he pinched and played, cleaning off the dirt and literally turning me into an absolute wet noodle of lust.

"Do you like spaghetti?"

He tilted his chin, confused. "What?"

"Nevermind, just kiss me."

And he did. And I melted. This is what it must feel like. To be loved. To feel treasured. His hands worshipped me, washing off the dirt from the haunted hotel, the stain of too many men who'd treated me like the grime that now swirled around and down the drain.

I never wanted to feel that way again.

"Are you done making me wait?" It came out a gasp, a whisper of pure need against the lobe of his ear. Don't get me wrong, showering with an Adonis or David or whatever was definitely a recommended experience, but my body screamed for release.

A smile quirked the corners of his mouth up, and I couldn't help returning it. This was so right. This was where we belonged. Together.

He turned the metal handle, and the water shut off. He flung the shower curtain aside, so hard it almost fell off again. If being soaped up was an erotic experience, being toweled off was even better.

I closed my eyes, letting him rub the nubby fabric all over my sensitive skin.

"Does that feel good?" He breathed the words into my ear as he rubbed the towel down my legs.

"If you make me wait much longer, you're going to regret it."

"Oh, is that right?" An impish grin, and I was over his shoulder, squealing as he carried me, caveman style, into the bedroom.

I giggled until he set me down, and then they stopped, the bubbles in a fancy champagne gone flat.

This was happening.

Jack and me. We were about to cross a line that couldn't be uncrossed. This was it. This was the big leagues.

This meant something.

At least, it did to me.

"Are you okay?" Jack set me gently down on the bed, as carefully as though I were a precious object, fragile and breakable and he was scared of damaging me.

I was scared he would damage me, too.

His lips sought mine, and I arched into him, my bare nipples rubbing against the smooth skin of his chest. He trailed kisses down my jawline, slow and torturous and absolutely perfect.

A sigh escaped my lips, and then his mouth found my nipples, and my nails bit into his back.

He paused at my belly button, his dark brown eyes locked on mine. "Are you sure?"

I bit my lip. Was he not sure? Was I doing it wrong, that he thought I wasn't?

"Please, please, please," I said instead. And then all rational thought vanished as his tongue worked down to the line of my bikini bottoms.

This was it. There was no turning back from this point. Gingerly, I lifted my butt, scooching my bottoms off as he watched, a man entranced. Propped up on his arms, his ridiculous biceps bulging, he looked at me as though I was the best thing he'd ever seen. It nearly undid me.

At least, I thought it had, until his tongue found my clit.

Heaven. *Heaven*.

Jack knew all the right places. He knew just what to do, and I moaned, raking my hands through that gorgeous brown hair. When he lifted his eyes, meeting me, I exploded against him, grinding into his mouth.

Fireworks. Perfection. Choir of angels.

Jack was it.

I gasped for air, breathing like I'd run a marathon. He shucked his shorts. Of course his penis was perfect. Like it was a surprise. Everything else was.

The best orgasm of my life. The first time someone had cared enough to get me off before he did.

And then he hopped off the bed.

"Wait, wait!" I screeched. "Where are you going?"

"Condom," he answered, an eyebrow cocked. There was only one cock I cared about.

"Hurry." I closed my eyes, reveling in the aftershocks. The

sound of a condom wrapper tearing. And then he was there. In me. My eyes flew open to find his, meeting mine. Locked on mine.

He thrust, once, twice, and then his fingertips found the center of my pleasure again, and I arced off the bed, hanging onto those ridiculous shoulders as I matched his thrusting, desperate.

"You feel so good," he whispered, dark eyes holding mine.

"Jack," I breathed, lost to it, lost to the rhythm of our bodies, the way it felt so fucking right, like coming home.

I lost track of time, track of anything but sensation, of anything but the need and desire in his touch, in his gaze.

He reached between us again, teasing and I moaned as another orgasm rocked me.

"Emma, babe…" Jack groaned, pinning my hips down as he found his own release.

His mouth found mine, and the kiss had lost its urgency, but none of the tenderness. I clung to him, my hands beneath those perfect, strong shoulders.

I closed my eyes. This was everything. Jack and I. *Finally*.

"Are you okay?" he asked, his breath tickling my neck, finally sliding out.

"Am I okay?" I echoed, flummoxed. "I'm perfect. I'm a cooked spaghetti."

"I knew I should have made you eat." He groaned. "Food on the brain."

"I could eat the rest of that sandwich."

"You *did* like it." His tone was accusatory.

"Of course, I did."

Post-sex, he looked even better. That gorgeous hair was all mussed, still damp from the shower.

I rolled on top of him, melting into his chest. I pressed my cheek to him, savoring the delicious smell of him. My Jack.

"Babe, are you hungry?"

I lifted my head. "Depends what is on the menu." A wicked smile curved my lips. I kissed down his chest, pausing to suck a nipple before continuing south.

Jack moaned, his fingers running across my back.

He tasted like me.

I liked it that way.

27

———————

EMMA

I collapsed next to him, and we lay there, our chests rising and falling in unison.

Jack rolled towards me. "Seriously, Em, are you hungry?"

"I'm perfect." I ran my hand across his cheek, and he smiled. I lived for it.

I couldn't get enough of him. Would never.

"I am hungry."

His smile was slow and sensuous and everything. Everything.

"Well, I made this amazing, beautiful, smart girl this sandwich earlier." He stretched, and his body did very interesting things. I rolled onto my stomach, matching his smile. "But, you know what? It was so strange, she didn't eat. She ran away, into a haunted hotel, instead of finishing this sandwich I made with love for her."

Made with love.

It drugged me, those words. Until I remembered. I'd run

away because of the message on his phone. From Caroline. I buried my head in the pillow. They were broken up.

I *wasn't* the mistress to a relationship.

I knew that. But *he* didn't. He didn't know I'd read his texts. He didn't know that I knew they were broken up. *He didn't want me.*

"Shit," Jack breathed. And for a second, I thought he knew exactly what I was thinking. That we were lying.

"That was amazing." Jack's arm wrapped around my naked body, and I squirmed, uncomfortable. Because, what did this mean? This perfect, blissful, orgasmic moment? And secondly, because I needed to pee.

Code yellow.

And I needed to deal with the fact he thought I was cheating with him.

What, and I cannot stress this enough, the fuck.

My post-orgasm bliss dissolved faster than I could enunciate the sentiment.

"I have to pee." *Brilliant, Holmes.* Nothing sexier than that after mind-blowing, fireworks style sex. And yet. It wasn't false.

I rolled, hopping off the bed, tucking an arm over my breasts. I glanced back at him, slightly mollified and slightly embarrassed by my absolute nudity. No matter that we were intimately acquainted with each other's bodies. Without the urgency of his hands on me, stark reality came crashing back in.

"You okay?"

"Mmhmm." I pulled the discarded towel over myself, nearly tripping on my way out the door.

"You don't have to be like that, Em."

"I'm not being like anything. I have to pee. Real bad."

It wasn't a lie. I did.

"Okay."

I shot a glance over my bare shoulder. Jack's arms stretched overhead, framing his handsome face, the jawline I'd kissed, lips swollen and satisfied.

We'd slept together.

I'd never understood that phrase. Neither of us had slept, there was no sleeping at all. We'd banged. Made love? No, too personal.

Uncertainty crept through me, and my feet scuffed against the well-worn wood floors, then cold tile. I swallowed, squeezing my lids shut until the world dissolved to black with dancing polka dots.

Peeing relieved some of the pressure, for sure.

I'd just had good sex. No, *great* sex. I opened my eyes. I didn't look any different. Well, my lips were fuller, cheeks flushed, hair damp and wild.

But a niggling in the back of my head told me I'd made a mistake. I shoved it down. Soap foamed across the back of my hands. A deep breath rattled my chest. No matter what we called it, things between Jack and I would never be the same.

God, I hoped that was a good thing.

The door opened a crack, and I jumped, yelping.

"Hey, it's just me." Jack stood there, lines of concern etching his forehead. "I can tell something's wrong."

My stomach grumbled, and I released my white knuckle grip on the counter, shifting my towel. The corners of his mouth tugged up, and his arm snaked out and caught me around the waist. Dipping his head, his lips brushed across the lobe of my ear, and I shivered.

"I knew you were hungry."

That must be it. Low blood sugar. Eating would make me feel better. My stomach growled again, as if seconding the motion.

"I could eat." I tilted my chin, reveling in his embrace, the way his eyes were soft and warm and without judgment.

His lips found mine, and just as a fresh flood of lust swept through me, he broke it off.

"Leftover sandwich?"

"Mmm." Like I could concentrate on any type of meat other than a bratwurst.

His hand tensed around my chest, and I squirmed.

"Shit. *Shit.*"

"I can just eat a snack, it's not a big deal if you finished it."

"No." His eyes were wide and wild. "No, I left the bag at the damned hotel."

My skin pebbled, and my appetite vanished.

"I'm not going back to get it." I said. "And neither are you."

Jack tucked me into his chest, and I closed my eyes.

"Of course not. We've got plenty of food here."

My eyes fluttered open, and I caught a glimpse of our reflection in the mirror. Jack smoothed my hair, absent-minded, his eyes fixed on a distant point.

Thinking.

Thinking about going back.

A trickle of water from my still-damp hair crawled across the nape of my neck. A shiver shook me, and I leaned into him. His chest warmed mine, and I leaned my check against his bare skin. Inhaled him.

"You're cold."

Overcome with possessiveness, I wrapped my arms around him, curling my fingers into his back. Cold? Sure, a little. Freaked out by the doll of the damned and the haunted hotel? More so, that.

"You believe me now?" The words whispered across his skin, as though the very utterance might summon bloody Mary in our bathroom mirror.

"Babe. Em." He ran a hand through my hair, pulling me closer, and I snuggled in. Reveled in the attention. Knew he would agree. The thrumming of his heart soothed me, and the aftereffects of all the orgasms started to take their toll. I nearly forgot I was waiting for an answer.

"About the ghosts?" I prompted.

Jack's hand paused. I cracked an eye open, then settled back into him as his hand roamed across my shoulders.

"I don't know."

My breath caught. It felt like a slap. How could he be unsure? The goddamned doll had been at the stupid hotel, with its weird glassy eyes. We'd gone through a fireplace into a secret room, for crying out loud.

And then the door shut. On its own.

What did he want? A neon sign screaming "LOOK HERE, HAUNTED AS FUCK! GHOSTS STAY FREE"?

Hmm, maybe if I did buy this property, I could use that in my marketing campaign.

I bit my lower lip. He didn't believe me. It wasn't a big deal. My fears weren't real. It was *nothing.*

"Em, you ready to eat?"

"Mhmm." It was the only noise I could manage, drowned in disappointment as I was.

"Okay, I'm gonna let go now. Why don't you get dressed and meet me in the kitchen?"

I opened my mouth to object, to press the issue.

To argue. Like always.

But one look up at his face, the dreamy smile, the mouth I'd wanted to kiss half my life parted in soft curves, and I capitulated.

So he didn't believe me about the ghost.

At least I'd get a sandwich out of it.

I'd already gotten the meat.

28

———————

JACK

There wouldn't be normal after *that*. I stretched, contemplating the contents of the fridge. Trying to be normal. Eggs, maybe? A bacon, lettuce, tomato with a fried egg on top? Simple, good food.

As though bacon and eggs could make up for the fact I was going to have to convince her to abandon this property, this whole grand scheme. Although I might not even have to try, considering the state of the old hotel and the fact she'd convinced herself it was haunted. Knowing her though, that could go either way.

But I'd let her believe I was still with Caroline. I'd lied about even wanting to hear her damn business proposition.

And I was lying to myself about damn near everything.

I closed my eyes. Leaned my forehead against the cool surface of the freezer door. *Idiot.* I needed to break it to her. I needed this deal to make partner, needed to sweep the rug crocheted from her hopes and dreams right out from under her. But maybe she wouldn't care now, maybe I could be enough, convince her to come to Houston with me, and I could take care of her.

We could never be partners, anyway, never go into business together.

I refused to repeat the mistakes of my parents. From the moment my father convinced my mom to quit the job she loved and work for him as a secretary, guilting her into it, into *helping* out the family, as if her taking care of us and cooking and cleaning and still working full time wasn't enough. Her nightly crying binges after he chewed her out over some miniscule mistake, after not respecting his authority.

The way the tears turned to ice. Frozen over anger when she would skip out to watch my brother or I play basketball. Until neither of them came to watch. Until the ice consumed them both, all of us, and our family broke apart into cold, jagged pieces. Neither of us deserved that kind of pressure.

I pulled a package of bacon and the container of eggs, laying the strips in the pan one by one. Methodical. Calming.

I just had sex with Emma. More than sex. That was... unbelievable. Life changing. My body responded to the mere memory of hers on mine, under me. Her soft, perfect curves, athletic legs and strong arms, and those lips.

Em and I had sex. I turned it over in my head, flipping the now sizzling bacon.

The culmination of years of friendship, and suddenly we were in make or break it land. Something pale flickered on the corner of my awareness, and my gaze swept to the window behind the sink. Squinting, I tilted my head mid-bacon flip.

What the hell was that?

Was it the same thing I'd seen in the forest?

A chill ran down my spine, adrenaline punching through my system like a punch to the gut.

That was no raccoon. Em might be right. Something might be well and truly fucked about this place. Whether it was vermin or the weird locals or...

The bacon popped, and a low swore tore from my mouth as I hastily pulled a paper towel off to absorb the grease.

Crack the egg, nice and easy. The whites bubbled on contact, and I spooned the leftover bacon grease on to the tops.

Or what? I refused to think it.

Ghosts weren't real. Ghosts hadn't locked us in that small room in the hotel.

Fucking creepy place, to be sure, but not haunted.

I jerked my head to the windowpane, the sense of being watched raising my hackles.

No. This wasn't a haunting. Someone was behind this. A real person. Someone who didn't want Em to get this property.

The woman, Tara, from the kolache place said the ghost stories were good for business. Maybe she was behind this. Although, with pastries like that, she couldn't be too hard up for customers.

And Earl, that asshole, owned the only other place to stay overnight for miles. Maybe he didn't want the competition.

Or maybe it was all in our heads, and I was letting Em get to me. Em, who probably started looking for an excuse not to commit as soon as she leapt out the door of my Bronco. Hell, she'd called it a *murder cabin* before anything weird started happening.

I clamped my lips shut, wrinkling my forehead. The egg began to turn golden on the edges, and I lifted it out of the pan and sat it on the paper towel next to the bacon before cracking a second egg in the pan.

This is your brain on ghost stories.

Something was definitely off. The discount Em kept referring to, the prize for lasting an entire weekend at the cabin.

What kind of scheme was this? Was the owner in on it? Was someone getting their rocks off on freaking us out?

Who? Why?

I wasn't sure.

But I was going to find out.

29

———

EMMA

The silence was broken only by the scrape of forks across plates. My brain tripped over itself, trying to work out what it meant. We'd done it. The deed. The dirty.

Made love.

Because what the *hell* did it mean?

My fingertips drummed across my thigh, my foot shaking on the floor. The plates rattled across the tabletop.

"That was weird, huh?"

The dishware stopped moving. It was weird? My breath stuttered. His skin under my hands, smooth over hard muscle. The hot whoosh of his breath in my ear, lips brushing against my neck.

Weird.

"I..." I didn't know what to say. My skin felt too tight, and a collar of panic tightened around my throat. He didn't want me. As far as he knew, he thought I was cheating with him.

"Wait, Em. Not *that*." Jack's warm hand encompassed mine,

the pad of his thumb running over my palm. He was close now, plates forgotten. On his knees, his arms circled around me, and he rested his cheek against my chest. "Never that. God, your heart's beating so fast. Like you just ran a fifty-meter dash."

My stomach twisted, didn't stop. He didn't mean it. Otherwise he would've told me something by now. Something about the fact that he was single. That he didn't have a freaking girlfriend.

Because for once, our timing was right.

But I snorted, sending his hair flying. My hand pressed against his shoulder, and I pushed him away. I rolled my eyes, staring up at the ceiling. Blinked. Refused to cry.

"Only *you* would bring up the fifty-meter dash right now."

"You were robbed that day."

I huffed out a laugh. "It wasn't my finest moment."

"She never saw the Gatorade jug coming. Priceless." He shook his head, and I finally looked down at him. He'd seen me at my worst. Being with Jack would be effortless. He knew my whole story, backwards and forwards, with just a few chapters ripped out, getting us closer to the here and now.

Pages I'd bled onto, kept from him.

And now he was keeping things from me.

"No, Em. I meant the house in the woods—the hotel." His thumb circled my palm again, and I shivered. He pulled me close again, and the heat between us became a living thing.

It should have been quenched. Should have had the edge taken off. Especially since every rational, logical part of my brain screamed that he was lying to me.

But I still wanted him. Would *always* want him. I should tell him.

"It was weird," I said instead.

"Listen, are you okay?" His cheek was still on my chest, and I wondered if he heard it there. The song my heart sang for him. The fear that he'd rip it out and crush it, let the blood run down his arms and laugh.

The Jack I knew would never.

The Jack I knew wouldn't lie to me.

"That freaked me out."

"The hotel." It wasn't a question. But then again, I hadn't really answered. Maybe I should just clear it up. Tell him I knew.

Tell him I knew he thought we were cheating?

And ruin this. But how could I ruin something that wasn't real?

"It's not real, you know that," Jack said.

I stiffened.

"Ghosts, I mean." He pulled back, lifting a hand and pushing a loose hair from my face. I leaned into it, and he cupped my face. "It was just... bizarre."

It felt so good to be touched by him. I could almost forget what I knew.

Maybe I should forget. Just live in this moment. For the next two days, just exist with him. Take it for what it was, then get my life back on track when we left. Use the memories of us— what we could have had—as fuel to push through.

Finally finish something. Finally stop flitting around from place to place and job to job and dick to dick.

Be good enough.

"Earth to Em."

"Hmm?"

"You really think it's haunted, don't you?"

Oh. That I could answer.

"Hell yes, I do." I scooted my chair back, the legs whining against the floor. Being tangled up with Jack... I couldn't think straight. I needed air. I needed to breathe.

He blinked, eyes wide and owlish.

"I don't know why you can't accept that it could be." The

words grated out of me, high and squeaky. Why couldn't he just believe me? "How else do you explain that freaky doll showing up all over the place? Huh?" I jabbed a finger at his chest.

Jack narrowed his eyes, chewing over my words. Or maybe he just took another bite of food. It made me madder. Him, chewing, at a time like this.

"How else do you explain that storm blowing through and then us getting stuck inside that room behind the fireplace? How do you explain any of it?" I threw my hands up, my fingers curved like witch's hands.

"As for the storm, it's Texas. That's what it does here. As for the 'freaky' doll, I have no idea, Em. It doesn't make sense."

I scrunched my mouth up and stared at him.

He pivoted, pacing around as the floor creaked beneath him. "The way I see it, there are two possible explanations. One —" He held up a finger. "—someone is playing tricks on us. I don't know why, but it is a possibility."

"And the whole town is in on it?" I objected.

"Is it any harder to believe than ghosts?" Jack glanced sideways at me, a half smile pulling up the corner of his lips. God, I loved when he smiled like that. And that dimple, phew. But I wasn't ready to surrender, so I threw my shoulders back. Great, now I looked like a puffed-up chicken ready to fight.

"Stop sticking those out at me." Jack waved at my chest, a full smile on his face now. "It makes it hard to concentrate."

Ha! Not if it gave me the upper hand. I slinked closer, shimmying a little as I stepped. "So you admit it's far-fetched to believe that the whole town is in on whatever prank this is?"

"No, I think people believe rumors. Wouldn't be hard to spread 'em and keep people guessing about that creepy place."

"So you admit it is creepy." I punched the air, exulting at my win.

"Em, I still can't believe you didn't finish law school."

And just like that, the wind went out of my sails.

"But—" Jack held up a number two. "—explanation two." He waited a beat, focusing on my face with such intensity that my breath caught. "Explanation number two is that you're right, and there are things we can't explain."

It should have made me feel better, to hear him agree with me. To hear him say that I might be right. Instead, it sent a thrill of fear through me.

Because if I was right, and door number two was the explanation, that meant we had a serious ghost problem.

Or demon doll problem. I screwed my lips up, thinking hard. *Whatever*.

"Salt." The word popped out of me before I had time to think it through.

He craned his neck toward me, tilting his head slightly as though he hadn't heard me right.

"Salt. That's what they do on all the shows. We need to make a salt circle around the house to keep the ghosts out."

"What shows have you been watching? Is it that one with the two brothers that you loved in college? I thought you stopped watching horror movies."

"So what if it is? Can't hurt." Hell yeah, I loved that show. Those brothers were hot as, well, really hot. Plus, they always won. They always beat the big bad in the end.

There was something really comforting about that.

Jack turned, reaching for the pantry. "Lucky for you, there's a shit ton in here."

"It's a sign." Had to be. I nodded, agreeing with myself.

He produced an old-fashioned ice cream maker. "Yes, a sign that they were ready to make delicious, home-made ice cream at a moment's notice. Probably stocked up on supplies for when the mood struck."

"Yeah, ice cream, or..."

"Or what?"

"Or sorbet."

He laughed, but I raked my hands through my hair. This trip couldn't get any freakier. We were being haunted and...

"We just had sex," I blurted. Yep. Definitely meant to say that.

He turned, a box of rock salt in his hands. Brown eyes met mine. I squirmed, wringing my hands and wishing I'd kept my stupid mouth shut.

His mouth opened, and then he bit his lip.

What was he going to say? Did he regret it?

"That wasn't *just* having sex." His voice was a throaty growl.

I blinked.

He leaned against the frame of the pantry door, dwarfing it. Heat rushed through me as I replayed the way he'd felt on top of me. Inside me.

"It would never be *just* sex with us, Em." In two steps, he closed the distance between us, claiming my mouth with his. "Now come on, let's go make your salt circle around the house."

He smiled at me once, like he'd won something. Triumphant.

Then he stalked off, and I was left blinking after him.

30

———————

EMMA

"We could just leave, you know." Salt trickled out of the box in his hands. The wind in the pines surprisingly loud, a sign of fall finally beginning its descent.

"And lose the discount we get if we stay the whole weekend? Hell no." I replied. "Besides, we're almost done." Huh. Was this why they'd offered a discounted price after staying the whole weekend? To terrorize any potential buyers? Or to really make sure I wanted the place?

Assholes, either way.

"What the hell are you two doing?"

We froze, and I groaned, eliciting a chuckle from Jack. Caught salt handed.

A thick layer of salt ringed the house. Three boxes lay abandoned and empty at the top of the steps, and Jack and I sat on the bottom step, shoulder to shoulder. The late afternoon lost its edge, the heat of the post-storm sun weakening into a watery light as it crept towards the horizon line. Night would be upon us soon. In the trees, fireflies flitted back and forth, blinking phosphorescence.

"We're taking precautions," Jack offered, and a smile crept across my face.

"Have y'all been killing slugs?" Lena eyed the salt. "Wait a minute, did you let her talk you into this?"

Jack stood up, almost all humor gone from his face. "She didn't have to. We all need to talk. Either that, or we need to leave."

Goosebumps pebbled my arms. The fear returned, temporarily banished by the silliness of making a salt circle. "I'm not leaving." I wasn't afraid of no ghosts!

Okay, I was, but I wasn't about to just pack it in and give up on this. Something about this place—it still called to me. The hotel was going to be a handful to fix up, sure, but I could do it.

I *knew* I could. I straightened my shoulders and lifted my chin, meeting Jack's gaze.

"If it's not safe, I'm leaving, and you're coming with me," he said. "And you two, too."

Lena's face froze, and she looked to Jen for support.

But Jack's tone brooked no argument.

"What happened?"

"Don't step on the salt line!" I called, my voice whipping out of me, stronger than usual.

Lena and Jen froze, wild-eyed.

"This isn't funny, Em. You know this kind of stuff freaks me out." Lena crumpled into Jen, who glared at me.

"She's not doing it to be funny," Jack barked, half standing, pulling me to my feet along with him. White dust coated our hands and legs, evidence of our hard work.

"Yeah, for once!" I added lamely, thinking back to the time I hid in Lena's closet for hours just to literally scare the piss out of her.

"Where did you even get all this?" Jen asked, looking askance at the now empty salt boxes.

"Ice cream supply hoarding."

"Ooh, is there ice cream?" Lena clapped her hands, making a speedy recovery.

"Not yet," I said, stomach grumbling. "We need to talk about the shit we saw today, though."

"You know what this is, don't you, hon? They're playing a prank on us, just like they used to. This is supposed to keep demons or something out. And you know what, it's not funny, Em." A muscle at Lena's temple pulsed angrily. Man, people said I was the impulsive one.

"It's not a prank," I retorted hotly, stopping just short of stamping my foot. Okay, a smidge impulsive.

"It's not," Jack said. "Get inside. We need to talk."

Lena went white under her tan, clutching at Jen's arm as they stepped into the circle. Hair fell into my eyes, and I blew at it. Jack pushed it back behind my ear, and I smiled up at him.

It hurt. It hurt to have him look at me like that, remembering what he'd said about Caroline. I frowned. Or didn't say. I rolled my shoulders. We didn't just need to talk about the ghosts or not-ghosts.

We needed to talk about us. About whatever was happening between us.

Later.

We filed into the house, the screen door slamming behind us. Lena shot me a dirty look, and I stiffened, pressing into Jack's solid warmth.

"Well?" Jen sank into a chair, leaning forward, elbows on his knees. He always looked like he needed a smoking jacket and a pipe to me, like he'd been transported out of a time decades in the past.

"We found the hotel," I said.

"The hotel?" Jen asked.

Lena's eyebrows arched, and she perched next to him. "So what?"

Oh. I forgot they didn't know half of it.

"This cabin used to be the owner's lodge," I told Jen. "It's part of an older, larger property, and I kind of stumbled onto the rest... the hotel today." Literally. "I think... we think something bad is going on here."

Lips pursed, Lena shot another look at me. Judging. Disbelieving. Jen rubbed her back, and I hugged my arms around myself. Jack wouldn't rub my back like that. Not in front of them.

"We went into town," I added. I had to distract myself from thinking about Jack. "With the key we found under the bed. Earl, the hardware store owner, said this place is haunted. The key went to the hotel." Jack stepped away, and I hugged myself tighter. "There was a storm. We sheltered there while it hailed—"

Lena stared at me as though I were a speck of dirt on a clean shirt.

"And we found this," Jack finished.

The book slammed onto the coffee table, and Lena and Jen jumped. I chewed the inside of my cheek, rubbing my hands across my arms. Suddenly, I wished Jack hadn't believed me. Had told me I was an idiot.

"What is it?" Jen squinted at the book.

"None of this explains why you two wasted all that salt," Lena said at the same time.

I swallowed, tired. So tired of explaining myself to her. To everyone.

"We got trapped. Somehow, we found a room. And a door that shouldn't have been able to close without human help—" Jack spread his hands apart. "—closed." He cleared his throat, looking at me. The lines around his eyes softened, and he was reaching for me, pulling me closer.

"Em and I got out when the storm broke, but we found this book and took it. And there's something else. The same doll that was here last night? It was there."

His fingers pinched into my arm, and I braced myself against them, the nagging feeling of wrongness, of the suffocating feeling of being trapped in that room drowning me all over again.

"You two are out of your minds if you think we're going to believe this bullshit." Lena tossed her hair. "Jen, come on, I'm hungry."

"Wait." Jen pulled the book closer, opening up the dusty leather cover. "You heard what they said at the diner this afternoon." She thumbed the page, flipping it to the next.

Lena sniffed. Well, that explained where they'd been, at least.

"What did they say at the diner?" I asked. My sister stared up at me, her face white.

"They said this place was bad luck. That bad things happen here."

"Will you look at this?" Jen said absent-mindedly, absorbed in the book in front of them. Jack looped his fingers through mine and squeezed. Lena's gaze darted from the book to our hands, her eyes wide, then accusing.

She *knew*. How could she not? We were holding hands.

He had a girlfriend. Or at least, that's what he'd made us believe. And now she thought I was the other woman.

Blush heated my face. Shame. I'd done nothing wrong; I knew that. But they didn't. Not that it would change their opinion of me. Nope. I was the fuck-up little sister.

In her mind, this was probably par for the course.

"What does the book say?" I pulled my hand away from Jack's. Ignored him. The carpet was soft underneath my hands, and I traced the pattern, unable to look at him.

"It's a journal. Well, no, it's not. It's a guest book. But each guest journaled about their stay." Jen flipped through it, skimming the pages.

Lena stared at me, and I jutted my chin out, narrowing my eyes at her.

I dare you. Say something.

"Here." Jen stopped, and I drew my eyes away from Lena and back to the book. "The last entry." He cleared his throat, and I was aware of Jack sitting next to me, his thigh pressing into mine. His hand traced a pattern on the small of my back, and it took every ounce of willpower to not arch into it like a sex-starved cat.

I leaned into the table instead. Away from Jack and his troublesome, delicious hands. "What does it say?"

"It's hard to read. 'The hotel has—" He paused, craning his neck towards the book, running a finger across the yellowed pages. "Has offered me some small comfort. As much as could be found when one's family has died during their stay here. I return every year, searching for them, for the memories we made before the accident..." Jen's voice trailed off, and he frowned. "I can't read this part. Okay, then it says, 'I miss them everyday, no more, no less, just the same sharp ache of regret that will never be filled. Only poor Charlotte's doll seems content here, where new children can play with her all the time. Charlotte would like that, I think.'"

I blew out a breath. My stomach churned.

"What else does it say?" I managed.

"That's all I can see." Jen shrugged, scooting back into the chair.

"This is fucked up, even for you, Em," Lena spat out. "You know I don't think this kind of stuff is funny, and I could've sworn *you* felt the same way. And now you make us all come out here, feeling sorry for you because your ex cheated on you, and you decide to pull some prank?"

I shrank back.

"That's enough." Jack's voice was low and rough. "It's not a prank. Em and I have barely spoken since college, you think she'd just call me up and we'd decide to ruin your holiday weekend for fun? This is serious to her. And her pitch was amazing. Emma is brilliant and talented and could make this place come alive. You think she wanted to get cheated on by that loser?"

"Hmm," Lena said, her gaze drifting between the two of us meaningfully. "Cheating certainly seems to be contagious, doesn't it?"

Hurt gave way to anger. Rage unfurled in my chest.

"How dare you?" I spat at her. "How dare you?"

Lena jutted her chin, defiant. "You two aren't as secretive as you think you are." Oooh, she got bitchy when she was scared, but this was next level.

"You're an ass." I threw my hands up in exasperation. "How in the world do you think I'd be able to make this all up? Plant this book? The people in the diner?" The diner I made a mental note to check out soon. Maybe we could collaborate on something once I bought the place. I squeezed my eyes shut, trying to slow down the random thoughts pinging around my skull.

"I don't know why you do the things you do. I don't think even *you* know."

My hands shook on my leg, and I squeezed my palms together, hot tears crowding for a way out of my eyes. Lena thought I was a cheater. Just as bad as my ex. A joke.

"You're right, okay? I'm a mess. Congratulations, you win the award, you're absolutely right, as usual, Lena. My boyfriend screwed some rando, which was so fun for me! I finally decided to make something of myself, do something after the goddamn crash took out my dreams, but I don't have enough money to go it alone, so I brilliantly talked the guy I've been secretly in love with since high school into coming out here to help me, hahaha, how hilarious! And now we're fucking!" My voice rang out, high pitched and manic. "And now I'm here, having this fight with you, because you think I'm such a screw up I'd want to ruin *our* relationship even more than I already have. Ha!"

My vision blurred, and I wiped away hot tears with the back of my hand. "Tell them the rest of it, Jack. I'm done pretending I'm fine. I'm done. I'm going to take a bath and read a book. Good night."

I stumbled into the hallway, shedding my clothes in the bathroom and turning the faucet, letting the tears run freely.

It wasn't until I sank into the hot water that I realized what I'd said.

Once I remembered, the words wouldn't stop echoing in my head.

Secretly in love with since high school.

In love with.

Love.

31

─────

EMMA

Voices filtered from outside, the roaring flames from the backyard firepit casting strange silhouettes through the windows. I pulled my knees up to me, watching light and shadow dance across the room. My chest felt hollowed out, scraped clean, all the ugliness I'd felt at Lena—at myself—gone. Purged.

I buried my forehead in the awkward cradle of my arms and knees. Jack's voice rose above the rest. Maybe he'd missed what I'd said. About loving him. Maybe he'd forget.

Maybe he wouldn't.

I sucked in a breath, my wet hair leaving chilly tracks through the soft fabric of my t-shirt. A knock sounded, and before I could react, Lena's pale face appeared, framed by her dark hair.

"Hey." Her voice was soft. "Can I come in?" She bit her lower lip, an arm crossed against her chest.

It hurt to look at her, my eyes stinging like I'd been the one sitting by the fire. But I nodded, resting my chin on my knees.

The bed creaked as she sat next to me, and for a moment, we were as one, watching the red gold flames surge across the yard. The smell of woodsmoke clung to her hair.

She sighed, and I knew she was looking at me. As though she were an extension of my own body, a phantom appendage I'd long forgotten how to use. I turned my face toward my sister, finding my nose and my eyes looking back at me. Instead of ruddy freckles, her skin was smooth and tanned.

"I'm sorry." A deep exhalation, a furrow between her brow. "You didn't deserve that. I was scared, and pissed, and what you do with, well, with *anyone*, is your business. I was a total bitch."

"You were," I agreed.

She lowered her eyes, tracing one of the geometric shapes scattered across the quilt like stars. "I didn't take you seriously. About this, I mean. The hotel. I should've. Jack showed me the presentation you put together. It was... incredible. I should have known, after what you've done with the restaurant on social media. And did you know grumpy Jim only ever asks for you? You have a way with people, and all this talent, all this creativity and I just—"

"Was a total poophead?" I used to call her that when we were little, and it earned a small smile.

"Ugh. See? You always try to make everyone feel better, even when we don't deserve it. When I don't deserve it." She rolled her eyes, the smile fading. "Why didn't you tell me off before now?"

I shrugged. "I didn't want to fight. And I shouldn't have yelled at you like that, either." I hadn't. I hadn't wanted to fight for a long, long time.

"What happened to us?" She drew her legs up to sit criss-cross on the rumpled bed.

I swallowed against the chafing emptiness. She was right here. Asking for forgiveness.

"I'm sorry, too," I managed. A non-answer. But it was a start. "I've been… mad. No, not mad. Jealous."

"Jealous?" Her eyes widened. "Of what?"

"Lena, you've got it all together." How could she not see it? "You have a great job, a great fiancée who loves you, you know what the hell you're doing. You have your own place to live. Meanwhile, I'm just floating around. I'm a floater." I picked at a loose thread on the hem of my shirt.

Lena snorted, then sobered. "I don't have it all together. I'm still figuring everything out. I don't even like my job. And I've been jealous of *you*. You have all this freedom, could do anything. You always know how to make people laugh, how to make them love you. I'm not good at that." She gnawed her lip. "And I miss you. You never want to hang out with me. I didn't think you even *liked* Jen. Jack was the one to call and ask me down here. It should've been *you*."

I stretched my legs out, plopping onto the bed, knowing I'd leave a damp spot and not caring. She was jealous of me? I chewed it over, the fan spinning lazy circles on the ceiling. I'd never thought she'd feel that way. Sure, I made friends easily, but when I needed them most, I didn't seem to have many. Lena clambered next to me, her head next to mine on the pillow. We curled into each other like we were nine and ten years old again, up past bedtime and giggling into the darkness.

"So we've both been idiots," I said.

"And I've been an asshole," she added.

"And I've been a funny asshole."

She laughed quietly, pulling a smile from me. Lena pressed her forehead against mine, staring into my eyes. I was struck with a realization. For all our differences, we were two sides of the same coin.

"Your breath smells like wine."

"Shut up." She laughed, smacking my arm.

"I want wine."

"Come outside. There's no ghosts."

"Not yet," I grumbled, trying to play off the fear that lurked just under my skin.

"Know what I was thinking we could talk about over the rest of the bottle?" She sat up, grinning wide.

"What?"

"How this might be the perfect place for me and Jen to have our wedding. I don't want to pressure you, so feel free to say no, but if this works out... I can't think of a more beautiful setting for us to get married."

My mouth dropped open. "Lena."

"You got this, baby sis. No one has the imagination you do. Clearly. Besides, I can pester you till you follow through." She gave me a sly wink, but the hurt I expected to follow never came.

Lena thought I could do this. My mouth must've still hung open, because she tapped my chin before pulling me into a hug. A shocking, deep sense of calm swept through me. Lena and I were going to be all right. It would take time to heal the fracture between us.

But this was a start. Something in my chest loosened.

I hadn't even realized how much it had ached.

THE BEDSHEETS TANGLED AROUND ME. Lulled by the tenuous peace between me and Lena, I'd fallen asleep as soon as I'd hit the bed. Thanks to helping her polish off the bottle of wine.

Oh, and probably the after-effect of being scared out of my mind.

And orgasms. Those too.

Something woke me. Fuzzy-eyed, I brushed a wayward strand of hair out of my nostrils. Why did it always end up in my nostrils? Argh.

I lurched up, half-drunk with sleep, then rolled to my right and punched the pillow. Flopping it onto the colder side, I nestled into it, eyelids fluttering closed, the fan whirring steadily overhead.

"Fuck me sideways," I yelped, springing up and onto the balls of my feet.

The window.

Something was out there. Something pale.

A whitened face pressed against the window.

Watching.

Balancing on the creaking mattress, pillow between me and the window, I stared. Ready to slap the shit out of anything with my pillow. Pokey feathers could do some damage. Maybe.

My breath came in quick huffs and pants, adrenaline kicking my body into overdrive.

At this rate, I needed a physical to make sure my glands were all functioning properly after this absolutely relaxing and totally normal holiday getaway.

The door swung open, and I leapt off the bed. Stretching the pillow between my hands, I barreled into the attacker, forcing fluffy white down over their face. *Take that!*

"Yippee cai-yay, mother..." *Oh.*

The air whooshed out of me in one breath as I hit solid, warm, delicious smelling man.

Jack's arms caught me, and one hand scrabbled for purchase along my ass as the other caught the doorframe. As for my pillow, it plopped out of my hands and onto the floor.

It wasn't the protection I wanted anymore, anyway.

"What, what happened?" Lit solely by moonlight, Jack's face was even more handsome. My legs didn't want to unwrap from around him. Despite my best intentions, there they stayed, firmly forcing us together.

"I saw something. In my window. A face." My voice was husky. Deeper than usual.

"What?" So was his. Sleep drugged. *Or something.*

"I don't know." I ran a finger down his cheekbone, stubble rasping against it.

Now that Jack was here, it didn't seem important. I was probably half dreaming it, anyway. There was enough bullshit going on to give me nightmare fodder for the next three decades or so.

But being in Jack's arms?

My legs wrapped around him?

That was the stuff of wet dreams. And the best part? It was real.

His hand drifted from the base of my lower back, found ass cheek, and squeezed. I arched back in response.

"Do you want me to stay?" Heavy-lidded, his eyes met mine. "Consider me protection against what goes bump in the night."

"Yes," I said. Who cared that he'd been lying to me?

He was warm and real and I'd happily bump him all night.

His lips were on mine. Again. I moaned into his mouth, and he seized my parted lips as an invitation, sliding his tongue against mine.

A frisson of electric heat jolted through me, and he stepped forward, shutting the door behind him. The rumpled sheets were still warm underneath me. All I cared about was the heat of the man on top of me.

"Emma." My name on his lips—a prayer. I closed my eyes, blissful. Jack kissed my cheek, my neck, and I shivered, hot and cold and wanting him all over me at once. My head lolled to the side, giving him better access to the sensitive skin where my neck met my shoulders.

I opened my eyes, running my hands over the hard curves of his biceps.

Distracted, my gaze slid to a flurry of motion.

At the window.

My forehead smashed into Jack's. He staggered back, eyes

unfocused for reasons completely opposite of lust. As far as I knew, he wasn't into pain. At least, not the headbutt kind.

"There's something out there."

He froze, then tilted his face towards the window. "Besides trees?"

I dug my nails into his arms. "Jack, I can't take this anymore." I needed to figure out what the fuck was going on at this cabin. And at the hotel. Done didn't begin to cover it.

Jack's eyes met mine. Softened. His lips parted, and a soft exhalation blew across my forehead.

"I know. I know."

Thank God.

"Okay, good." We could leave my car at the mother trucking repair shop for the rest of my life. I was going to have an absolute meltdown if I didn't get out of this situation—

"I broke up with her. Caroline, that is."

The world slammed to a stop. Time stretched, and the fan seemed to move more sluggishly.

"What?"

"I broke up with her," he said again, a smile stretching across his face. A kiss landed on my forehead. My eyebrows. The corners of my mouth.

My brain scrambled to catch up. I knew this already. Why did it feel like a revelation?

"What does that mean?" I struggled to sit up, trying to maintain focus.

"It means the timing is right for us, Em. Finally. I haven't wanted to scare you off. I mean, I needed to figure it out, this—" He smoothed a hair off my face, tucking it behind my ear. "This thing between us. See if we could be good together. If you were even interested." Another kiss landed on my ear lobe, and I squirmed, half sitting up, under his weight.

Under the same spell he'd put me under over a decade ago.

"Why didn't you tell me?" I regretted the question. Then I

didn't. Well, fuck, why *hadn't* he told me? And why hadn't *I* told him I *knew*?!

"I was scared…"

A white shape outside the window grabbed my attention, and I froze, forgetting Jack. A chill struck me, and I shivered.

"Are you scared?" he whispered, his stubble nuzzling against my face.

"Yeah, like I said, there is something right outside." Goosebumps pebbled across my skin.

Jack's weight lifted off me, sending a fresh wave of chills down my back. I pulled my knees to my chest, and my hair fell around my shoulders in an unruly tangle.

"Oh," he said.

Shit. I missed something he said. Something important.

"Jack, I'm sorry, but listen, I'm not joking around. Let's have this conversation later. This place is freaking me out. I mean it." My voice had jumped up an octave, and I hugged my knees, pulling the quilt up to my neck.

Half-crouched on the bed, Jack surveyed the window.

"I don't see anything." His hand snaked around my waist, and I melted a little bit into his warmth. "I promise I'll keep you safe. Haven't I always?"

My gaze stayed out the window, at the unremitting darkness around the cabin, the silence in the woods.

The silence.

It hadn't been quiet since we got here. Sure, it was quiet in the way that any place outside a city or big suburb was. But not like this.

Where were the cicadas? The odd rustle of squirrels and owls calling and wind and—

"See?" Jack asked, tipping my face back to his.

"That there's nothing out there? I mean, I don't see it now but, it was there. I swear, Jack."

He sighed, a throaty noise of deep disappointment. "This is

why I was afraid to say anything." The faded blues of the cotton quilt disappeared as he fisted it in his hand.

My mouth dropped open, my stomach tying itself in new knots that had less to do with the specter of the past and everything to do with the way I'd fucked over this conversation.

"I'm not, no, hey..." I couldn't form the words.

"Emma, it's fine. I know how you are. When you're ready, we'll talk. And if that's never, at least we had today." His lips smiled, but his eyes were downcast.

I opened my mouth again, ready to say something. Couldn't. He pressed a kiss to my forehead, then my mouth, and it tasted so bittersweet.

Jack stood up, the bed protesting the sudden shift in weight. Shoulders slumped, he took a step toward the door.

"Stop right there," I blurted.

Something like hope flitted across his face as he turned back to me.

The quilt and sheets flew across the mattress as I launched myself out of it. I'd wipe that hangdog look off his face. The floor chilled the soles of my feet, and I shifted my weight to the balls and pranced to him.

My hands caught in the soft mass of his hair, pulling his face down to mine, covering his mouth with a fervent kiss. His hands swept underneath my shirt, massaging and kneading the small of my back. A groan left his mouth and I pressed more firmly against him before breaking it off.

He bent to kiss me again, his eyes confused, but I put a finger to his lips. My mind was made up. Something was going on here. I'd prove it to him. And then I'd prove that I was worthy of him. Of this entire place. Of all my dreams.

"I'm going back. You're coming with me." I needed him to believe me.

"What?" His hands squeezed against my waist. "You're leaving? You don't have a car."

I found a pair of jeans and shimmied into them, tying my hair back in a quick jerk of motion.

"I'm not leaving-leaving. I'm going back to the hotel." I rummaged through my duffel until I found the lone dilapidated sports bra. Turning back towards the bed, I tugged it on through my shirt. Even if I'd wanted to leave, I wouldn't have. *Three nights, three days.* Or no deal.

"It's twelve o'clock at night; I can think of other things we could do."

"No. I'm going now. There is something out there." I narrowed my eyes at him, trying to ignore the tempting bow in his lips. "You and Lena and Jen don't believe me." I stopped myself from saying *I'll show you* like a nine-year-old, but just barely.

He rubbed a hand over his face. One eye peeked out at me from between his fingers. "This is so typical."

"What is? That I like to be right?" The bed creaked under my weight, and I tugged my shoe on, trying not to see the pained expression on Jack's face.

"No. Yes, obviously, but no, that's not... nevermind."

I scrutinized him, my eyes fully adjusted to the dark.

"Never mind what?"

"You always have an excuse, Em. This is why I didn't want to tell you we broke up. Because it's always about why *now* is not good."

The words flew out of him, raw, hard, slapping me across the face.

Because he wasn't wrong. I'd been a hot mess, and he deserved better.

But I *could* be better.

32

———

Hot mess express, party of one, that was me. Sure.

But I also wasn't wrong. I threw a shirt at him. He caught it easily, shaking his head slowly.

"Are you coming or not?"

"See? You can't even deny it." He shrugged the shirt on, and I licked my lips at the way his stomach bunched and his pecs—

Nope.

"We can talk later. I want to talk about it—about us—later. I promise. I want that." I pressed a hand against his cheek. He briefly closed his eyes, his expression softening.

"As usual, I don't see how I have a choice, Em. You're not going alone, in the middle of the night, to a condemned hotel that may or may not be haunted."

"Good. I knew you'd see things my way." Besides, if we didn't leave now I'd lose my courage and I was too pissed at the cockblocking ghost to *not* go.

He huffed out a breath and buttoned up a pair of pants. "I'll grab the flashlight from my truck."

"I'll get the supplies."

"Supplies? For what?"

"I don't know, that's what they always say in those ghost hunting shows." I tilted my chin, considering. "Maybe there's something good in that spell book."

He half snorted, half grunted, as he barreled out of the room and into the darkened house.

Outside, something rustled beneath the trees.

And I'd be damned if I wasn't going to find out what it was.

On second thought, maybe that wasn't the best way to think about it.

The hallway stretched before me, and I kept one hand on the wall for balance, focusing on not rolling my ankle and ruining my ghost capturing adventure. Gotta be hale and hearty before getting scared to death. No reason to give supernatural monsters or demon dolls the upper-hand. I was gonna murder their pale, wispy asses. Or burn them.

Starting with that freaky ass porcelain doll.

Yeah!

"What's going on?" Lena's low-pitched, sleep drugged voice filled the silence.

I gasped, grasping at my chest as though it would slow my speeding heart. The wall offered staunch support, and I leaned against it, blowing out a breath and closing my eyes.

Some rough and tough ghost hunter, that was me, all right.

"Why are you dressed? It's the middle of the night."

"I am sick and tired of these motherfuckin' ghosts in my motherfuckin' vacation rental." I cut her off.

When in doubt, cover up real emotions with humor: The Emma Way. For six small payments of $69.99, you, too, can become emotionally unavailable.

A sharp pain wound around my chest as Jack's disappointed puppy-dog eyes flashed before me. Lena scratched at her head, watching my face.

"I'm going to the hotel. With Jack."

"Emma, I'm worried about you." She scrunched her eyes up, giving me her patented big sister once over. "Fine. We're coming." Lena looked over one shoulder. "Get dressed Jen, we're going on a ghost hunt."

Jen made an indistinct sound accompanied by the squeak and creak of exhausted bed springs.

"I'm leaving in five minutes, ready or not," I hissed. *Worried about me?* She needed to worry about herself. I was fine. Perfect, thank you very much.

Sex with Mr. Right, check.

No idea where I stood with Mr. Right, check.

On my way to a haunted hotel full of ghosts and possessed objects, probably, check.

Totally in a great headspace, ha ha ha, check.

Fine. *Maybe I should be worried about me, too.*

Lena gave me one more look, full of meaning, before turning on her heel.

"Five minutes." I repeated, the words bursting out of me, hot air from a deflating balloon.

Matches were in a drawer in the kitchen. They went in a grocery bag. Rock salt followed, three quarters full. Did salt even burn? *Huh.*

I located the spell book, abandoned on the living room coffee table, and flipped it open. "Hmmm. Where's a good spell when a girl needs one?"

My forefinger ran down the index, before I found something that might just work. A spell to banish unfriendly spirits. I thumbed to the page listed, sixty-nine. It said nothing about getting rid of all ghosts, just the naughty ones. Made sense, relinquishing the naughty ghosts to page sixty-nine.

It would have to do. Besides, it only needed some of the herbs we'd bought at the grocery store. Sage, thyme and rose-mary all went into a massive mason jar. I squinted at the recipe. Water poured by silvery moonlight?

Mmkay.

Well, the moon was out. Tap would have to do. Water filled the heavy glass jar, and my eyes widened at the nice floral scent. I screwed the lid on and shook it up seven times.

Worst come to worst, I'd smell good as I gave my body up to naughty ghost possession.

Oh, and the guest book, I definitely wanted that. Water seemed like a good idea, but so did wine. *Both is good.*

I chugged a near empty water bottle, then filled it up with wine. Then I chugged the remnants from the bottle. Lena leaned against the wall, watching me.

"Make yourself useful and grab the book."

"You're salty." She did it though, holding it slightly away from her chest and eyeing it with apprehension.

I shook the box of rock salt at her. "Salty AF."

That earned a small smile, and the bonus of an eyeroll. "How come?"

"Because I'm tired of being scared."

Lena's sleepy eyes opened a bit wider, and she blinked at me owlishly.

It was true. I was sick of being afraid. Afraid of failing. Afraid of losing Jack. Afraid of doing anything that would show someone who I was underneath the bravado.

And of the demon doll, sure. Also definitely afraid of that ramshackle old hotel Zoolander would no doubt dub 'derelict'. Perhaps it could be the star of the third movie no one asked for. The setting of the final runway show.

A manic giggle escaped from my lips, high pitched and weird.

Lena pursed her lips, her head tilting slightly. "All right, then. Let's go hunt some ghosts."

Jen rounded the corner into the kitchen, looking for all the world like he was ready for a business casual job interview. Pressed khakis and all.

My eyes scrunched up. "Did you do your hair?"

"Ready?" Jack's head poked around the door. "What, they're going too?" He looked at me, lines creasing his forehead.

Lena held out the book, disdainful. "Oh, we're going. If you two are hunting ghosts, we're not about to stay here and go looking for your dumbasses in the morning."

Thanks for the support, Lena.

"Besides, if my little sis is gonna tackle her fears, better believe I'm gonna be at her side."

"That is completely irrational," Jen said, but not before I felt a little curl of sisterly love.

"Who cares, Jen?" we both asked.

"Well, I've got two big flashlights. Everyone have on walking shoes?" Trust Jack to make midnight ghost hunting as safe as possible.

"I've got the salt," I said. "And a mason jar full of ghost juice."

"I don't want to know what that means," Jack muttered.

"I've got the book," Lena added.

We looked at Jen.

"Jen did her hair." I smiled at her, and she rolled her eyes before smiling.

Jack looked skyward, as though that would be of assistance. "We sure about this?"

"Stalling?" I arched an eyebrow.

"No, Em, I'm done stalling. I've decided to go for what I want." There was a world of meaning behind the words, and I blinked at him, trying to figure out what he meant. Trying not to get my hopes up so high.

He gave me a tight smile, reaching for my hand. I let his fingers curl around mine, dry and warm and... absolutely terrifying in how right they felt.

"Let's go," I said. What was the point in staying safe?

FLASHLIGHT BEAMS BOUNCED around the tree trunks. A few times glowing eyes blinked, then disappeared back into the brush. The moon hid behind dark clouds, occasionally peeking through before returning the night to pitch black.

"Did it take this long the first time?" I huffed. A branch cracked underfoot, and my heart rate sped up.

"You walked it twice," Lena said. I didn't have to look at her to know the expression that went with that tone of voice.

"I was pissed the first time. And the second..." I trailed off, my face suddenly hot. *And the second time I'd been horny and motivated to get back fast.*

"The second we were in a hurry to *come* home." Jack put a special emphasis on the second to last word, and I was grateful for the fact no one could see my blush.

We marched along the narrow path, brambles pulling at my jeans. Had I really come this way in only a bikini less than twelve hours ago?

An owl hooted in the night, and the hairs on the back of my neck stood up. The moon reappeared, soft yellow light filtering through the treetops. And then the clearing.

We were here.

At night, the house looked like something out of a Grimm's fairy tale. Dark, foreboding, the bright yellow of the flowering vine leached by the lack of light. The broken door gaped open, a tragic maw, telling a story of decay, of secrets kept and lost.

I shivered. A fine mist pervaded the clearing, just enough to add an otherworldly film across the rigid tree trunks, partially obscuring the house.

Jack tucked my hand behind his back, dropping it in favor of putting his arm around my shoulders.

"Holy hell, Em, you went in there by yourself?" Lena's voice seemed especially shrill without the cover of trees.

In the dark face of the looming mansion, it seemed altogether too loud.

"Well, it was during the day. It didn't look quite so..." I didn't need to finish the sentence. The hotel did it for me. Our two beams of light splayed across the surface of the house, dissecting the moldering shiplap as sure as a scalpel in a surgeon's hand.

I took a step forward, jutting my chin out. My stomach tied itself in knots, and a chill ran down my spine.

A breeze lifted a stray strand of hair, licking cold against the adrenaline flushing my skin. The flashlight was heavy in my hand. I blew out a breath and stalked toward the cadaverous hotel.

The railing on the porch steps was rough and grimy under my hand, all peeling paint and dirt. Jack's hand swept across my back, and I closed my eyes for a brief second, relishing in his touch.

My foot tested the steps up to the once-grand wrap-around porch. The wooden step creaked but bore my weight. I took another step. Somewhere deep in the house, a door slammed shut. I froze, my blood turned to ice. I looked over my shoulder, to where I felt Jack's breath on my neck, for reassurance.

He stood at the perimeter of the house. Not anywhere near me.

Definitely not within touching distance.

What in the name of Sephora touched me?

"Did y'all hear that?" My teeth chattered slightly, and I clamped my mouth shut before anyone heard bone clacking on bone.

Jack walked toward me, face unsure, eyes narrowed. "I heard it. I'm right behind you, babe."

Babe.

It dispelled some of the chill, and my teeth resumed their normal stasis. There. See? It was all in my head. Well, except there was definitely a ghost. But I had backup. I wasn't doing this alone. I'd had everyone I needed with me this whole time, and if I learned to let them, they'd help. Sniffling slightly, I shifted the weight of my grocery bag, motioning for Jen and Lena to follow.

"Come on. Don't chicken out now."

Lena looked at me like she knew I was talking to myself. Which I was.

She rolled her shoulders and stretched her neck. Her tell. She was freaked out too. Jack passed me on the stairs, in neat, careful strides to the front door.

"Hold the light for me."

I did, shining it through the odd opening. Mouth dry, I swallowed, then followed him through.

Jack squeezed me to his side, and I rested my cheek on his chest. The steady sound of his heart calmed me. A little.

Lena and Jen followed us in, and we all spent a minute in silence, sweeping our flashlights around the former lobby.

Two pairs of footprints led to the fireplace.

"Is the key there?" I whispered.

Jack stiffened, his fingers tightening on my hip, as I swung the light across the mantle. The key was there.

But not in the hole where we'd left it. It lay neatly on top of the fireplace, the ratty ribbon swaying gently in a phantom breeze.

The same breeze that rifled my hair.

"Look," Jack said, pointing to the ground. He took the flashlight from me, moving towards the fireplace. "Another set." A third pair of footprints led from the staircase to the fireplace, then stopped.

"I don't like this," Lena snapped, her voice loud.

I fumbled with the bag. "Have some wine." I fished out the former water, now wine, bottle. "It'll help you relax."

She held her hand out, but I heroically twisted the cap off and took a long swig before handing it to her. The wine burned my throat.

I coughed, wiping my mouth with the back of my hand and passed it to her. In the dark, I could barely see her, but if I knew my sister, I knew that bottle was going to be half-empty.

"It tastes like bad choices," she sputtered.

"What do you want to do, Emma?" Jen asked.

Leave. I wanted to leave.

I shook the bag full of spices at her. "We're gonna do the spell." I pulled out my special naught ghost potion in a jar, and Jen's flashlight illuminated the herbs inside.

"Does it involve roasting a turkey?"

I scowled, blinking at the sudden light. "It has most of the herbs we need." I paused. "And some we don't." But whatever. I had a feeling this ghost wasn't picky.

"Well, we don't need to summon anything." Jack's voice was low and steady.

Something about the absolute neutral tone sent a fresh wave of panic through me, and I tightened my grip on the over-sized glass mason jar.

"Why?" I squeaked out, turning towards the fireplace. Behind me, I heard the distinct sound of crinkling plastic as Lena swigged some more wine from the bottle.

Jack's flashlight illuminated the porcelain doll, who perched on the mantle with the same frozen rictus of a smile on her creepy doll face.

My skin crawled.

"Em, I believe you. Either someone is pulling an elaborate prank, or..." He let the silence fill the unspoken words in. The hairs on the back of my neck stood up, and I licked my lips, frozen in place.

"That's the demon doll?" The floor creaked as Lena stormed towards the fireplace. "She's cute. Not my top pick for a kid's toy, but you know, everyone's different."

She reached her hands out, Jen's flashlight glinting off her perfect pink manicure.

"Lena, don't…"

Too late. She took another step, picked up the doll, and time stopped.

The floor, rotted beyond the limits of safety, opened up beneath her. A cloud of dust exploded from around the fireplace.

"Lena," Jen shouted, racing towards the debris. Where Lena had been, doll in hands, there was now nothing.

My sister was gone.

33

EMMA

My stomach churned. I'd gotten my sister killed. Death by demon doll.

"I'm okay," Lena called out, coughing. "Ugh. Seriously, Em, this wine is terrible."

Jen's flashlight pierced the hole in the floor, and Lena, sprawled on the floor, shielded her eyes against the light. The doll was laying on one side, little porcelain hand outstretched, starched skirts askew.

"You're okay?" I bent over, breathless with relief. Tears pricked my eyes, and I blinked rapidly.

She shifted, casting a dark look at the doll next to her. "Honestly... my foot hurts pretty bad." She stretched it.

Jen paced the side of the hole like a cat, hair slightly disheveled. Frantic, she glanced at me, then Jack.

"Jen, stop," I said, but it was too late. She jumped in, landing in an awkward crouch next to Lena. The flashlight caught something glinting in the wall.

I scooched closer to see better. Jack threw his arm out,

blocking me from falling over the edge. Footsteps echoed overhead, and I swallowed, queasy with fear.

"What *is* that?"

Jack shrugged, tucking me into his side. Protecting me. Making me safe. Making me want him again. *As if.* If we got even close to kissing, I was pretty sure that meant we would be the first to die a terrible death at ghostly hands. It was like, horror movie rules. I detached myself from him.

Needed to think straight.

"Are you okay?" I shouted down to them. Seriously, how deep was it?

"Lena's ankle is messed up," Jen reported, swinging her flashlight around. "The wood's nearly rotted completely through—it's not safe. You two could fall through at any moment."

I backed up, Jack beside me.

"Is there any way out?"

Jen and Lena were silent, their flashlight waving around the opening.

"Not that I can see. This looks like an old bar." Jen disappeared from view, and Lena whimpered as she tried to put weight on her bad foot. "A speakeasy, maybe? This is pretty cool, actually. Well, except that we're stuck."

I didn't like this. Even now, I thought I heard footsteps. Felt someone watching.

"Yeah, there's all kinds of crap down here, old." Jack and I looked at each other.

"Wait," Jen said, followed by a scraping noise. "Some of this stuff..."

I burrowed into Jack's chest. This had been a mistake. We never should have come here.

"What do you mean?" Jack's voice had an irrepressible growl to it, an edge.

"Good grief," Jen said, her voice low and tight.

Another shiver ran down my spine. My heart stuttered, then raced.

Jack pulled me even closer.

"Is that showing what I think it is?" Lena asked, peering into the dark corner Jen disappeared into.

"We need to get the fuck out of here," Jen said. "And fast. There's a live video feed of the house. Someone has been watching us come and go."

I squeezed my eyes shut. Jesus. This was worse than the time me and half the basketball team got caught breaking into that old house. The night I'd gone to jail and lost my college scholarship in one fell swoop, taking the fall for everyone after Jack dared us to go in. *That* seemed like high school silliness now. Like absolutely no big deal.

"Hold this." All business, Jack pressed the heavy flashlight into my hands. "Jen, can you lift Lena up to me?"

"Yep. We got you, love, don't worry."

I'd never heard Jen sound so, well, so sweet. So concerned. Whatever she'd seen down there freaked her out. That made two of us.

Jack lay down on the floor, dangling halfway into the hole. The floor groaned, and I hugged my arms around my torso, the ghost potion mason jar cold where it met my skin.

"Please be careful," I muttered, holding the light steady.

"You worried about me, babe?" Jack grunted, heaving Lena out of the hole.

"Got her?" Jen called up. Behind me, the floor creaked, and I spun on my heel, certain the ghost had materialized.

"I'm fine." Lena's voice wavered, and I didn't have to look at her face to know she was near tears.

I didn't look at her, because my field of vision had narrowed to a pinprick.

Focused on one thing.

The man standing directly in front of me, holding a shotgun at his side.

"Well, well, lookee here." A wad of chewing tobacco distended one of his cheeks, making him appear like a lopsided chipmunk. *Alvin, Simon, The-o-dore!* "Didn't expect you four to be dumb enough to come snoopin' around after dark out here."

Behind me, the scuffling stopped.

He tilted his head sideways, sending a ferocious gob of tobacco and spit careening onto the floor. "Now don't be gettin' too hasty, big boy. I just came out to make sure y'all weren't gettin' into trouble too big for your britches."

"Big boy?" I repeated. *Britches*? Had he taken a page out of the handbook for idiot villains?

I should have been scared.

The man had a gun, and if that failed, a mouth full of tobacco and an apparent penchant for suddenly expectorating.

"Tha's right. Everybody jus' calm down, now." He lifted one hand in the universal sign for supplication. But his other hand still gripped the gun. As I watched, the barrel slowly crept up. *Son of a bitch.*

Talk about mixed signals.

And I wasn't scared. That rational thought had fled. What I was?

Furious.

"You realize if you want people to calm down, the last thing you want to do is tell them to calm down. Calm down?" The words burst from me. "Has that ever worked in the history of the world?" He opened his mouth to talk, the barrel still aimed at my legs, but I raised my hand, taking another step closer. He must not have liked what he saw in my eyes, because he flinched back slightly.

"The answer is no, no it has not," I answered. Adrenaline punched me, and the sound of my teeth grinding rang in my ears.

The man stared, and a bolt of recognition hit me.

"You." The word hissed out of me, and Jack took a step closer. *Safe.* "You!" The part of my brain responsible for witty comebacks malfunctioned, apparently. *The only place in town to buy hammer and nails.* And he owned the *only* other goddamn hotel in town.

"You're from the hardware store," Jack supplied, inching toward me.

"Earl," I added, and then I put the pieces together. "You."

"You sure say that a lot. Ya know, you should respect your elders. And people with guns, missy."

Missy. *Missy.*

"Missy!" I huffed. My eyebrows shot into my hairline. "Are you *threatening* me?"

He chuckled, though the sound was devoid of humor. The hairs on the back of my neck stood up.

"Now, now, not threatening, no ma'am." Earl scratched a hand through the grizzled grey scruff on his chin, eyes glittering oddly. The words didn't match his actions, the gun now aimed at my stomach.

What an asshole. *Ma'am?*

"Ma'am is *worse* than missy." I stuck a hand on my hip, heart pumping so fast my smart watch no doubt was recording the entire exchange as cardio.

He rolled his eyes skyward in frustration, as though that would stop me from being ridiculous. *Hell* no, it would not. I wore absurdity like armor. And it was clearly the chink in his. Well, I'd wriggle into that exposed area like a freakishly large insect and sting him until he dropped dead of irritation. My specialty.

Eyes still on the ceiling, Earl heaved a sigh.

That was about enough of *that.*

"Not threatening? Not threatening?" My voice climbed an octave, and another door slammed shut. Earl looked up, eyes wide. "You have a gun. You came here to intimidate me. The competition." The floor creaked underfoot as I stepped closer to him.

I was tired of being bullied. Tired of ghosts. Tired of laying down and letting everything stop me from getting what I wanted. Tired of getting in my own damn way. And at the moment, real fucking tired of Earl.

"Emma, don't," Jack whispered, moving on the periphery of my vision.

But I only had eyes for Earl.

He nudged the weapon upward at me, his eyes wide with disbelief, clearly stumped that I was dumb enough to keep coming. He didn't note the heavy jar full of ghost potion in my hand. Should've.

"Step back now, I don't want anyone to get hurt, 'specially not someone as pretty as you." He leered, his tobacco wad threatening in a different way. "And you're not competition, darlin'. Never will be."

But I didn't step back. I stepped closer, floorboards creaking underfoot. "Doesn't seem like that's something you'd say if you came to check if we were okay. How'd you know we were out here, anyway?"

The shotgun slackened at his side, my being stupid enough to not listen to a man with a gun probably taking him by surprise as much as it was taking me by surprise. More adrenaline jolted through me, along with a flicker of surprise that my kidneys could produce any more of it. I bounced from toe to toe, gaining momentum.

Something wild howled upstairs, another door slamming. And another. The hairs on my arms were never going to stand down.

Earl's eyes were wild, his mouth open in surprise. He raised the gun up, blowing a shell straight into the floor above. At whatever caused the doors to slam. Wind, most likely. Still distracted by the noise I sincerely hoped was an army of raccoons above, Earl loaded another shell into the gun.

"What the hell kind of hogwash did that devil woman Tara tell you to work tonight? What kind of evil did you all let loose?" The shotgun blast nearly deafened me.

"Fricasseed devil, bitch!" I screamed it at him. Then I swung the jar as hard as I could into his temple. His face went slack, his eyes glazed. I swung again, my arm jarring with impact.

"That's for scaring me with a gun." I smashed the jar on his head, and it finally cracked. The smell of fresh herbs and water poured by moonlight filled the air. "And that's for climate change, you asshole."

I lifted my arm again, incensed to the point where I half-expected steam to pour from my ears.

My arm stopped, and I looked up. Jack's face appeared, eyes wide and face white.

"It's okay." His hand circled my wrist, and I swung my gaze back to the crumpled figure of the man on the floor. Still holding my arm, Jack bent and recovered the rifle. Bemused, I watched, teeth chattering slightly.

"*Yeah*, it's okay. I got him." I stared, shocked. "And he would've gotten away with it too, if it hadn't been for us meddling kids!" A sob wracked my chest. Adrenaline? It was gone.

"You are the bravest *idiot*." And suddenly, I was in his arms. Surrounded by his scent. His warmth. *Safe.* My stomach clenched and threatened to expel its contents as the truth of his accusation hit. I sagged, totally overcome.

"What were you thinking?" Jack asked. Jen was huddled on the floor, face white. Lucy was still in the hole, I supposed. With Lena.

"He did this." The words came out quiet. "He did this." Louder. I motioned to the whole of the hotel, the gaping hole in the floor.

"He has been trying to intimidate us." I looked up at him. He hugged me closer. "He didn't want us to buy this place." My brain tumbled over the 'ghost', the noises, the doll that appeared and reappeared, the pinwheeling fear of being locked in the room behind the fireplace.

I was an idiot. My bottom lip ached, and I realized I was biting it.

"I wondered," Jack admitted.

I didn't even have the energy to scowl at him.

"What the hell is going on up there?" Lena's voice echoed up from below our feet. "Are you guys okay?"

I waved a hand, feeling the fool. "He didn't want competition. Or something. I can't believe I called him a bitch." Knowing someone wanted us out of the picture, was afraid of me—I'd never wanted anything more than to buy this whole haunted place and shove it down everyone's throat.

Jack narrowed his eyes at Earl's crumpled form. A shrewd, calculating look formed on his face. "We need to call the police."

"I did that to him. Holy shit." Earl's chest rose and fell. Still breathing, the jerk. But I'd done that. Nausea roiled through me, the anger and shock not so much wearing off as vanishing without a trace. I sank down, rocking back on my heels.

Jack's hand massaged between my shoulders, his phone in his other hand, thumb arcing over the screen.

I stared at his fingers. They worked.

Mine, on the other hand—they shook.

34

───────

JACK

Her self-defense classes must've been pretty damn good. Fury and concern warred for attention. Outrageous anger at the idiot with the gun. Irritation that Em decided to attack said idiot with a gun. With a mason jar. Pride at her success. Relief she was ok. *Intense* relief.

What the hell had she been thinking?

"911, what's your emergency?"

How the hell did he explain this?

"We're at an old hotel property, and a man threatened us with a gun—"

"Are there gunshot victims?"

Disbelief rocked me. We were okay. Em was okay.

"No, but the man needs medical attention, my girlfriend beat him up, and there are two others who are hurt."

"Sir, I need you to tell me the address."

I swallowed, closing my eyes. This weekend was an absolute disaster. I rattled off the address Em gave me, assuring the woman on the end of the emergency line that Earl was, in fact, breathing. A purple lump swelled on his forehead, and I kicked the gun away from him.

Rage ripped through me for the second time that night. Em shouldn't have had to hit him. I should've done that. I should've protected her.

Should've known something else was going on here besides that damned raccoon or something as absurd as ghosts. And acted on it.

I answered the questions the woman asked me as best I could, thoroughly distracted. My breath came in cold puffs, and I watched the small clouds with a detached interest, hugging my arm around Em, where she rocked back and forth on the floor, making odd moaning noises.

"I think my girlfriend is in shock," I added, staring into Em's beautiful wide eyes.

This was my fault.

"Help is on the way, sir. Please stay on the line until they arrive."

My judgment fell to pieces around Emma. It always had. There was no way we'd ever be in this situation if it weren't for me enabling her whims.

Which I loved about her. Her back was warm against my hand, and her chattering teeth filled my ears. I loved her.

I loved how she barged through life, unafraid to say what she meant and to say it like she meant it. I loved how her funny, whip smart brain worked, derailing my train of thought. I loved the way she looked in the morning, the sun gilding her wild hair. I loved how she looked with lips swollen from kissing me.

I loved her.

And there was no way I could take this dream away from her. But I couldn't go into business with her, either.

Not when I loved her this much.

This absolute shit show of a night was enough to prove that.

And if we were meant to be together, if we could work together at all—she would understand that.

She knew my past better than anyone in my present or future could.

How had I ever thought I could be *'just friends?'*

Em was my *best* friend. And more. I squeezed my eyes shut, memories flooding through me. Em, smiling back at me while we raced our bikes in middle school. The way she stood up for everyone. Her fingers, coated in salt from Cheez-its. The way her heart was bigger than anyone I knew. Em, dancing wildly on a table at a college party. Cramming for finals and eating pizza together. The look on her face when I made her favorite birthday cake. Em, naked and gleaming in the shower and in my arms. Em, a fucking super-hero with a mason jar, saving the day.

Just like she had in high school, taking the fall for everyone.

I wasn't going to ruin us again. I wouldn't let her ruin what we had, either. But I couldn't lie to her anymore. I needed to come clean. Explain the disaster decision to act like maybe I was in a relationship.

Explain that I couldn't help her buy this place.

If we were meant to be, she would understand.

Her teeth chattered more loudly, and I pulled her closer, sitting on the dusty floor and lifting her onto my lap. Jen and Lena's voices floated up from under the floorboards, words unintelligible. I leaned my face against her head, her hair soft against my cheek, the delicious scent of her overwhelming me.

She'd understand. I'd support her in a different way. I wrapped my free arm around her, and she leaned into me. Taking my shared strength.

Em would understand that I couldn't ruin us by going into business with her. Because there was no way I could lose her. Lose this.

And as far as undercutting the bid and making partner? No

way in hell. Robert would have to find some other place. I rubbed the back of my head.

"First responders are at the cabin address now and heading your way." The woman's voice brought me back to reality.

"Em? You all right?"

She nodded, teeth still chattering, breath coming in puffs.

The noisy growl of ATVs echoed weirdly across the clearing and into the hotel. They must've brought them knowing we were pretty far out in the woods.

"You're squashing me," she squeaked, and I loosened my grip while she wriggled.

A high beam flashlight lanced through the dark, followed by several harsh barked directives not to move. My heart thrummed in my chest.

"It's going to be okay," I murmured into her hair.

35

—————

EMMA

Police stations were not my favorite place in the world. I wrinkled my nose, the scent of stale coffee barely overwhelming that weird institutional cleaner smell you get in hospitals and schools and, apparently, police stations.

The Styrofoam cup still steamed in my hands, which were finally steady. Well, steadier, at least. They'd separated me for questioning. Considering I'd had blood on my hands and had beaten the ever-loving shit out of good ol' Earl, I couldn't blame them. Besides, I had nothing to hide.

Still, guilt and fear curled in my gut.

I closed my eyes, trying to relax. Trying to hang on to the fact that everyone was okay. Lena's ankle was swollen and iced, a sprain, they'd told her, she'd been lucky. Jen hovered over her like a mother hen. Jack looked at me like... words failed. He never had looked at me like *that* before.

Now that I was out of my old hotel, I was finally warm.

There was no ghost. *Probably.*

There was only Earl. And a mason jar to the temple.

The door handle squawked, and I opened my eyes as a cop smiled disarmingly at me. His dark blonde hair was flecked with silver, beard cropped close. He shouldered his way into the room, holding two cups of coffee.

I raised an eyebrow and smiled back.

He scooted the chair closer to the table with a foot, and it ground across the floor. "I'm Detective Harrison."

"You look more like a Steve Rogers." I grimaced, then braved the burnt coffee in an attempt to shut myself up. The resemblance was uncanny. And after the weekend I'd had, I now considered myself an expert in the uncanny.

He flashed white teeth. "My first name *is* Steve."

"Shut up."

His eyes narrowed.

"I mean, uh, Steve is really your first name?"

"I'll be asking the questions."

I clamped my mouth shut.

He let out a barking laugh, and it echoed off the walls. "I'm just kidding with you. Steve's not really my first name. That would be funny though, huh?"

I tried a chuckle. It got stuck in my throat. The detective was shaking with laughter.

"Okay, so—"

"No really, my name is Steve." He stopped laughing.

"Is it though?" Was it? This was getting weird. I thought my sense of humor was weird. Steve—or maybe not Steve—was definitely weirder.

He shrugged one shoulder, and the remnant of his grin disappeared. "Mr. Earl Gleason is going to be fine, by the way. Slight concussion. He's up and talking and—" He leaned forward. "—mad as a wet cat."

I blew out a sigh of relief. "I still can't believe it. This whole weekend has been..."

Steve Rogers—er, Harrison—leaned more heavily onto his

forearms.

"Has been what?"

I paused, considering. A lot had happened in a couple of days. Weird. Good. Scary. Fucking orgasmic. Heat creeped into my cheeks.

"A lot," I answered lamely. "Look, do I need a lawyer?" My pulse skyrocketed. I didn't want to go to jail. Again. And besides, Jack and I were finally... He'd called me his girlfriend. Girlfriend. *Me.*

And I could buy this property. The ghosts weren't real. I *wanted* it. Something that could be completely mine. Something to be proud of besides perfectly executed spreadsheets or keeping my parent's customers happy. I could keep my own customers happy, sell and deliver the ideal vacation. Relaxation. Peace.

It was like all my dreams were coming true at once. Jail would definitely get in the way of that. Jail didn't figure into them.

Officer-Detective Steve snorted, pushing back off the table, crossing his arms. "I should've led with that. Earl confessed. Said he'd been messing with that property for years. Easy enough to see, considering all the equipment we found at that hotel."

It was my turn to lean in. "Messing with it how?"

Steve narrowed his eyes at me, then ran a thumb over the edge of the coffee cup. He looked up at the ceiling, then leveled his gaze at me.

"We've had more complaints about that old cabin and all that acreage—not to even mention that hotel—than anywhere else in this town. Double, triple even. Never could find anything. Never any reason. Earl said he put audio equipment in there to scare buyers off. Messages." He shrugged again. "It's worked so far. You two are the first to stay longer than one night. We found a whole bushel of digital tape and cameras in that old hotel where your sister fell. Evidence." He fist pumped, but my stomach sank. Earl had camera footage of us? "We can get him on criminal trespassing and we're going to be taking a good look at his own finances for his little inn. Odds are if he was doing this, he was probably doing something else illegal. Not to mention what he did to y'all last night."

Last night? Was it already morning?

"Wait, what do you mean by camera footage?" I felt nauseated. I pushed the coffee cup away, leaning heavily onto my arms.

"Just a few filming the outside of the property, one in the kitchen. Nothing untoward. Earl was a creep, but he wasn't a perv."

Relief washed over me, and I sagged in the chair. "Thank god." I pushed my hair off my forehead, blinking back tears. My brain snagged on what he said.

"None in the bathroom? Or the small bedroom?" A memory of dripping words in a fogged mirror replayed through my head.

"No, ma'am."

"Call me Em," I said automatically. "You sure?"

"Sure as the sun shines in summer," he drawled.

"I thought it was ghosts," I admitted, stretching my hands across the shiny silver tabletop.

He snorted. "There's no such thing as ghosts."

I thought of how Jack haunted my thoughts, regrets pinging around me as I cleaned my apartment. Of how I let fear of him, of myself, stop me from going after what I wanted for so long. Of good ole Lucy, the doll that kept popping up like an unwanted roommate from hell.

"Of course not." I smiled again. "Did he tell you how he managed to move the doll around so fast?"

Steve fixed me with an odd look, lips a thin line.

I shifted, my chair suddenly uncomfortable.

"What doll?"

36

———————

JACK

The still of early morning blanketed the cabin, random bird calls the only interruption of absolute quiet. In the seat next to me, Em dozed, her lips parted and face blissful in sleep. The black vinyl upholstery and plexiglass barrier of the cop car provided an odd backdrop to her angelic features.

My thumbs flew over the touchscreen keyboard, replying to Robert's last email.

I won't be offering on the New Hopewell property. I have a personal conflict of interest.

Apologies,

Jack

The email chimed as I hit send, and I sagged against the seat. Lightheaded with relief. Em and I could make this work. The phone dinged again, with Rob's reply displayed across the screen. Later. I'd deal with him later. I tucked it into my pocket.

"She's one tough cookie, huh?" The Captain America looka-like peered back at me in the rearview mirror.

Tough cookie? I squinted back at him and nodded. He even sounded like Steve Rogers. Or my grandmother. "You have no idea."

His eyebrows raised. "Renovating the old hotel, huh? That'll be real good for New Hopewell. Bring some life back into it. I've been thinking about opening up a place downtown, on the square, a brewery or something." Steve grinned. "Little nightlife out here might go a long way."

"I bet a brewery would do great." Something like jealousy slithered through me. Once, in college, Em half convinced me I should open up a brewery. But stability and money seemed the smarter bet.

And look what I had to show for it. *Nothing.* Lying to the woman I loved.

"Are y'all gonna go for it? Buy the old place?"

I shrugged, worry flickering. I had no intention of buying the place. Not when I could have Em instead. My parents showed me I could never have both.

She would understand.

"Some uniforms swept the cabin and packed up the AV equipment last night. It's all in evidence now, you two lovebirds should be good to go." He gave me a thumbs up.

I nodded, trying not to focus on last night.

"Come on, Em. We're here." I rubbed her arm, and her lashes lifted.

"Hi." She blinked sleepily, a soft smile banishing any apprehension. "Mmph." She closed her eyes again.

A grin tugged my cheeks up. I kissed the tip of her nose, and she wrinkled it.

"Fine," I said. I eased out of the backseat and walked around the cop car. Carefully, I opened the door, scooting Em into my arms. Her head tumbled limply against my neck and shoulder, her lush fall of auburn hair tickling the skin on my arms. "Thank you, Officer."

"You've got my card if you need anything." I'd stuck it in my wallet, wondering why I felt the need to keep it. "Feel free to call if something comes up." The small town cop dipped his head and shifted his cruiser into reverse.

Good. I didn't like him calling her a tough cookie.

She was mine. He could get his own tough cookie.

Em's head lolled, and I adjusted my arms to keep her from getting banged up. The gravel path crunched under my foot. Our salt circle glistened in the morning light, like some kind of fairy ring from a children's story.

What a night. What a weird night. I owed Em an apology for not believing her about the ghost. Not taking her seriously. I would try not to make that mistake again. A crow cawed in the distance, and a flock of blackbirds took wing above the treeline.

There was no ghost, sure, but that old asshole sure was trying to make it seem that way. I shook my head, tightening my grip on the sleeping woman on my arms as I stepped onto the porch and searched my pocket for the key. The night's events caught up to me, and a wave of exhaustion crashed over me.

Then Em's arm snaked around my shoulders, trailing a soft fingertip across the base of my neck. My body snapped to full attention, suddenly extra aware of the curve of her hips and ass in my hands.

"Hello there, handsome," she purred, batting her eyelashes.

I snorted, jangling the knob until it opened. "Sleeping beauty awakes."

"And my handsome prince, carrying me over the threshold of our castle." Her smile grew.

Guilt stabbed me. Not *our* castle. I shoved the guilt aside. This was for the best. For us. I was going to turn down her business deal for us. For our future.

"Although, I think *I* was the knight in shining armor in this fairytale."

"You definitely were." I hesitated before setting her upright onto the floor. I rubbed the back of my neck, already missing her soft touch. Em pouted before circling slender arms around my waist and burrowing into my chest. She inhaled deeply, and the press of her breasts across my torso nearly undid me.

"How tired are you?" I breathed the question into her hair, the hair I loved, flaming red-gold in the sun and soft as silk, wild as the woman herself.

She tilted her chin up to me, a devilish grin on her face. "Not that tired."

Her hand ran down my back, and she lifted up my shirt, tracing shapes on the bare skin of my lower back.

I swallowed. "I have to tell you something. Before we—"

Her fingers stopped, still there, warm, pressing into my skin. Driving me crazy.

"I already know what you're going to say."

"You do?"

"Yes. And I'm pissed, don't get me wrong. I was furious. Now I'm just pissed." She started tracing shapes again. Long vertical stroke. Short horizontal stroke. A circle.

"I understand." My mouth was dry, my body so flooded with lust I could hardly think straight. Couldn't believe she still wanted me. "How? When—"

"I saw the text from Caroline before I ran to the hotel yesterday. That's why I ran." She cocked her head at me, the tracing stopped. Her eyes widened, and I knew that look.

"Don't cry, Em." I hugged her to me, furious with myself. Furious I'd lied. Furious that this wasn't even half of what I wanted to tell her. "I should've told you we'd broken it off." A rasping laugh escaped me. "She broke it off, to be honest. Told me I cared more about work than her. Called me cold."

Another pang of guilt clenched my chest. I *had* cared more about work than Caroline. But that wasn't why I felt guilty.

Say it. Tell her you can't go into business with her.

But her hands were tracing shapes again, and I closed my

eyes, lost in the sensation. In her scent, her body pressed against mine.

"I forgive you. And you aren't cold." Her voice was a whisper. She nestled deeper into me, and all I wanted was to be deep in her. "You're so warm. Hot, even."

A diagonal slash. Another diagonal slash.

"Em, what are you—"

"Remember that game we used to play in elementary school? Where I traced letters on your back and you had to guess the words?"

Three short horizontal strokes. A long vertical one.

My eyes shot open, and I tugged her chin up to me, staring in her eyes.

"Love."

Her eyes widened. "You were always shit at that game."

I crushed my mouth to her, her full lips so soft, inviting as they parted. I hoisted her up, and she wrapped her legs around me. She squeaked, the sound melting into a moan as I worked my hands across her back.

"How long do you think we have before they get back from the hospital?" Jen insisted Lena get x-rays. Now it seemed like the best idea the woman ever had.

"I don't know." She smirked up at me, and I ran my thumb across her lower lip, berry red and swollen from the force of our kiss.

"I need to—" I wanted to tell her. To break off the idea of our partnership. If I played my cards right? She'd never have to know I originally planned to steal this property out from under her. My stomach twisted.

"Shh." She took my finger in my mouth, sucking it, making a promise. I groaned, all rational thought driven out of my mind. Guilt gave way to lust, and I all but ran with her to the bedroom.

37

EMMA

I wanted this man. I wanted all of him. I slid down his chest, tugging his shirt over his head, the heat in his eyes igniting me completely. Reverent, my hands slid across his chest as I lowered myself onto my heels.

"How are you so..." I trailed off, my fingers tripping over the button and zippers.

"Built? Incredibly hot? Fit? Close to perfection?"

I bit off a laugh and peeked up at him. "Something like that, yeah."

He flexed his arms, planting a kiss on one bicep.

I couldn't hold it back. Laughter pealed out of me, and Jack, if anything, looked even more pleased with himself, chuckling along with me.

Then I unzipped his pants, and he groaned, the sound turning me on even more. His hand wound through my hair, and I blissfully closed my eyes at the feeling of his fingers tracing along my scalp.

"You don't have to do that if you don't want to." Jack grated out.

I cut him a sly look, before tugging his pants and boxer shorts down to his knees.

"I want to. I've thought about for a long time, as a matter of fact."

"Is that right?" His voice was hoarse.

And his cock? Well. It was right in front of me. Slowly, I licked the tip of it, and it jerked up as I blew a cold breath across it.

"You like that?" I asked, a devilish smile on my face, before taking him in my mouth.

"Dammit, Em."

"Do you want me to stop?" I stroked the surface of him, loving how he responded to my touch.

Feeling powerful. Beautiful. I looked up at him, waiting for his answer. The look in his eyes scorched me, and desire ravaged through me.

"I want to make love to you."

The words brought me up short. Something in my chest clenched, and I had a sudden urge to cry. We'd wasted so much damn time.

"I want to make you happy."

"Oh, Em. You do." He tugged me up, and I teetered forward before he clamped his arms around me, throwing me on the bed. Kissing me, his smart tongue and big hands blazing across my skin.

We worked together, and our clothes came off. His big body pressed against me.

I shivered. Everything in me was condensed to a searing need, a want. I wanted him so badly it almost hurt.

"Are you cold?" he whispered, kissing my earlobe, his fingers teasing the peaks of my nipples.

"No. I'm on fire." His head dipped to my breast, and I gasped as he sucked.

"What do you want? Tell me."

I wanted it all. I wanted him.

"Make love to me," I said, and his eyes jerked up to mine, serious. "I want you to do that," I added lamely, feeling like maybe I'd killed the mood.

Instead, he took my nipple back in his mouth, and I arched into him.

"Like that?" His words caressed my sensitive skin, and I moaned.

"It feels so good."

"I'm glad." He shot me a self-satisfied smile, kissing down my stomach, his clever fingers touching, stroking, finding the secret parts of me no one had cared to find in such a long time.

He moved down between my legs, and I let out a small gasp as he stroked the peak of my pleasure there. He looked up at me, and I writhed against him. Need. I needed him.

"I'm glad it feels good, because I love you. I want to make love to you, because I love you. I've always loved you."

Emotion surged over me, and tears welled in my eyes. "I love you, I love you, too. I love you so much."

He grinned a knowing grin, before putting his lips to work. And his tongue. I lost track of time. The only thing that mattered was sensation. Was him. And me.

He *loved* me.

He loved *me*.

"Jack," I breathed, the tension building. "I want you. I'm ready."

He nodded, reaching down for a condom packet, somehow managing to tear the packet so quickly that I didn't have time to recover before he was plunging into me. "You're so wet for me. I won't ever stop wanting this. Wanting you."

My heart was so full, it felt as though it would burst. I sat up on my elbows, and Jack kissed me hard, light stubble raking across my cheeks as he slowly pulled in and out.

Everything was perfect. Perfect.

"I love you," I breathed into his ear, wrapping my arms around him, my legs.

Giving myself to him.

Perfect.

38

———————

JACK

Her hair fanned around us, gleaming in the sun streaming through the slats of the small window. Despite my arms circling her, pulling her close, I wanted her closer. I wanted to be like this forever.

Emma and me.

"That was pretty good." She cast a glance at me from over her shoulder, and I pressed a kiss to her temple.

"Just pretty good, huh?"

She shrugged, turning back and snuggling deeper into me. "Four and half stars out of five."

I launched up to my hands, caging her in my arms against the bed. "Four and a half out of five stars?" I repeated in disbelief.

"Would recommend." She nodded nonchalantly, making a show of examining her nails. Trying to hide a smile.

I bent my elbows, skimming my chest over her bare breasts, and she squeaked in surprise.

"What would it take to get the last half star?"

"Well now, I don't go giving five-star reviews to just anyone." She smirked.

I made a noise of mock exasperation, kissing along her slender neck, and she sighed beneath me. "I had no idea you were running a sex Yelp."

She snorted, then caught my face in her hands. My breath caught in my chest. *So beautiful.* I was so lucky.

"Girl's gotta make a living somehow."

And with those words, reality came crashing back over me. I rolled off of her, instantly regretting the loss of her body, her warmth. Her satin smooth skin.

Regretting what I was about to say.

"Hey."

She propped herself up on an elbow, draping a languid, long leg over my hips. "Uh oh. Listen, I could make an exception for the last half star."

I grinned at her, catching the hand that ran over my chest and kissing her knuckles. *My funny, brilliant woman.*

"I want to talk about this."

She retrieved her hand and walked her fingers back down to my groin. "We can *always* negotiate a new rating system." Em waggled her eyebrows meaningfully.

"I love you. I meant it, Em. I love you. I want to be with you."

Her forehead smoothed out, and she launched herself on top of me, pressing her face into my neck. A muffled noise came from my collarbone area. I smiled at the top of her head.

"What was that?"

Her eyes met mine, my whole body aware of hers. Her perfection. Her expanse of smooth, freckled skin, constellations that all pointed me to one conclusion.

"I love you, too. I'm just so glad I called you. I am so glad you're here. Even though I thought maybe we'd die this weekend." She traced letters across my skin, branding me forever.

No one could ever take the words her finger melted into my body away from me.

"Hey." Her eyes met mine, laughter in them. "Hey, look at us. Who would've thought?"

Catching onto the reference, I shook my head, chuckling. "Not me."

Had I ever laughed like this before sex? After it?

I wanted to laugh with Em like this always.

Which was why I had to tell her.

"What I was trying to tell you earlier..." The words stuck in my throat.

"You don't have to apologize about the Kitty 7.0 drama. It's whatever. You wanted to protect your virtue from me, I get it."

I let her talk, drinking her in. Wanting to make it last forever. I rolled to my side, the sheets tangling around my legs. I couldn't tell her naked. This conversation required pants.

I sprang out of bed. Couldn't stand to look back at her until I got the words out.

"I love you." A pause, as I dived into a clean shirt.

"Why do I get the feeling there's about to be a big but attached to that." I looked over my shoulder at her, where she waggled her ass on the bed. "A big butt, get it?"

Distracting as hell.

Which was exactly why I had to tell her now.

Something in my expression must have told her something, because her butt stopped moving, and she pulled a sheet up to her chest, her face shuttering.

"I want you to be my girlfriend."

Relief smoothed out the worry. A smile bloomed.

"But I can't—I won't—be business partners with you." I turned away, but not before catching the way her face crumpled up, lips becoming a thin line, devastating me. Breaking me. But I had to be strong. "I know what happens to couples who try to go into business together. Em, you know that, too."

"Goddammit, Jack." The words exploded out of her. "Your parents aren't the rule. And even if they were, we aren't them."

"We can be partners in life. I love you." I turned back to her, tugging my pants on. "I can't do business though."

"Do you think we can't do it? Do you not believe in me?"

"No, Emma, that's not what this is about."

"That sure as hell seems like what this is about."

"You could come back with me, and I could find you a job you like better."

"What the fuck, Jack?" Color rose across her collarbone and up her throat, blotchy and angry. "I don't need you to *find* me a job. Are you ashamed of me? Worried that I won't fit into your neat little world?" She took a breath, eyes filling with tears. "Answer the question: do you believe in me?"

Where was this coming from? I rubbed a hand over my face. I was making a total mess of it. My phone began ringing, and I had a sinking feeling I already knew who it was.

"Of course, I do, and no, Em. No, how could I be ashamed of you? You're incredible. I thought you weren't happy, that's why you came out here." Tears tracked down her cheeks, and I raked a hand through my hair, words tumbling out of me in an unstoppable deluge. "I thought you wanted a change. You know, that you were sick of living at home. *I* could be that change. Besides, you weren't going to be able to buy this place once my company put in their offer—"

Her face pinked, her cheeks flushed with more than the post-orgasmic glow I'd given her. With rage. My stomach clenched. I'd just fucked it up.

39

E MMA

"ONCE YOUR COMPANY DID WHAT?" My pulse raced wildly, and I rubbed the ridge of my collarbone, sure I'd misheard. Sure I was wrong.

My brain, always too fast, skipped along like a hamster on a wheel as Jack's mouth opened and closed.

He didn't think I could do it. He was *ashamed* of me. It all made sense. That's why he didn't tell me about Caroline, he knew we would *finally* bang it out—but I wasn't good enough for him. Not the perfect little corporate wifey.

And now he didn't want to be business partners either. Never even intended to give me a chance. Intended to buy my dream out from under me.

"I don't understand, Jack." I spread my hands wide, mad at his t-shirt for covering up his stupidly hot body. Mad at him. Mad at myself. "I don't understand why you agreed to come at all if you weren't serious about going into business with me." I swallowed, trying not to openly sob. "If you planned on... What the hell did you plan on?"

I found a hair tie on my wrist, maturely resisted the urge to shoot it into his face and instead hastily piled my hair into a bun.

"I was serious." But his gaze skittered away. *Lying.* "I wanted to help you see that this wasn't a good investment, not that you couldn't do it. Of course you could do it. It's just not a smart investment. Listen, was I supposed to outbid you on the place? Yes. Em, look at me," he pleaded.

My stomach churned. "I can't." I'd really start crying if I had to look at him lie to my face again.

"Emma, I called it off. I told them I wouldn't outbid you. I see how much it means to you, how great this would be for you. How great you would be at it. How much it means to you."

"Enough." My voice was a whisper, but it felt like a roar.

"I'm so sorry, Emma. I never should have led you on about business, never should have lied. I made a mess of everything. I just, I wanted a chance, I wanted you."

Laughter bubbled out of my mouth, incongruous and sick sounding.

"I'm not joking, Em. It's not a joke. Just look at me."

"You're right, it's not a joke." I couldn't look at him. Look at the face of the friend and lover I'd pinned so many hopes on. Disbelief and shock melted within me, replaced by white hot anger and shame. I slept with him. I *thought* I loved him. "We had sex, and now you're telling me that's why you came here? That you never actually considered being partners with me in any way but the biblical way."

It sounded dumb when it left my mouth, but I let the words hang between us. A small part of my brain told me to stop, but I was too mad. As for Jack, he loomed in the way only a man well over six feet could do. His temple twitched, and I knew his teeth were grating against each other.

"And what now, Em? We love each other, at least, you said you loved me, until I told you the truth." The fight went out of his gaze, the words said so softly—but somehow ringing through me like a hammer. I was vaguely aware of his phone ringing, but he ignored it.

"That you don't trust me enough to be partners? That you were going to snatch all this away from me? For work? That's not what you do to someone you love." My voice was louder now. I swept my arm across the bed, gesturing towards the entire house. The house I wanted. The property I would buy. The hotel I wanted. The future I wanted.

The future I *needed*.

"I fucked up," he said slowly, his eyes searching, looking for something I wasn't sure I had to give. "I didn't know I still loved you. I didn't know that coming here would only prove how much I need you in my life. You've been my best friend for so long, and when everything fell apart between us, it left a huge hole. I don't want to make that mistake again, Em. I refuse to. I know I hurt you again, by not telling you, but I won't lie again. I can't hide how I feel from you anymore, and I won't lie and tell you I can go into business with you. But if this is what you want, if this hotel and this property are what you want, then I will support you however I can without being your business partner. I won't do that with the woman I love, I won't risk us. But like I said, I told my firm I was out. I won't be bidding on their behalf."

"This was all really fucking sneaky of you, Jack," I said, my lower lip trembling.

"I swear to God, Em, I will spend every day of my fucking life trying to make it up to you. I don't want to hurt you. I don't want anything *but* you. I don't like who I am without you. You make me want to be better. I am so sorry." His dark brown eyes filled with tears, and my heart squeezed as he took a step towards me.

"No—" I held up a hand, mustering a strength I didn't know I had, sucking back the tears that threatened. "I am hurt, Jack, but I understand. Or I can try to. This is a hard line for you. I can understand that. I want us to work. I want *you*, too. But this hotel, this dream... This is important to me. I know not ending up like your parents is important to you. If we want to have a chance at an *us*, then I think we both need to understand those things."

"Em," he breathed, my name a whisper on his lips. He stepped closer, his hand tracing softly over my cheekbone. "I fucking love you. I will make this work."

His phone rang for the third time, nearly buzzing off the dresser. His gaze slid to it, and before I could stop him, his fingers flew across the screen as he picked up.

"Hey—"

An angry male voice sounded on the line. I couldn't make out what was being said, but whoever spoke was pissed. Oh, God. Jack's boss.

"Listen, I have a good explanation—" Jack turned towards the corner, where I couldn't see his face.

"Uh-huh. Right. I understand. Yes. Yessir."

When he turned back around, a cold mask slipped over his features. Jack Colson in business mode.

With that, he straightened, a strange look on his face. "I need to get back home."

"What? Now?" I sat bolt upright, flummoxed. "Why?"

"I have some things to figure out." He raised his phone, his face melting into weariness. My heart ached.

"Jack, what? Why are you leaving now? Is it me? Is it something I said?"

He rolled his shoulders, then planted a kiss on my forehead, leaving me staring after him. "I need to get back to work."

"But it's the *weekend*—"

"We're going to make this work, babe. But there are some things I need to do. I promise, this isn't about you. At all. Well, it kind of is. But I need to figure this out before I can make us work. I need to figure my shit out." He grinned at me, and the corners of my own mouth twitched in response, even though my heart sank so low in my chest it made my stomach hurt. "I will call you. Every night. Every morning."

"I want you to stay," I whispered, my throat closing in. Why did he need to leave right *now*?

"Trust me, it's better if I get the ball rolling on this sooner than later."

"Jack, you're not making any sense." I clutched the blankets closer to my chest.

"Don't worry, babe, it will make sense." His eyes flashed, slightly manic. "Now you get that discount, and you get this plan of yours off the ground, do you understand?"

"So what, we're just going to do long-distance?"

"Long distance is nothing compared to all the time we've spent apart the last five years." He angled his head, eyes raking over me like he memorized the lines of my face. "Do you trust me?"

"I mean, yeah, of course, I do, Aladdin. But I want you to stay."

"I will, love, I will. Just give me some time." With that, he snatched his cell phone and keys from the dresser. I flinched as the front door slammed, followed by the sound of the Bronco tearing down the driveway.

What the *fuck* just happened?

40

EMMA

How was it that crying made my entire face hurt? My eyes stung, my cheeks felt raw, and my whole chest hurt.

It felt like Jack squeezed my battered heart until it stopped beating entirely.

I mean, that was a *bit* dramatic. Considering I was still in my cozy little murder cabin, I probably shouldn't even *think* about the walking dead. My fingertips fluttered to the skin on my neck he kissed a mere day before. Found my pulse.

Deep breaths. In and out.

My chest shook, and for a moment, I half-expected more tears to flood out of me. But nothing came.

I was cried out, the tears starting as soon as he left. He said that he'd call. He hadn't. Not yet. I spent the day sleeping, woke up to eat. Nothing fancy, I couldn't stand the thought of cooking. Spending time in that kitchen felt too raw. Too painful.

Scrambled eggs and toast.

I needed him. I rolled over, my hair catching on my lips. I blew, trying to dislodge them, catching the tell-tale scent of Jack all over the sheets I'd been too tired to wash.

It smelled like him. Like us.

My head hurt too, the Sunday morning sun too bright. Had it only been four days?

Four days since we first got here. One day since Jack ran out, saying he loved me, and then forgetting to call.

Swinging my legs over the edge of the bed, I groaned and stretched my toes to the floor, finally shuffling across the floor. I flung the bedroom door open, wincing as even brighter sunshine spilled across the hallway.

Shower. Brushing teeth.

A few zombie-like steps took me to the bathroom, and I opened the door. My hands acted like they belonged to someone else. Sobbing and sleeping had left me disassociated. Light and heavy all at once.

The shower turned on, pipes rattling a bit before calming. Water rushed from the head in a torrent. I sat on the toilet and waited for steam.

Shucked my clothes. Got in. Washed. On autopilot. Shampooed. Conditioned. Cried a bit more.

Got out.

The words on the mirror were back.

You are not alone.

"Oh, fuck off, ghost." I sighed, rubbing the mirror with a hand towel. My reflection was blotchy, eyes puffy. I looked like hell.

I didn't care.

I'd been through it.

"We have that in common, ghostie," I said, chuckling. It hurt to laugh. Maybe that wasn't how ghosts worked, really, who knew. Irritation welled in me. Why hadn't he called? He could have at least texted. It made me feel cheap.

Still, I didn't think he'd been lying.

Jack was just never great at peopling, which was why we stuck together like glue. I was enough people person for us both. But if he wanted us to work, he was sure as shit going to have to fix that right quick.

My irritation ebbed, washed away in a steam filled room definitely still haunted by some encouraging and odd ghost. I'd broken the jar at the hotel. Maybe the ghost potion actually worked. Whatever hung around now? It wasn't mean.

We'll be partners, me and the ghost.

"I need to stop drinking," I told to my reflection.

"Em, are you okay?"

Lena and Jen returned in the early afternoon yesterday. I heard them come in. Completely avoided them. Couldn't bear to talk about it. About Jack. Didn't want them to think I'd fucked up and driven him away. Again.

"Em?"

"Just communing with the spirits." I raised my eyebrows in the mirror.

Ha ha.

I flinched back as the words dripped across the top of the mirror, a still-steamed section I hadn't felt like cleaning with my towel. Better late than never.

"There's someone here to see you," Lena called through the door.

My reflection looked as confused as I did.

"Tell me it's Jack." His name burned as it left my lips. I squeezed my eyes shut, gripping the sink as though it would take away the confusion I felt.

Who said they loved someone, then ran away?

"No, it's a sweet little old lady." Lena cracked the door open and peeked in at me. I wrapped the towel tighter around myself. "You look terrible. What happened?"

"We... he..." I spread my hands wide, choking on the words. "Little old lady?"

Brow furrowed in concern, Lena nodded in affirmation. "I can tell her you're sick."

I sighed, and it hurt. Everything hurt. "No. Just let me get dressed and I'll be right out." I would see this through. Despite everything, I wanted this place. I wanted to prove to everyone—to myself—what I was capable of. What I could give people with this place.

She nodded, clearly unconvinced that I should be talking to a little old lady when I was so clearly not ok. She was a good sister. Lena moved to close the door, and I stopped it.

"Thank you, Lena."

"Of course." She shrugged, her hurt foot hovering above the floor.

"No, I mean it. For everything. I love you."

Her lips twisted to the side. "Now I *know* you're a mess. I love you, too. And whatever happened, you're tough. You'll get through this."

Fresh tears welled. Damn it. Just when I thought I was out of them.

"Don't make me be mean to you to keep you from crying," she threatened, lips pursed.

I huffed out a laugh, wiping my eyes with the back of my hand.

"Just like old times."

"Something like that," Lena answered, and we both knew it wouldn't be like old times. Because we weren't the same. They would be better than old times.

Except Jack wasn't here.

MY WET HAIR curled around my shoulders. I eyed it with distaste. It was going to dry frizzy and weird. Not like I was trying to impress anyone.

"Are you quite all right, dear?" Katherine, the old woman from the grocery store, sat perched, prim and proper, on the edge of the sofa, a structured purse stowed in her lap. Her hands lit atop it, fragile like birds.

"I'm fine, thank you." I wasn't. But I had coffee now, and it was fortifying, at the very least.

"And where is your strapping young man?" She peered into the kitchen, as though Jack might appear at any moment. My heart hurt.

"He had something to... do." And it wasn't *me*.

"All right, then. Hmmm." She plucked her rhinestone spectacles off her chest, where they hung on a similarly sparkly cord. Emma opened her purse, pulling out a sheaf of papers. "It shouldn't be a problem." She bit her lip, pouring over the papers.

I edged closer to her, anticipation welling. God, it felt good to feel something other than absolute depression.

"Charlotte doesn't seem to think you buying the place by yourself is a problem."

I blinked. "What's all that paperwork?" I finally asked.

"Why, the deed, of course. Legal contracts. Nothing out of the ordinary." She gave me a withering look over her glasses. "Are you quite all right?"

"No," I answered, not sure what else to say. Done with lying. "Are you Charlotte's lawyer? Where's Susan, the realtor?"

"Oh, oh, yes, Susan is such a doll, isn't she? Well, I do have power of attorney, but no, not an attorney. I'm Charlotte's great-grand niece."

Lena hobbled around the corner, settling herself on the couch and giving me a concerned look. Jen hovered in the hallway, neat and pristine as always.

Charlotte was Katherine's great-great aunt? There was no way she was still alive. I covered my confusion with an introduction.

"This is my sister, Lena, and Jen, her fiancé." My heart was beating loud enough. I could almost hear it.

"Very nice, dear." She waved a hand, dismissing them both. "Charlotte thinks you'll be perfect. As such, I have a quite a deal for you, if you're still willing."

I nearly stood up in distress. Unless it was a really, really good deal, as in *free*, there was no way I could afford it without a partner. Without Jack.

"My funding has—" I began, but she cut me off with another little wave and a harrumph.

"Charlotte has impeccable taste. And we're quite excited to part with the property, especially now that awful man's scheme has been found out. *Earl*." Her tone dripped with acid. "Good work on that, dear Emma. Yes, we think you'll be up to the job here. Quite a lot of strange things happen at this old place."

She retrieved a stub of a pencil from her purse, licked the tip and lightly circled something on the paperwork. Holding it out to me, she looked just past my shoulder and smiled.

I shivered, suddenly chilled.

Then I took the ream of papers, and Katherine positively beamed at me.

Lena's eyes were huge, also fixed behind me. A shiver ran down my spine. I had a feeling I already knew what was there. *Who* was there?

Despite any lingering misgivings, I looked slowly to where Lena stared.

"She comes with the house, I assume?" My voice sounded high-pitched and strange, and a chill washed over me, before a slow sense of calm descended.

"She does as she pleases," Katherine said. "She won't be a bother. She just wanted to make sure the right person was here for the Gertrude Akins. And, my dear, that person is you."

My eyes shot to the circled number on the paper, and I

stood up. Disbelief snaked through me. Seeing was believing, though, when it came to ghosts *and* amazing discounts.

"You can't be serious." Despite my new roomie, it *still* seemed too good to be true.

"Oh yes, quite serious, mmhmm." Her eyes were bright, a wide smile on her face. "In fact, if you have the money with you, which I assume you might, then we can consider this all wrapped up as soon as the ink is dry."

I moved slowly, as though underwater, to where my ratty purse hung from a hook. My fingers shook as I pulled out my waller, fishing out a crinkled five-dollar bill.

"What about Susan? The realtor I spoke to?"

She took it with a smile and held out a hand to shake. "Oh, she helped draw up the papers. Don't worry, we paid her commission already."

"I guess we have a deal." I grasped her palm, her papery skin warm and somehow comforting. I would stand on my own two feet. I was buying this place, all on my own.

So what if it had a ghost or two?

I was pretty sure we all did.

41

————

JACK

S weat clung to me, dripped down my back. The gym faded away into nothing, the pounding of feet on tread-mills echoing the beat of my heart. My entire body screamed, asking for mercy. I kept going. Ten more reps. Twenty more.

Until I couldn't think straight. Couldn't think about *her*.

I gripped the bar tighter, grunting with effort. I'd called her every day this week. Texted her. Sent flowers to her little cabin, imagining the place chock-full of roses and carnations and whatever the hell else the florist told me would look pretty.

I knew Em's new address by heart.

I missed her, loved hearing her voice every night, even though I wasn't ready to tell her my hare-brained schemes. Didn't want to get her hopes up in case they fell through. She sounded distant, like she couldn't believe it when I told her I loved her. Like I'd hurt her when I left.

I knew I had.

I knew I'd messed up again.

But I'd messed up so I could make it right.

Up, down. Up, down.

I set the weights down, equipment rattling as it bounced against the gym floor. Closed my eyes against the sting of sweat. Of tears. My heartbeat thudded in my neck, in my temple. All I could think about was the biggest flaw in her plan. What was out in New Hopewell that would bring anybody all the way out there besides Em? That Tarot Kolache place, the one greasy spoon in town, no bar, no nightlife...

I'd refused to bid on it, and knew at least Robert hadn't gotten the property, that my company failed to land the deal. Robert was pissed. No, pissed didn't even begin to cover it. Robert was furious. I closed my eyes, resting against the bench, overcome. Messed up things with Emma, failed to get the promotion. Not that I cared about my job anymore, not like I used to. Like I used to *live* for it.

All I cared about was not being such an idiot when it came to my personal life. When it came to *her*.

Emma was going to soar, and I was determined not to be the one to weigh her down.

"You done?"

The words jolted me out of my reverie, and I opened my eyes, nodding and getting off the bench for the next gym bro. I cleaned the equipment with a wipe.

"Looked like you were punishing yourself, man."

"Maybe." *I deserved it.*

All I wanted was her. Wanted her, came close to losing her, couldn't sleep without her, couldn't think straight. Couldn't risk getting her hopes up with my plan only to dash them if mine fell apart. Emma made me realize I'd been living life too carefully, proving I'd grown as cold as Caroline claimed.

Fiery Em made me realize I'd barely been living. I refused to give up on us. Again.

"Seems like you need a beer."

A beer. That was exactly it. *A beer.* Holy shit.

Holy *shit.*

My cheeks ached, and I realized I grinned from ear-to-ear. "Thanks, man, enjoy your workout." I gripped his shoulder, filled with something besides anger at myself. *Hope.*

The guy's brows furrowed in confusion, but I was already moving toward the locker room.

❧

DELETE, delete, delete. Where was the pitch? I dug through my emails, powering through a tasteless meal at the small desk in my apartment. Emma sent the pitch, I was sure of it, watched her smart fingers send it straight to me and pulled it up to show Lena the next night. I'd no reason to pass it up to Robert, but I knew it was in my inbox somewhere.

A new idea took shape in my mind. A post-workout beer sweated on my desk, condensation pooling around the bottom.

All I needed was to tweak the numbers in her pitch, figure out my own way forward. I knew exactly what real estate was up for grabs in the small town. It was time to nut up and make a go on my own dream.

Aha, there you are.

I sucked in a breath, running a finger across the screen of my laptop. This pitch, the Piney Woods Inn… this was truly something special. Just like Emma. I frowned, thumbing through it, past the images and plans. Where is the spreadsheet and graphic?

My phone lit up, a quick succession of texts from Aiden buzzing through.

Aiden: tacos tonight? It's Tuesday

Aiden: I've got a new pale lager to try, crisp with a hint of lime. Nice citrusy nose, little bit floral

Aiden: or are you still a complete ass to be around

I paused, hand hovering over the laptop. My mind spun out, possibilities playing out around me. My gaze darted between the phone and the screen.

Aiden could wait.

The video recommendation letter Em skipped over last Friday was cued to play, an older gentleman frozen in a grin on screen. Salt-pepper hair set off his dark complexion, and the man could pass for Morgan Freeman's brother.

I pressed play, unable to resist hearing someone else sing her praises. I raised the beer to my lips and drank deep. Not a bad IPA, but I could make a better one. Used to practically be able to do it in my sleep.

"I'm Theo Rockberry, former owner and operator of the Rockberry Inn and Spa in Pflugerville, Texas. Like most of us independent boutique hotel owners, I was bought out by a big chain. It was time to retire, anyway. But we never would have been half as successful in saving up our nest egg without my girl, Emma. Wish I could do more to help her get started, but I trust her taste in investors. Never worked with a smarter manager."

Emma's old boss, Theo, continued to sing her praises. I rubbed a hand across my chest. Theo saw Emma as the woman she was, not the teenager she'd been. He detailed her strong work ethic, her charming manner with guests, her quick smile and quicker wits. I swigged the beer.

The video ended with his contact information.

Suddenly, I knew exactly how I could help Em. I could *prove* I believed in her. Put my money where my mouth was. That would have to be enough for now, knowing I was helping her, trusting she would eventually understand why I'd had to leave and forgive me for being cagey.

I rewound the video and scribbled down Theo Rockberry's number, too. I had two calls to make, and everything to gain.

I'm coming back, Emma.

I made the easiest one first.

"Hey, Aiden—"

"Why the fuck are you calling me? Can't you text like a normal human being?" He laughed, but the surprise was clear in his voice.

"I wanna talk about that business opportunity we used to dream about. I'll bring the chips, queso, and tacos, you get that lager ready for me. I might also be bringing an apology with me."

A long pause, and for a moment, it felt like the world hung in the balance.

"Hell yeah, man. You know I'm down. I guess you removed that stick from your ass?"

"It wouldn't budge, but I think it might be looser now." I snorted into the phone. "See ya tonight."

"You can't be serious."

I met Robert's expression of absolute shock with a grin. "I am."

"Take a beat. Take a week. Hell, take a month, man, but don't do this."

"I need a change. This place has been..." I glanced upward, the words not coming. At least, the right ones. Meat grinder hardly seemed the appropriate term. "It's been a ride. And I'm thankful for all you've taught me. But I need a change."

"Yeah, you said that already. What the hell are you planning to do?"

"Take a beat." It felt bizarre to be leaving. But I couldn't go back to this. To being cold.

It had been two months. Two absolutely miserable, completely fucking shit months. The only thing keeping me going were the projects I was involved in and trying to make things right between Emma and me. We talked every night, every morning, but we hadn't said I love you again.

I knew I'd broken her trust by leaving. By lying to her for nearly the whole weekend.

It wasn't much, but it was enough. Enough to keep me moving towards her, towards my goal. Without Em, the possibility of her, my ordered world didn't mean anything. And with that thought, the grin slid off my face.

"There's the shark I know." My boss rocked back in his chair. "You'll have to sign a noncompete."

I snorted. "I'm not planning on building a new business—" I paused, rubbing the back of my neck. It was a lie. And I was done with that. "Not a business that competes with you, at least."

It was a plan I immediately set to work on. Pulling funds from long term investments, liquidating assets and my personal real estate investments. Filing for licenses, permits, more state paperwork, hiring employees, and the best part, the tastings. And even more paperwork. Research. Construction.

Aiden's expertise and reputation were the cherry on top, and I was having more fun than I'd had in years.

"What the hell kind of business are you going into?" Robert steepled his fingers, his head cocked to the side.

I fished in my pocket for the shiny new cards and flung one onto his desk.

He reached for it, eyebrows shooting into his hairline.

"You've gotta be fucking with me." He looked from me to the card, and back to me again.

"Nope. I've needed a change for a while."

"This place... New Hopewell? It's in the middle of nowhere. Wait, isn't this where I sent you out to view that property? The one you refused to offer on?" He set his feet on his desk, eyes fixed on the card, then flashed back to me.

I nodded slowly. "Sure is. And nowhere can be a good thing. Maybe we'll put it on the map."

Robert's eyes narrowed in silent appraisal then gave a slight nod. "So there *is* a we?"

I sucked in a breath. "Not exactly. Not yet. But there will be."

"There will be?"

"I hope so. If I have it my way."

"You've always *made* it your way." Robert smiled, rubbing a finger over the letters and logo on the business card. "Great name for a place. Give me a call when it's ready and I'd love to swing by. Or if you need more seed money." A calculating light played in his eyes. "Always smart to diversify."

"I'd like that, Robert." I paused, thinking of Emma, her wild red hair shimmering in the morning light. "There's a great hotel being renovated there, too. Perfect place for a corporate retreat or a family vacation."

The words echoed Em's pitch, and I *knew* she was going to do it. Come hell or high water, that hotel was going to be successful. Theo sent me updates on the construction progress regularly, even when Emma got tongue-tied about it. She didn't want to talk about business with me.

We had that in common, at least.

I only hoped my faith in her wasn't too late.

And that she would forgive me for being an absolute ass. If she forgave me, really did, not just took my calls and made nice, then just maybe I could truly fix the shit I'd messed up between us. I told her I loved her as much as I could, and while I could hear her smile through the phone, she hadn't said it back yet.

As soon as I left Robert's office, I was on the phone with Aiden.

"How much longer?"

"Hello to you too, Jack. Inspector should be by any minute, and I'd like to do a walk another through with you and have at least a half-day tomorrow to finish training employees. And you know my schedule is tight, so the sooner you can get free and get your ass down here, the better."

I refrained from rolling my eyes. I didn't need a walk through, I knew the place like the back of my hand.

Like the back of Em's hands.

"I just put my notice in. I'm taking vacation as my last two weeks. I'll be there tonight, and we'll refine the details. How's the site look?"

There was a pause at the end of the line. "It looks pretty good, Jack. A lot like the mock-ups, but even better. Have you talked to her about it yet?"

I winced, taking the phone from my ear and looking at the screen for a second before swinging it back up to answer. "No. No, she hasn't... The timing hasn't been right."

"You still think it's the best idea to surprise her with it, don't you?"

I blew out a breath, squeezing my eyes shut. "I don't know if it's the best idea, but maybe I'm more of a coward than I'd like."

Maybe this was a fool's errand.

"I can't say I'd thought I'd ever hear you say that," Aiden said on a laugh. "Well, she'll be surprised, that's for sure."

"Think it will be enough?"

"I sure hope it is, for both our sakes. I know only too well what a moody fucker you can be when things don't go your way."

"I'm sorry." I paused, gritting my teeth. "You don't deserve that. You never have."

The silence on the other end spoke volumes.

"Thanks, man," he finally said. "It's... you know what, it's not okay, but I appreciate you owning up to it. I have high hopes for this place, and for that stick getting clear of you once and for all." He cleared his throat. "We got the sign up out front, and I confirmed with the local paper from Kilgore and another from Dallas. The whole town is buzzing about us. Emma called our business line and wanted to hash out details for some kind of business arrangement. I told her she'd have to take it up with my partner." A laugh. "I don't think she even recognized my voice? I can't believe how long it's been."

"Good. That's great, man." I couldn't be relieved, though, not yet. I'd bought the property under an LLC, adding Aiden as a board member.

Emma didn't have a clue who actually owned the place. I grinned.

I couldn't wait to see her face when she figured it out.

If my new business succeeded, it would help her. Even if she didn't accept my apology, I would be helping her.

Worst case, that would have to be enough.

42

———————

EMMA

It was coming together. So quickly it hurt, growing pains of splinters and nail guns and sandpaper. The hardhat slipped over my forehead again, and I pushed it back up, annoyed. A frigid breeze whipped through the revived lobby, the plastic sheeting over the gaping holes where the windows should be flapping loose. Again. One of the crew paused to reattach it.

Sighing, I turtled my neck into the soft fleece collar of my jacket.

It turned cold after Jack left.

October swooped in, all dark clouds and flocks of grackles. Absolutely perfect for what I planned this weekend. Moping around the cabin and continuing my social media campaign. Campaign or, you know, onslaught. Hearts and minds and explosions. Okay, no explosions unless they were glitter cannons.

If only he were here.

The first few weeks, the thought of him, sparked fiery indignation.

But I struggled to see past his lies. I'd mentally replayed our last conversation so many times I could make a Spotify soundtrack to match it for every mood. I'd put words in his mouth. Hadn't even stopped to consider that no matter my intentions, the first contact I'd had with him in five years was to ask him for money.

That was pretty messed up of me. *Selfish.*

One of the crew was nailing a four by four, the pneumatic gun punctuating my thoughts.

Jack and I had both made mistakes. I could admit it to myself. I would admit it to him. And I wouldn't let five more years go by this time. I'd just needed a little more time, to prove to myself I could stand on my own two feet.

And so I kept him at arm's length, taking his phone calls, looking for his early morning texts. My heart fluttered every time he sent fresh flowers, which honestly, was way too often. My house smelled like a greenhouse.

My house. The thought made my heart lighten.

A crow perched on the window frame, cawing loudly and cocking its head, beady black eyes fixed on me.

"Shoo," I said half-heartedly. Honestly, crows were the least of my worries where this place was concerned. At least they were corporeal. Unlike Jack, the memory of his touch haunted me.

At least I *had* happy memories.

And I'd make more.

But I missed him. Missing him was an ache I couldn't soothe, no matter how much I poured myself into this hotel, this town, this work. Even a month later, still woke up, touching the sheets next to me, wondering where he was.

A small smile surprised me.

The contractor was still talking, pointing to the blueprints and clearly seeking input. *Oops.*

I held up a hand, interrupting him. "I'm sorry. I zoned out."

Colton's eyes narrowed, nodding. "You've got a lot on your mind with trying to get this place up and running, I'm sure. Are you taking care of yourself?" His East Texas accent twanged slightly, and I shrugged.

"I'm doing the best I can." I held up the cooling cup of coffee from Tarot, Kolache, and Coffee as proof. I'd been swinging by most mornings. Tara, the owner, was quickly turning into a good friend. Though she'd been weirder than usual today, all secret smiles and meaningful looks.

Whatever. She'd probably read my tea leaves or looked in a crystal ball or communed with the spirits or something.

"I was saying that the windows are due to be delivered Monday morning, and we need you to sign off on the purchase order again. Trim and flooring come Monday afternoon. Should be done in time to start work on the new construction on that parcel of land that sold next door to you."

"We're getting close, huh." It wasn't a question. *This was happening.* The thought left me breathless.

"Just need to make final selections on lighting and hardware." Colton nodded, grinning at me. "How you feelin'?"

"Excited." I was. But not as much as I thought I'd be. Nervous, and a bit queasy, and so tired. And lonely. So fucking lonely. "I'm gonna miss you when this is done."

"Don't get soft on me now."

I put a hand to my heart, gasping in faux shock. "I wouldn't dare."

"Besides, I expect to be hearing from you when you break ground on the barn. And the tiny house retreats, and the docks, and—"

"You've made your point." I grinned.

"Well, the gang's all here." A new voice rang out from the front door. Theo, my old boss, stood in the doorway. Light limned his silhouette, turning him every inch the guardian angel. Behind him, work on the new circular driveway was well underway, bright red stones fitted in place. "Gotta say, this place is looking mighty fine."

"Theo! I am so freaking glad you came down," I squealed, running and giving him a huge hug. "Finally ready to see what all your money's been up to?" He'd contacted me out of the blue after Katherine basically gifted me with the property, said he'd like to be a silent investor. Wanted to help with the cost of renovations. Wouldn't take no for an answer.

Now, in the foyer of the Piney Woods Inn, Theo shifted from foot to foot, not quite meeting my gaze. "Honey, you know I trust you implicitly. Never had a doubt about it. I have loved getting all the pictures from you, though."

I narrowed my eyes at him. Huh. He was hedging. I knew him well enough to see that right away.

Why?

But Colton coughed, and I turned my attention back to him. Out of the corner of my eye, Theo snagged a hardhat and trekked up the stairs.

"Be careful up there!" I called out, and he waved at hand at me, shaking his head.

Colton and I shared a look. Upstairs was nearly done, too, but... but things went missing up there. Tools moved around, left in one place, found in another in the morning. Doors banged open and shut, no matter how many times we'd checked to make sure the floor was level.

"Still thinking about hosting a ghost tour here at the end of the month?"

I nodded. "Will it be safe by then?" Visions of a Halloween festival danced in my head.

"Should have windows in at least. Light fixtures?" He

shrugged. "Maybe they'll come in early. If you can make up your mind between the samples I sent."

"The transitional brass ones."

He blinked. "Okay. The transitional brass ones. Got it."

"Good." A resounding thud echoed down from upstairs and we winced.

"Heard a new place is opening up downtown for drinks."

"I heard that, too." I squinted at him, surprised by the non-sequitur. He didn't seem like a nightlife kind of guy. In fact, getting any personal details out of him was near impossible. Unless we were talking business, the man was a serious grunter and monosyllabic monster. But he didn't care about ghosts, he was honest, and that was all I really needed.

And his crew didn't seem to mind things getting moved around in the middle of the night. Only one had quit, at least.

"It'll be good for business, having a bar and restaurant in town. They've got reporters coming out. Maybe you should go and tell them about this. About that ghost tour. The whole shebang. They'll eat it up."

I chewed my lip. I'd hardly stopped working in the past month. A few movie and wine marathons with Tara didn't count as going out. Lena and Jen visited once. Said they might be down this weekend. We *could* all go to the new place together.

"Maybe I should."

"Wear something cute," Colton said.

I did a double-take. "Excuse me? If you're asking me out on a date—"

"No, just thought since you might have your picture taken or something." Colton had the decency to look chagrined.

"Thanks for the fashion advice, didn't know I was paying you for that." I grinned at him.

"First one's on the house," he replied, completely straight faced.

I laughed in surprise. "Was that a joke?"

He grunted, refusing to make eye contact, focused on rolling the blueprint back up.

Ah well, back to normal.

❦

"Wear something cute," I mocked under my breath, rifling through the few options I hadn't jettisoned in my Marie Kondo phase of moving. I threw a few things on the bed. Cute jeans, chunky little booties, an off-the shoulder teal sweater that set off the red in my hair.

Lena knocked on the door as I shrugged it on. "You ready? Jen and I can't wait to go check out this place. Hard to believe there is going to be a decent brewery to hang out in all the way out here."

"It'll be good for business." My heart just wasn't in it, not tonight. I'd been running circles around myself, triple checking everything for weeks. Tonight I'd be scoping out a potential new partner, someone I could work with to order beer from or arrange hotel excursions too. I should be excited. Should be thrilled, even.

Something about breweries would always remind me about Jack, and even though he was just a text away, it wouldn't be the same without him.

"Wait." Lena paused, eyeing me critically. "You look like a ghost."

"So?" I fit right in. My new natural habitat.

"Put on some eyeliner and mascara. And blush. And some lipstick won't hurt."

My nose wrinkled. "Rude."

She shrugged, holding her hands up. "Do what you want, but I think you should look extra nice tonight."

Suspicion curled through me, and I tilted my head. "You know, Colton said something like that too."

"Probably because you look like death warmed over and there's going to be press there."

"You're being so rude."

"I'm your big sister, I'm supposed to be. Come on, where's the goods."

Muttering curse words under my breath, I yanked out my makeup bag and held still while she went to work.

"I hope there's tweezers in here."

My eyes shot open. "You are *not* plucking my eyebrows, they're finally filled in."

"If you want to keep this chin hair, go right ahead." She raised an eyebrow, staring at my chin. "We could name him."

"I've grown quite fond of Fred. He keeps my face warm."

"Too bad there isn't someone else keeping your face warm." She muttered.

I closed my eyes again, my stomach falling. "The tweezers are in there."

Her hands tugged on my chin, and I opened my eyes.

"Did you ever think about maybe stopping being so proud and admitting you forgive him? He's getting his life together for you. *For you!*"

I squirmed, not ready to talk about it. Not ready. "I want to prove..."

"Prove what?" she challenged. "That you're the most stubborn person on the planet? Trust me, we've all known that for a long time."

"No, Lena, I want to prove *I* can do this. That I am not flighty or dramatic or high strung. Prove that I want him because I *want* him. Not what he can do for me." I raised a hand, then let it fall. The ache in my chest eased a little, like the words had been fighting to get this whole time. "Or with me."

We'd both said things we hadn't meant. And we'd said things we meant, too.

I love you.

Then acted like scared teenagers instead of the terrified adults we were.

"Okay, then."

That was it? I'd expected another hot retort, a dressing down.

"Close your eyes," she commanded.

I complied, afraid she might stab me with mascara if I didn't. She scrubbed a brush over my eyelids, followed by the cool touch of liquid eyeliner.

"So you admit you *do* want him. Look up."

And there it was. I stared at the ceiling, heaving a sigh as she brushed on mascara.

"It's always been him."

She tilted my face, examining it before coating my lips in red. I smushed them together.

"Good."

I wasn't sure if she was talking about her handiwork or Jack.

It didn't matter, either way.

43

J ACK

"I STILL THINK the name is weird." Aiden leaned on the polished bar, surveying the crowd. People of all ages were seated at tables, mingling in groups, a live band on the small stage in the corner.

"I know." I sipped the whiskey in my hand. More for something to do than any real desire to drink. Despite being the new owner of the hottest spot in New Hopewell.

Also known as the *only* spot in New Hopewell.

"It turned out nice."

"You did good, Aiden." I couldn't quite smile.

He grimaced. "Weird hearing sweet nothings come out of you when you look ready to smash someone's face in."

The door opened again, a blast of cold air sweeping through the place, and I stepped forward. Hope bubbled.

"Calm down." Aiden clapped me on the shoulder. "It's just

the Avengers." Steve, the cop, stepped through, grinning around like the huge goofball he was.

"Don't make me snap my fingers," I grumbled, rewarded by my new business partner's thin laugh.

"She'll be here. Relax. Colton and Lena are on it. Theo's got you covered, too. How's the new house coming?"

I grimaced. "Colton won't break ground until he's done with Emma's hotel." Her name burned like hot sunshine in my throat. Sweet and painful all at the same time. Necessary.

"You had a big part in that, too."

"No I don't," I ground out. "It's hers. I just found someone to donate to the cause." The last thing I wanted was to take away her pride in the place. The only thing I'd done was give Theo the idea to invest, insisting he reach out to Em. She trusted him.

An overwhelming sense of panic gripped me. What if she took my help the wrong way? What if she took me working with Aiden the wrong way?

For all my talk about not going into business with a friend, I'd turned around and done just that. Except, Aiden and I weren't romantic.

And that's *exactly* what I wanted with my Emma.

All I'd wanted was to show her I trusted her, that I believed in her. I ran a hand through my hair, frantic. Holy shit. This might go completely sideways. Would my grand reveal completely backfire?

"What now?" Aiden sipped his drink. A signature craft beer, the first batch concocted immediately after I signed the lease on the bar. We bought the equipment dirt cheap at auction. Our first red Ale, dubbed the Emma.

"What if she hates me for not telling her?"

"That's a possibility. I told you it was from day one."

"Damn it."

"Jack, you know her better than I do. Than anyone, it sounds like. What do you think will happen?"

I hoped it meant I'd close the deal with the *only* woman of my dreams. My face must have said as much, because he grinned and shook his head.

"Play nice with the locals, okay? Enough of the brooding mystery man look." Aiden fixed me with a stern expression before tightening his grip on the glass in his hand and pushing off the bar to greet our patrons.

A tall brunette sauntered over, clad in a wine-colored floor-length dress showcasing impressive cleavage. Her face was vaguely familiar, but I couldn't quite place her. She smiled brightly at my attention.

I groaned inwardly. *Not interested, keep moving.*

"Hi, I hear you're one of the owners?"

"That's me." I took a long drink of ale, admiring the industrial chic lighting I'd picked out. At least, that's what the designer told me it was.

"Jack Colson, right?"

I turned my attention back to her. "Are you the reporter from the Dallas News?" Maybe that's why she looked familiar.

"Nope. I'm Tara." She pointed to the door. "I work right over there. I own the coffee shop. Remember?"

Recognition dawned. "Oh, of course. Sorry... I'm distracted."

She grinned, her cat-like eyes watching me.

"What can I do for you, neighbor? I've been meaning to come by and grab some kolaches."

"I just wanted to say welcome, best wishes, and if you mess with my friend Emma again, I'll curse you." All this was delivered in a cheery alto, made all the more unnerving by her megawatt smile.

I choked on my beer.

Tara's eyes narrowed, and she gave me a satisfied nod. With that, she produced a business card out of nowhere and laid it on the bar between us. A magician's trick.

"She's here, by the way. Good luck."

I swallowed my response, nearly forgetting to breathe. Tara was forgotten. Auburn hair shimmered in the dim light near the entrance. A hint of smooth skin, her shoulders.

My mouth went dry, and I set the beer down hard on the soapstone bar top.

She was here.

Shit.

My entire body tensed. Would this be enough? Too much?

What seemed like an amazing plan two month ago now reeked of idiocy, of desperation. I turned back to the bar, burying my face in my hands. A liquid sound filled my ears, and I looked up to find the bartender refilling my drink.

"Don't mess it up now," he said, pushing the glass towards me.

"Does everyone know?" I demanded, the glass cold in my palm.

He shrugged. "Small town."

What if she didn't forgive me?

What if she did?

I swigged the beer, the sweet butterscotch flavor coating my tongue.

Enough what ifs. I hadn't come this far to ruin it again. I took one step, then another. Her back was to me, facing Lena, who looked positively gleeful, and Jen, who looked, well, like Jen always did. Theo stood behind them, a huge smile on his face. He winked, shooting a finger gun at me.

I grinned back, but my excitement quickly fizzled, turning to fear.

My chest expanded, and I sucked down a breath. Squeezed my eyes shut. Touched her bare shoulder, heat exploding inside me at the contact.

She turned, a half smile frozen on her face. Replaced

quickly by surprise, then hurt, then something that looked like...

Hope.

"Hey," I managed.

"What are you doing here?" She glanced back at Lena, who nodded and gave her a shove towards me.

My cheeks hurt. I was grinning like an idiot. I shrugged, nonchalant. All right, failing at nonchalant.

I wasn't going to play it cool.

"Can I borrow you for a drink? Outside?"

Lena gave her another shove, and Emma nodded slowly. Jen gave me the geekiest thumbs up ever, and Theo crossed his fingers, shaking them high overhead, behind Emma's back.

I offered my arm, and to my absolute relief, Em took it, her hand resting delicately in the crook of my elbow. Pleasure licked through me. I leaned down and whispered into her ear.

"I missed you."

Her eyes widened, her lips parting with a soft "oh."

Those perfect, plump lips. I missed them too. The feel of them on mine, on my body. I swallowed a groan, continuing to lead her to the back patio.

My pièce de résistance.

44

EMMA

I couldn't breathe. Could hardly think. My whole body was taut, tense, thrilled. Waiting. Wanting.

My fingers gripped his forearm, the thin Henley doing absolutely nothing to disguise the fact that the man was pure muscle.

What was he doing here? Why hadn't he told me he was coming?

I couldn't think straight. It was his smell—the tell-tale spicy cologne making me weak kneed, a Pavlovian response from high school that I should probably go to therapy over.

"What cheap cologne is it tonight?" I winced. An inadequate and bizarre question. On brand, for me.

"Kraken. Why release the beast when you can stop your BO?" he answered.

"Are they paying you to advertise now, too?" On brand for *us.*

He let out a throaty chuckle, then whipped my hand out of

his elbow, ducking his head to kiss my knuckles, his chocolate brown eyes never leaving mine.

I swallowed. "It's hot. It's uh, it's really hot in here." I looked away, taking in the massive silver cylinders fenced off from the crowd. Huh. A bar and a brewery? Whatever was New Hopewell coming to?

Coming to. My face heated, and my gaze darted back to Jack.

He cocked an eyebrow, as if he knew I was barely keeping from ripping his tight shirt off and climbing him like a damn tree, a spectator sport in this random crowded bar.

"Good."

"Good?" I echoed.

"Mmhmm." Was I imagining the look he was giving me? "I have the perfect place we can go and keep that beautiful blush from getting any redder."

Then he was leading me by the hand to a back door marked "Private Event."

"Hey, don't you think we shouldn't—"

"It's okay, I know the owner." He threw a wink over one shoulder, and I tried not to salivate.

Drool is not cute.

He pushed the door open, holding it for me. A gentleman Jack.

I full on gasped, sucking a surprised breath down and almost choking on it. A lone sprawling oak, draped in twinkle lights. A gorgeous patio, scattered with tables and chairs and candles, and in the middle, a huge brick fireplace with two chairs set in front of it.

The wind was cold, but the fire blazed merrily, crackling and leaping and smelling like everything in the fall should. In a trance, I settled myself in one of the chairs. Jack followed, hands in his pockets. Watching me.

"What do you think?" The way he said it—the smug tone, the pride—my brain clicked along, putting it together.

"Did you organize this? Plan this?"

He nodded, his eyes never leaving my face. "Something like that."

"Lena was in on it."

He nodded again, his white teeth flashing in the firelight.

"Colton?"

Another nod, and then he turned, producing a growler of beer and a couple stemless glasses. A cheeseboard. A...

"Is that a fur throw? And *how* do you know Colton?"

He placed the blanket on my lap, tucking it under my thighs and around my waist. Fires ignited where his fingers brushed my skin. "Theo introduced us. He's helping me with some construction."

"Theo?" I blinked. *Theo?* I felt like I was right on the verge of understanding something, but Jack was too much, smelled too good, I'd *missed* him too much...

The cheeseboard sat on the small table between the chairs, and Jack perched on the other one.

"Jack, what is going on?"

"Emma, why haven't you told me you loved me? I haven't heard it from you since the day I left."

I studied him. In the firelight, he looked even larger than normal. His muscles seemed bigger. He looked rugged, a slight shadow of stubborn stubble shading his jawline. I took a cleansing yoga breath, as though that would somehow summon my courage. My pulse was so quick I was half-sure this counted as cardio.

"I needed..." Even now, the memory of him leaving twisted my stomach.

Jack's face fell, his eyes shining with emotion. "And?"

I felt like a champagne bottle. Uncorked, the words fizzing out like drunken bubbles. Unstoppable.

"I wanted to prove—" I paused, taking a deep breath, trying to find the right words.

He waited, knowing me. Knowing I needed time.

I closed my eyes. Heat from the fireplace bathed my face, my bare shoulders.

"I wanted to prove I could do it on my own. I wanted to show you that you weren't." I stabbed a wedge of gouda with a cheese knife. "You've never been a means to an end, Jack. You've been the endgame."

"The endgame?" He breathed the question, and it felt like everything I wanted was right within reach.

I looked up at him, saw the tears threatening to fall from his eyes. "Jack…"

"Em, I *want* to be that. And I'm sorry. I am so sorry I made you feel that way. You are incredible. A force to be reckoned with. I was wrong to have said that, I was stupid and scared I never should have put my parent's failure on you. On *us*. I wish I could have stayed, but I had to make some tough choices, and I needed to make them in person. Needed to get things untangled before I could be right for you. For us."

The way he said *us* sent a thrill through me, and I stepped closer, no longer sure if the heat was from the raging fire or from pure lust.

"I love you. I have always, and will always, love you. For me, there is only you. I want to prove it to you, too. I want to show you every day. *That's* my endgame." He leaned forward, brushing a curl off my cheek.

I bit my lip and surveyed the romantic set-up, the selection of delicious cheeses and wine on the table. "How long have you been planning this?"

He shrugged. "I came to my senses about two months and one week ago."

I laughed, thumping his chest with both hands. "That was the last time I saw you, you dork."

"See? One reason to be my girlfriend. I'm a fast learner."

"Wait." I stopped, suddenly slack jawed. "This place wasn't here two months ago."

He nodded, that flicker of pride returning to his face. "No, it sure wasn't."

"Jack... wait..."

"You and I both know this town was in sore need of some nightlife. Your business will grow faster the more attractive the downtown area is. Your hotel will bring me business, too. And you, of all people, know this was always my dream, neighbor."

"You bought it." The words rushed out, all the puzzle pieces snapping into place. I'd always hated puzzles. Never had the patience for them. "You bought the bar, and... the land next door?"

A nod. I rubbed my fingertips across his stubble, and he closed his eyes, leaning his cheek into my palm.

"That explains the name."

His smile grew even more infectious. "Do you like it?"

The question was soft, as though the weight of the world was on it.

"The Salt Circle?" I leaned into his chest. "I'll never forget that day, that's for sure."

"That doesn't answer the question."

"I love it." I hesitated, taking a step back. "But we're going to have to discuss *other* boundaries."

The smile slid off his face. "Okay, Emma, whatever you need. I can wait, we can take it slow, whatever you want. You're in charge. But I still have something to tell you." His brow pinched, and he turned toward the fire. Shifted his gaze from me to the flames.

"Besides the fact that you started a brewery in the town I live in as well as the land next to me?"

"I gave Theo the idea. To help with the renovations, to invest." His eyes found mine, were narrow with concern.

"What?" I plonked down on the seat. My heart raced. I stuck a piece of cheese in my mouth to keep from talking.

Jack ran a hand through his hair.

"I know you wanted to do it on your own, and I can see now, how maybe getting in touch with Theo was too much, how you might take it the—"

My hand found his, and slowly, his fist uncurled. I threaded our fingers together.

"That money has helped make my dreams reality. How could I be mad at you for that? Jack, I always imagined *us* running the Inn. Together." I grinned wolfishly. Ha. And he thought he would surprise *me*. "Besides, I made Theo sign a contract that I'd pay back every cent. I cut him a check tonight."

Jack scrubbed a hand over his face, stunned. A smile grew, and his dimple appeared.

But I wasn't done.

"I paid him with the deposit from a company that booked the Inn's most lavish corporate retreat. For the next five years. Some guy named Robert said *you* recommended the hotel."

His eyes were wide, his grin infectious.

I held up my other hand, not willing to let go of his. "I do have one last thing we need to discuss."

"Anything, Em, anything."

I bit the insides of my cheeks. I was probably enjoying the groveling a little *too* much.

"I don't want any fences between our land. I want to be able to pop over whenever I want for a cup of sugar."

He closed the gap between us, circling one arm around my waist, his mouth dangerously close to mine, his other hand in my hair. "Sugar, huh?"

"It would be the neighborly thing to do." I batted my eyelashes.

He kissed me, so rough and fast it surprised a gasp out of

me, and then I moaned into his mouth as his hand slid down my lower back.

"I like sugar," he rasped out.

"Good, because I'm going to need a lot of it."

"Is that right?"

"For cookies."

He burst out laughing. "Oh, is that what you're calling it these days?"

I stared up at him, taking his face in my hands. "And Jack?"

"Mmhmm?"

"I love you, too."

I stood up on my tiptoes, not quite tall enough to reach him despite the heels, and kissed Jack Colson like my life depended on it. He took my breath away, so maybe it did, after all.

Worst case scenario, I knew someone who could ask a ghost or two.

FOR A BONUS EPILOGUE of Emma's soft open on Halloween weekend at the hotel, click here!

For the latest updates and to never miss a new release, subscribe to my newsletter.

ABOUT THE AUTHOR

Brittany Kelley writes spicy romantic comedy. Her goal is to make you laugh out loud and swoon so hard you see stars.

When she's not writing, Brittany's busy wrangling her three children, drinking her sometimes still-hot coffee, playing board games with her husband, and acting as a servant to a flock of ducks and a pack of cats. Oh, and reading books. All the books.

For the latest updates, subscribe to her newsletter or follow her on Instagram and TikTok.

Head to www.brittanykelleywrites.com for more!

9 79898 809 1042